MY MOTHER'S LIES

DIANE SAXON

Boldwood

First published in Great Britain in 2024 by Boldwood Books Ltd.

Cover Design by Head Design Ltd

Cover Photography: iStock

A CIP catalogue record for this book is available from the British Library.

Paperback ISBN 978-1-83518-060-0

Large Print ISBN 978-1-83518-061-7

Hardback ISBN 978-1-83518-059-4

Ebook ISBN 978-1-83518-062-4

Kindle ISBN 978-1-83518-063-1

Audio CD ISBN 978-1-83518-054-9

MP3 CD ISBN 978-1-83518-055-6

Digital audio download ISBN 978-1-83518-057-0

Boldwood Books Ltd
23 Bowerdean Street
London SW6 3TN
www.boldwoodbooks.com

For Beau.

1

PRESENT DAY – SUNDAY, 30 JUNE 2024, 3.30 P.M. – SIOBHAN

Siobhan Martin reversed her car into the only space she could find in the Wrexham Maelor Hospital car park, breathing in as though that would allow her car more room. Her mirrors skimmed through the neighbouring cars' mirrors by a hair's breadth, and she allowed herself to sigh out as she turned off the engine.

Without air-con, the car filled with stifling heat as the sun beat through the windscreen. She edged open the driver's door and sucked in again to squeeze herself out of the narrow gap. It seemed that in recent years car parking spaces had become smaller while cars were made larger all the time. She couldn't moan; her own SUV was too big for one, but then she needed it to transport all the feed and bedding for the smallholding she owned with her mum.

Her mum, who was currently in hospital, having broken her hip when she slipped over in the chicken compound. The heatwave had baked the ground so hard that Siobhan heard the crack of her mum's hip as the woman went down.

Frantic, Siobhan had called 999 and shielded her mum from the relentless sun with two large umbrellas and a sheet hung between them. Regardless of all the precautions she'd taken, her mum had still gone into shock and was severely dehydrated as Siobhan had been advised to give her nothing until she'd been through the hospital A&E process in case she went straight into surgery. Once she'd been assigned a bed to await her operation, which they'd delayed until the following morning, she'd been put on fluids. The last Siobhan had seen of her, she'd looked like a frail shadow of her former self.

Siobhan pushed the driver's door closed, locked it, looped the strap of her handbag over her shoulder and made her way towards the main entrance of the hospital. The light dress she'd slipped on after her shower an hour earlier already stuck to her as sweat beaded across her skin, caused not only by the weather but by panic and fear trembling through her veins. A sleepless night had also contributed to her sensitivity.

As an estate agent, it wasn't always easy to work from home, but she'd managed to organise a couple of days where she could work flexible hours. After all, she didn't want to use up holiday allowances until her mum needed her back home. It wasn't as though she worked for a large practice with people who could fill in for her, and her boss was not exactly the most understanding. It should have been her weekend to work. All day Saturday and a half day on Sunday. Ivan Brown was the kind of person who expected his staff to trawl their way into the office no matter how deep the snow or whether or not the car had broken down. During Covid, despite putting her on furlough, he'd requested that she go into the office every day just to pick up the post and deal with it. Requested was not entirely correct. Demanded, with some degree of aggression. What was she supposed to do? Lose her job?

Siobhan had been contemplating a move, looking at options, but unless she moved to the city, there weren't that many vacancies she could apply for in her area of work. All the estate agents knew each other. Her application would hardly be a secret. That was the way it worked in Wales. That being said, Tracy Hartridge of Hartridge and Carlton had been making noises about Sean Carlton retiring soon. She'd also been hinting at taking on someone younger, more driven. Someone who could perhaps take over the practice when she wanted to retire. An exit strategy. It was a prospect Siobhan had been contemplating. Another year and it was a possibility. Tracy was a nice woman. A good woman. Her clients came back to her time and again, her employees stayed. Always a good sign.

In the meantime, Siobhan had yet to figure out how she was going to cope right now. Her mum was the one who looked after the animals on their smallholding as a rule. Three pygmy goats, two donkeys, forty-two chickens, six cats and a dog. They'd have more dogs again soon, but they were waiting for the right ones from the rescue centre. Ones that would fit in with their way of life.

Siobhan's mum was thirty-five when Siobhan was born. Now sixty-six, she had led a quiet life dedicated to her smallholding in the last few years. It seemed her mum preferred to keep out of the limelight, spending her time in the company of animals rather than humans.

Of the forty-two chickens, two were cockerels. Neither liked Siobhan. Truth be told, she wasn't so keen on them either. The huge Buff Orpington observed her with murder in his eye. Siobhan was never quite sure why they had cockerels, but her mum reassured her that it was a deterrent to foxes.

Siobhan wasn't so sure.

Her mum raised income by delivering fresh eggs daily to the local corner shop and through the honesty box she'd set up at the side of the road. The latter method often proved to be a loss leader as, all too frequently, the honesty part of it failed and they would find someone had swiped both the eggs and the money from the box, leaving it empty.

Her mum persisted. The local shop took two dozen eggs daily and normally sold them all, but if there was a build-up and they weren't selling as many for any given reason, her mum was left with a glut.

Siobhan had spent the morning giving Beau, their black Labrador, a 5 a.m. walk down to the river before the heat of the day kicked in, feeding him and the six cats, and collecting the eggs from the previous day that had been abandoned due to her mum's accident.

The treadle feeders they used to discourage rats had needed to be refilled with layers' pellets and mixed corn, but that meant she had approximately five days' worth of feed in them, which was one less job to do daily. She'd cleaned out the housing units, the waterers, the goats' house and the donkey shed, which was the chore her mum had embarked on when her accident occurred. For Siobhan, it had proved a welcome distraction.

By lunchtime, Siobhan was overheated and exhausted and, no, she'd not managed to work from home. There'd simply been too much to do and too much on her mind to concentrate. Mucking out was mindless.

With visiting her mum, Siobhan would have to catch up later that evening. Perhaps she'd even treat herself to a weekend glass of wine while she did so.

She stepped into the cool, air-conditioned foyer of the hospital and made her way through the long corridors, using the stairs to go up one floor instead of the lift she knew would be stuffy.

She realised just how much hard work her mum put into keeping the rescue animals. All of them had come into their lives almost by accident. Her mum couldn't help saving lost souls. They'd rescued half a dozen chickens first and continued to do so, building their flock. The donkeys had been abandoned when an old man died with no one else to care for them.

In addition, her mum also ran a soup kitchen she'd set up for the homeless. She never turned away waifs and strays. She grew a wealth of food in their fenced-off allotment and instead of profiting from it, she put most of it into supplying those in more need. Siobhan had never questioned her mum's desire to look after the homeless.

She never had to cook for herself. It wasn't that she was incapable, but her mum always had an evening meal prepared when she arrived home from work. The freezer was laden with every kind of meal she could think of. All of them meals for two. She'd had spaghetti Bolognese the previous day and would again that night instead of the Sunday roast her mum would normally cook. The following two days would be fish pie.

She didn't want to deplete the freezer too much, though, as her mum wouldn't be capable of standing in the kitchen for some time once she was allowed home after the hip replacement she'd been about to have the previous afternoon. Knowing her mum, she'd insist on cooking. You couldn't keep a good woman down.

When she'd called the hospital early that morning, expecting to be able to visit, the sister on the ward had advised her to leave it until mid-afternoon before she came to visit.

She thought nothing of it.

Until she pushed through the doors into the heat of the orthopaedic ward, where the air-conditioning appeared to be switched off, to find the bed her mum was allocated the day before empty.

Her heart lurched.

Not just empty but cleared out.

2

PRESENT DAY – SUNDAY, 30 JUNE 2024, 4 P.M. – SIOBHAN

The sick feeling didn't subside even when the nurse at the desk quietly informed her that her mum had been put into a side room.

'Why?'

The nurse's soft voice penetrated her concern. 'I'm sorry, Mrs...'

'Miss. Martin. Siobhan Martin.'

'Siobhan.' The nurse edged out from behind the nurses' station, manoeuvring around the meds trolley to come and stand beside her, her features calm, but there was a flicker of something in her eyes that Siobhan couldn't quite place. Concern? Apprehension?

'They're just in with her now, making her comfortable.' She chinned towards a private room at the end of the long line of bays.

A trace of worry made Siobhan's stomach clench once more. 'Why? What's going on? Can I see her?'

'Yes, of course. Let me check if they're ready for you. Mr Carmichael is just doing his rounds, he'd like to see you.'

'Me? He wants to see me?'

Was that the normal way of things? Siobhan had no memory of either her or her mum ever going to their GP's surgery, let alone the hospital. She'd no idea what the process was.

'Would you like to come through to the office to wait for him? Can I get you a cup of coffee? Tea?'

'I...'

The heat in the ward swarmed over her and Siobhan pressed her fingers against her lips as she pushed down on panic that threatened to surge up and overwhelm her.

'Water, if you have some, please.'

She allowed the nurse to guide her into a tiny box room jammed with equipment and paperwork, a small computer screen almost swallowed by the piles of files surrounding it.

She sank into a plastic chair and allowed the quiet of the room to settle her. It wasn't silent, but the noise and movement from the main ward were muffled, blending into white noise, so she found the time to think.

Was this normal? She'd not noticed in her brief look around other visitors being taken to one side; they all appeared to be perched on the edge of chairs next to their loved ones in bays of beds that ran the entire length of the corridor.

Siobhan watched through the wide window overlooking the corridor as nurses hustled from bed to bed, bay to bay, under pressure and understaffed.

Her heart skipped a beat as a tall, regal-looking gentleman let himself out of the side room that the nurse had indicated to Siobhan. She wanted to spring to her feet and rush down the corridor to him, demanding to know what was going on, but there was nothing about his demeanour that invited that.

Weariness etched deep lines around steel-grey eyes as he made his way towards her. The slight bow of his shoulders indicated the exhaustion he must feel. Not a young man, Siobhan wondered at the toll the job had taken on him and why he would stay so long. He definitely looked over retirement age to her.

Covid had managed to dispose of so many of the experienced

medical profession, either by killing them, maiming them or simply making them give up as their eyes were opened to a whole new world of horrors.

Her mum wasn't there because of Covid, merely an accident. Normally a healthy woman, Siobhan had been surprised at the ease at which her mum's hip had snapped. She'd re-run the moment over and over in her head but still she couldn't get the sound of it from her mind.

Siobhan surged to her feet as the consultant stepped up to the door. Her breath halted as he paused, his hand on the door handle while a nurse in a navy uniform waylaid him. Possibly a sister. Siobhan didn't really care. She wanted to see him. She wanted answers.

The grim set of his mouth should have been warning enough as the doctor slipped into the small room and made way for the sister to accompany him as she sidled in behind him, but Siobhan held on to the hope that still gripped her.

How bad could it be? Would she need to get help in until her mum was back on her feet? She was going to have to work from home. It wasn't the easiest when she had to schedule appointments with clients and show potential buyers around homes.

Nothing mattered other than her mum. She closed her eyes and envisioned her mum, weak and pallid as she lay in the dirt in the blazing sunshine. Her heart quivered. Her eyes popped open as the doctor spoke.

'Miss Martin. I'm Mr Carmichael. Do take a seat.'

Finding herself in such an enclosed area with two other bodies, Siobhan was relieved to melt down into the plastic chair. Mr Carmichael perched himself on the edge of another chair, while the sister stood with her back to the door, hands linked at her waist.

Siobhan had never been in hospital before, barely ever been to a GP surgery. The man in front of her exuded a confidence that was almost overpowering in the enclosed space. He leaned forward in his chair, eyes direct so she felt obliged to burble.

'Is my mum okay?'

'Miss Martin, when your mother came into the hospital through A&E, it was our understanding that she'd broken her hip, having taken a fall.'

Siobhan nodded, although she felt like she was missing a key element of their conversation. 'Yes.'

'Were you there?'

'Yes.'

'Did you notice anything out of the ordinary? Does your mother take a tumble on a regular basis?'

'No.' She shook her head again, completely at a loss as to where he was going with the conversation, aware of the woman who stood at the door, her arms now folded under her breasts. Closed in. Uncomfortable.

'My mum is really very tough. Sturdy.' Her mum might not like that description, but it was true. She lugged small bales of straw and hay and twenty-five-kilogram bags of feed on a daily basis as though they weighed nothing. She may be small, but she was strong, muscular.

Siobhan fidgeted in the hard chair. What the hell was going on?

'Is something wrong?'

Mr Carmichael gave a long pull of breath, almost an inward sigh. 'Miss Martin...'

'Siobhan.' She was rarely addressed by her surname.

'Siobhan.' His brows drew together. 'I'm very sorry to tell you that your mother's condition is more complex than we at first believed.'

She drew in a breath to ask a question, but he raised one finger and stopped her mid-thought.

'It's my opinion that your mother's hip was already broken by the time she hit the ground. I believe the cause of the break was not simply the fall, but what came before.'

Siobhan's heart skipped a beat. 'What do you mean?' But she knew in her heart there was something wrong. It was those thoughts that had kept her awake all night. The sound of the crack as she hefted a bag of feed, and then the fall. Not the other way around. She'd thought she'd imagined it. Sweat broke out on her forehead, a sick anticipation curdled her stomach.

'I'm afraid that once we started your mother's operation, we discovered something far worse than a straightforward break in her hip and took the decision to bail out. Sadly, your mother sustained the injury because she already has a very serious condition. We've conducted tests that we're awaiting the results for, but... until then, we can do nothing further. We need far more detailed analysis before we continue, for your mother's safety.' He paused, sympathy lurking in those steely eyes. 'We're looking at whether this is secondary cancer. We are currently conducting tests to see whether and where the primary cancer might be.'

Cancer?

Cancer!

Siobhan raised a hand to her forehead. Her head swam with the overload of information and rush of fear-induced adrenaline.

Her mum had cancer? Cancer that had broken her hipbone? Wasn't that the hardiest bone?

Siobhan pulled in a breath, but it stuck in her chest. A burning pain lodged. 'I don't understand. Cancer. My mum has cancer?' She could barely process it. The word scraped like sand on her tongue.

'It appears so.' Mr Carmichael nodded. The sympathy in his eyes seemed to dissipate and was replaced instead with professional determination. 'We're conducting tests to see whether there's a primary cancer as bone cancer per se is quite rare. We're looking at the possibility of it originating in her lungs. It may seem a tenuous link, but bone fractures are not uncommon when lung cancer metastasises.'

Lungs!

'She's never smoked.' Not to her knowledge, in any case.

Mr Carmichael shook his head. 'It doesn't necessarily mean she won't get cancer. It could be anything.' A cynical smile quirked his lips. 'Life is not always fair. I've found over time that there's no rhyme or reason to cancer. Sometimes the healthiest living people are struck with it. Your mother may be one of those.'

'How?'

'Has she shown any recent signs of being… ill?'

Tiredness. Loss of weight. Lack of energy… interest.

Siobhan's chest squeezed. She should have noticed. She should have realised. Her mum had dropped pounds recently, delighted after being plump and square for so long.

Siobhan wanted to put her head in her hands but stared at Mr Carmichael instead as she thought of how gaunt her mum had looked recently and she'd done nothing. Said nothing. 'Yes.' The word fell from her lips. Her shoulders sagged into the curve of the chairback.

'Without results, I can't confirm this, but there's a possibility that what we found has metastasised from elsewhere into her bones, which is why her hip… crumbled. That's the most likely scenario. Until we get the results of the blood tests and scans we've carried out today, we can't know for sure.'

Siobhan let out a soft moan.

'I'm sorry.' He reached for her, placed a cool hand on the burning flesh of her upper arm.

Tears pricked the back of her eyes at that one small show of sympathy and she choked out the next words.

'Did you fix it? Her hip. Did you manage to fix it?'

Mr Carmichael leaned forward and shook his head. 'Sorry, as I mentioned earlier, we decided our best course of action when we saw what we were dealing with was to bail out immediately and give her a better chance once we understand what challenges we are facing. Currently, your mother is being kept comfortable. There is nothing we can do to fix her hip until we find out how much damage there is to her connecting bones. Once we know what margins we have to take, we can resume. Be warned, though, she has what we classify as post-operative delirium, caused partially after the fall when she became severely dehydrated. Her body is refusing to take on fluids, despite an intravenous drip. She is very confused. We are doing all we can to assist her, but I think it would be wise to prepare yourself for the worst.'

Worst?

What could be worse than this?

What could possibly be more terrible than being in this room, listening to this doctor?

Death.

Death could be worse.

3

PRESENT DAY – SUNDAY, 30 JUNE 2024, 8.55 P.M. – SIOBHAN

The soft sigh of her mum's breath was the only sound in the darkening room.

Siobhan had sat by her bed for hours, until the light began to fade. The soft whisper of respect as nurses came and went, from time to time, changing her mum's catheter or taking her blood pressure.

In all that time, her mum had never so much as opened her eyes, her cool fingers never gave an acknowledging squeeze of her daughter's gentle clasp.

Sleep had to be the best way, but Siobhan wanted her to know she was there. To acknowledge her presence.

She glanced at her watch.

She needed to go soon. The healthcare workers had brought her coffee and water, but she'd declined the package of sandwiches made with thin plastic-looking bread. She was starting to regret it, but she needed to go home to feed all the animals and bed them down for the night in any case. She could get herself something then. Freshen up and return later.

Mr Carmichael had said she could stay as long as she wanted. They'd find her a comfortable chair.

She peered around in the dusky light. That all depended on what their idea of comfy was, with the single plastic-coated chair in the corner of the room, made for hygiene, not comfort.

She could always bring a throw and a pillow back with her. A book, a flask of real coffee and a snack for later in the night if she wanted to keep awake.

Siobhan slipped her fingers away and felt a slight resistance from her mum's hand. Real? Or was it imaginary? Her own desperate need for acknowledgement. Awareness.

With her breath held, she leaned closer, coming to her feet so she could lean over and study her mum's features. Slack mouthed, her mum's sallow skin lay in folds around her chin. Something Siobhan had never noticed. Never considered. Her mum wasn't old. Had never acted anything but robust. Healthy.

No longer healthy.

Her bruised eyelids flickered.

'Mum?'

Siobhan touched the cool arm that lay on top of the white sheet and gave it a gentle rub.

Her mum's eyes slit open.

'Who are you?' The stilted murmur came through pale, dry lips.

'Mum, it's me. Siobhan.'

She gave the arm a gentle squeeze, concerned when her mum blinked. Blank eyes stared at her.

'Siobhan? I don't know a Siobhan.'

'Mum... Mum, it's me.' Siobhan gave her mum's arm another gentle squeeze. A prompt for her to recognise her. The woman stilled, her focus turning sharp as though a light had been turned on inside her head.

The door swung open and light from the corridor slashed

through the room. Her mum squeezed her eyes closed against the intrusion and rolled her head away. Siobhan turned to confront the interloper.

Mr Carmichael stepped inside and snapped the door closed behind him. 'My apologies. I've had an emergency to deal with and never got to catch up with you or your mother.'

Confused, Siobhan stared at him as he leaned over to click on a small lamp over the bed, throwing her mum's features into shadows from above that emphasised the hollows in her cheeks and the bruised look under her eyes, giving her a sinister death mask.

He glanced at her mum and then leaned his back against the wall. His face took on a haggard appearance, most likely down to the long hours he'd already worked.

He took in a long breath before he spoke. 'I'm sorry to tell you that my earlier thoughts on your mother's condition have been confirmed. Sister will come in shortly and give you any information you need and answer your questions.'

Was he implying that he didn't want to answer her questions now?

He pushed away from the wall. His face looked gaunt, making Siobhan wonder how many times he'd delivered this news in his career.

Pity stirred in her, because it was easier to think of the doctor right now than face her own desperate situation and her mum's diagnosis.

If she could throw herself across her mum's frail body, Siobhan would. She held back. Respect for her mum and a deep resolve not to destroy the woman by burdening her with her own terror. Terror of losing her.

Surely it was best if her mum never even knew. Could they let her slip away without fear?

'What...' She could barely find the words. 'What's her prognosis? How long...?' She glanced at her mum's listless body, eyes a moment ago open, now closed, face slack. Was it rude to discuss her condition while she lay there? What if she could hear?

Mr Carmichael must have been of the same mind as he opened the door and stepped into the corridor, gliding his hand through the air as an invitation for her to join him.

Siobhan hadn't realised how much she was shaking until she pressed icy fingers to her lips.

'I'm sorry. I should make myself clear. We've had results back on the bloods we took earlier, and the news is not good. Unfortunately, when your mother fell, we believe she may have suffered a blow to her kidney, or kidneys.'

She nodded. Could it get any worse?

Siobhan pictured her mum on the hard ground, partially on her side. When Siobhan had tried to roll her, her mum had cried out in pain. The only thing Siobhan could do was run inside, phone the ambulance, grab a pillow for under her mum's head and the umbrellas to shade her.

It had taken forty-five minutes for the ambulance to arrive and probably another forty-five until they decided they had her stabilised enough to move her.

'That, together with the dehydration she suffered...'

'Because they took too long to get to her?'

He shook his head. 'Not necessarily. It will be a combination of factors. The blow to her kidneys, the heat, the damage to her hip, shock. Sadly, it all adds up to her being a very poorly patient right now. We will do our best to make her comfortable, but it is a matter of whether her body has had enough.'

'Enough?'

'She may just give up.'

Siobhan shook her head. 'My mum is a fighter.'

The doctor gave her a grim smile. 'Even the toughest of people sometimes succumb to the elements conspiring against them.'

Siobhan's brow twitched into a frown. 'How long…?' She didn't really want to ask.

Dr Carmichael shook his head. 'It's not as simple as that. If we can stabilise her bloods, then she could be around for some time, otherwise…' He shrugged.

'Otherwise, what?'

A piercing sound in the quiet hallway had Siobhan jumping but the doctor automatically raised his hand and glanced at his bleep. Tiredness etched deep into his features. 'Looks like I won't be heading home for a while.'

He reached out a hand and gave her elbow a gentle squeeze. 'I'll see what I can do to make her comfortable.'

Siobhan watched the back of his white coat recede up the empty corridor, her chest squeezing at the thought of her mum leaving her.

Oh God, what was she going to do? How would she cope?

She loved this woman so much, she'd never even given thought to her mum's mortality.

Her mum had always been such a strong woman, always known what to do. So independent. She'd moved them around England for the past three decades, until they'd settled four years ago at their smallholding in Wales. Their forever home, as her mum called it.

Well, it may well be forever. For her mum.

She squeezed her eyes closed against the threat of tears and took in a long breath, letting it slide back out again before she was ready to face her mum.

She slipped in through the door, this time noticing immediately her mum's focused eyes upon her.

Forcing a smile, she stepped close to the bed. 'Hello, Mum.'

Puzzlement slid over the woman's pale face, and she withdrew the hand Siobhan reached out to touch. 'Who are you?'

What had they told her? That her mum had some kind of delirium. Post-operative.

'It's me. Siobhan. Your daughter.'

The papery skin over her mum's forehead twitched into a doubtful scowl. She settled her head more comfortably against the crackly medical pillow, letting out a low groan of pain as she adjusted her body. Her eyes when they met Siobhan's turned shifty, something Siobhan hadn't ever noticed before.

'I don't have a daughter. I can't have children.'

A small puff of disbelief carried on the air as Siobhan let out a laugh.

'I am your daughter.'

'No. You're not!'

The vitriol in her mother's tone had Siobhan rearing her head back as though she'd been struck. What the hell?

Siobhan reached for the call button resting on the bed.

Her mum's hand snatched at hers, fingernails digging deep into Siobhan's skin with a vicious intent she'd not imagined her mum had.

The woman's eyes narrowed as she reached up with her other hand, grasping Siobhan's long hair and pulling her face down to meet hers.

'You stupid little bitch.'

Siobhan gasped. She'd never heard such words from her mum's lips. Only when the paramedic tried to move her, and that surely was understandable in the heat and the pain. Her mum wasn't like that, though. Her gentle, sweet, caring mum.

'You don't deserve a baby. How could you even let him treat you like that? How could you leave that poor baby to weep and wail, while he...'

Her mum tossed Siobhan's hair away, hatred flitting across her face.

Shock took hold and Siobhan took a hasty step away from the bed, barely able to recognise her own mother. She pressed herself against the closed door while she stared at the frail old woman in the bed.

Where had that come from?

The glare in her mum's eyes struck terror through her soul.

This woman wasn't her mum, was she?

There was no resemblance to her.

Siobhan raised her hand to press it against her thundering chest. Oh God. What was she supposed to do?

The spiteful glare was still there and as Siobhan moved, the woman in the bed bared her teeth at her.

Siobhan fumbled for the door handle and stumbled from the room, fleeing the hospital as fear gripped her.

4

FIFTY YEARS EARLIER – 1974 – GRACE

I raise my hand and smooth shaking fingers over the hot welt on my cheek.

I hate my mum!

Isn't a mother the one person in life you should be able to rely on? For love, for life, for protection.

Not my mum.

She's an evil bitch from hell.

I know. You're shocked that an eleven-year-old child could even form that thought in their innocent minds. But my mind is not so innocent.

Not now.

Not since her latest boyfriend arrived.

Kev, she calls this one. A car mechanic she picked up at the local pub one night.

Greasy Kevin the sleazebag, I call him.

That's what earned me the slap on the cheek.

No, actually, that's not quite true. It was when I told her 'Uncle Kevin' (that's what she said I should call him), 'the sleazebag', had asked me to sit on his knee while she worked the night shift at the local mental asylum. Or mad house as she calls it.

Mum is an attendant. She cares for poor, tortured souls, she tells me.

I find that so hard to believe. Not the poor, tortured souls bit, but that she cares for them.

She's never cared for a soul in her life. No one other than herself. Not unless it's for money, in any case.

So, when I mentioned he slid his hand up the inside of my thigh and tried to slip his fingers under the elastic of my knickers, she refused point blank to believe me. Like I could make that kind of thing up. These are not the kind of things children know of. Not unless they've been through it.

'Grace, you horrible child,' she sputters through eyes filled with crocodile tears. 'Spiteful. That's what you are. You'll do anything to stop me having a relationship, won't you?'

It's not her relationship I'm worried about. It's the relationship Kevin would like to have with me I'm more concerned with.

I shrug. 'He's a dirty old man. A pervert.'

'Where did you hear such a thing? You're a lying little bitch,' she spits at me.

That's because she had no idea Kevin was in our house with me last night and truth be told she's dead shocked. Her shock shouldn't impact negatively on me. It always has, though.

She's left me alone while she works the night shift for as long as I can remember.

My first memory was when I was around four. Maybe five. After all, I have no real timeline to base it on, apart from I'd not long started school. Prior to that, I think she drugged me at night so I wouldn't wake and realise I was alone. I believe now she was probably slipping me meds she obtained from the old folk where she worked.

It's not unheard of.

Bad parenting, it was called back then.

Abuse, I think the term is now. Or neglect. I've heard the teachers talk about it at school. It amounts to the same thing when you leave your child alone and they accidentally set fire to the house, like little Gregory Charles did last summer. His face is still wrinkled from where the fire melted his skin and one of his eyes droops downward onto his left cheek. They say he'll never get any better.

Since then, I've been very careful not to turn the gas fire on when I'm alone. I'd never been scared about being alone before. Not until I started to read the newspaper Mum brought home after work. I read every page of it, sucking in knowledge, desperate to know more about the world and its dangers.

Like the child on the news who broke their neck falling down the darkened stairwell, or the one who sliced open a finger as they cut a sandwich for themselves with stale bread and rancid margarine their dad had left them while he worked. All of those factors fall into the same melting pot. Unless one of these things happens to me, she's safe from 'the authorities', as she calls them.

Anyway, no one knew. No one asked. No one cared.

Except at school when they wanted to know why I seemed so tired all the time. Which was when she stopped giving me meds. She wrapped my hair in her clenched fist, pulling me in close and explained that if I woke in the night and made a sound, she would slap me silly the next day. She drilled into me that the authorities would come and take me away, put me in a home with other naughty little children, and I didn't want that. Did I?

Looking back, it probably would have been the best course of action. A result for me. After all, I might have ended up adopted by the most incredible parents. Ones with money, luxury yachts and plenty of love.

Of all those things, love is the most important.

I crave love.

Not the kind Greasy Kevin is willing to offer me.

Even at the age of eleven, I know that's so wrong. It's not love. It's something dark and dirty. I don't want it. I don't want his motor-oil-stained fingers anywhere near me.

I'd leapt from his lap where he'd pulled me as I walked past where he sat on the settee the night before and darted upstairs, skinny legs flying until I crashed into the bathroom. I'd shot the bolt across the door as I slammed it closed so he couldn't get to me. No matter how much he pleaded. He threatened. He cajoled. His voice low and gruff so the neighbours couldn't hear through our paper-thin walls.

Short of knocking the door down, there was no way he could get me. And if he had, that would definitely have been a red flag to anyone who cared to ask.

Not Mum. She probably wouldn't care even then, provided her lovely Kev continued to hang around.

The neighbours may have had something to say about it. In fact, that was the main reason he took off. It was me who raised the alarm when I yelled, 'Go away! Leave me alone!' I banged on the dividing wall with the side of my fist, like Mum does when they play music too loud. The neighbour had hammered back, shouting, 'What the fuck is going on in there? Quiet down, or I'll 'ave the pigs on you.'

Now, Kevin is gone and hopefully will never return.

That's my fault. According to Mum. I've deprived her of adult companionship. Of a man who she loved.

She never loved him. But she did use him. At least he'd managed to do a few DIY jobs around the house before he showed his real self. The evil inside.

Now he is gone. Not because she told him to go, she'd have clung on to him despite his liking for younger girls.

No, he left because he wrongly believed she'd kill him. Of course she wouldn't. It was all my fault. I must have flirted with him. Given him the 'come on', according to Mum.

I have no idea what a 'come on' is, but I can take a guess and that was never my game. Not now. Not ever. I don't play games.

I refuse to meet her gaze as I cradle my burning cheek with an icy hand. After all, what will I gain from that? She's never going to believe me. She never has. I'm just a nuisance. She never wanted me, as she reminds me all too often. Never in public, though. Now I'm getting older, I notice that. She's different when we're in company.

There's a mask she has that slides into place as soon as there is another person around. I wonder if this is the mask she uses at work. Does it slip momentarily if she's in charge of one of the old folk? Does she give them a mean pinch when no one is looking? I wouldn't put it past her.

In the silence, she lights a cigarette and I feel her gaze on me, astute and searching. It's not something I'm used to from her. It makes me want to curl up in a tight ball as her narrowed gaze rakes over me. She's assessing me. As though she's only just seen me for the first time.

I wonder why.

Then I notice the glint of something in her eyes. It's jealousy. I swear it is. She can't actually disguise it. But why is she jealous?

Is it because she no longer sees herself as young and pretty and she's realised I'm just starting on that journey? That men soon will be looking at me with my tiny breasts that are just starting to bud. I know this because the boys at school already nudge each other in the ribs and stare at girls' chests with knowledge in their eyes that's come all too soon.

When she's not at work, I watch as she spends hours in front of the mirror, smoothing out fine lines she imagines she sees from the corners of her eyes, and that deeper one that has formed between her eyebrows. Age is not responsible for that. Discontentment is.

The scowl deepens as she stares at me.

It won't be long until I'm a teenager. My skinny frame will fill out and will she then have even more trouble snagging boyfriends for herself? Will they always have one eye on me?

I don't know how old she was when she had me; she's certainly younger than most of the parents at school. She says I took away her childhood. I ruined her life. She could have been married now, but what man wants to burden himself with someone else's child?

Burden. I know that word well. She uses it often.

I once suggested that it wasn't my fault she couldn't keep her legs together – I'd heard one of the parents say that about her as they picked their child up from school, while I made my way home alone.

I earned myself a slap that time too.

She's fond of reminding me that she never wanted children. She wished she'd got rid of me instead of going through with my birth. That was the other thing the parent had said that day as she walked home behind me.

'The only reason that woman didn't have an abortion was because she thought she'd get free housing. Shame she didn't know who the father was, she could tap him up for some money too.'

I don't quite understand the mechanics of how a woman gets a baby inside her. School showed us how a plant reproduces, but for the life of me, I can't translate that image into what happens with girls and women. I mean, where does the stamen come from to insert in a pistil?

Evidently, according to that woman, my mum collected lots of stamens and if you insert a stamen into the pistil, you can't blame anyone else for the fact that you end up pregnant. Knocked up, was the phrase she used.

With each day that passes, I know how much Mum detests my presence.

When I have children, I'll let them know every day of their lives that they are loved with every part of my being. They will be so assured that I wanted them that they'll never doubt for a single moment my love for them.

Never.

5

PRESENT DAY – SUNDAY, 30 JUNE 2024, 9.25 P.M. – SIOBHAN

Pain squeezed at Siobhan's chest until she could barely breathe.

The cherub-faced nurse, with cheeks ruddy through effort as she dashed around, had still afforded Siobhan the time to explain that her mum was suffering from post-operative delirium and that she shouldn't take it to heart.

How could she not?

Delirious or not, her mum had denied her existence. Surely that wasn't right. Did delirious people then declare quite coldly that they had never been able to have children?

She didn't know.

She'd never been in this situation before. Never had friends who had been.

Truth be known, she didn't have very many friends.

With moving around as much as they had in her earlier years, those bonds that others seemed to form with kids they grew up with weren't there.

Siobhan got along fine with the other girls at work, and some of the lads. She had noticed, though, that the married guys were always a little wary of her... or they were wary because their wives were.

They'd no reason, except Siobhan was attractive. She was aware that she was and exuded a confidence in herself that had been instilled by her mum. Her mum who told her almost on a daily basis how beautiful she was, how clever she was, how loved she was.

Tall with long legs she considered to be her best feature. As one boyfriend once told her, they go right up to her arse. Although she'd had a number of compliments about her eyes, too.

Siobhan wasn't vain, but aware. She knew men found her desirable. Women too. Not necessarily in a sexual way, but in that sideways glance women often do when they admire another woman's features.

Never one to slather on make-up, she only applied a touch of tinted moisturiser, especially this time of year. She had a thousand freckles scattered across her cheekbones and down her nose that insisted on joining up as soon as the sun came out. Less like a dot-to-dot and more like a map of the world smudged across her face. There was no point trying to hide them with foundation because once people saw her without make-up, they were shocked.

Arran was. He could hardly be called her ex because he was never her boyfriend in the first place. They'd never quite got that far, despite her misguided belief that they were stepping towards a permanent relationship.

'What the fuck's happened to your skin?' he had asked the first and last time he woke up in her bed.

She'd been awake for a whole hour before Arran had stirred that morning, debating whether he'd had a good time the night before. Back then, she wasn't massively experienced in the area of sex. Partly because Siobhan and her mum had moved frequently, giving her little opportunity to strike up relationships, and partly because her mum made sure she was well-educated about the pitfalls of unprotected sex – and to be truthful had probably frightened the living crap out of her – which made her unsure of herself.

What she did have was every confidence in her looks.

Her mum raised her to believe that everyone is beautiful.

She'd stared in the mirror after Arran had left.

Her skin was as smooth as silk. She knew that. There wasn't a spot or a blemish on it. Because her freckles were not blemishes and she was damned if she was about to allow some freakin' egotistical, sex mad, self-professed perfectionist get her down. No way.

Her mother had taught her better. Instilled in her an inner confidence.

Siobhan had booted him out of the door before he'd even registered the insult she reeled with as she'd quickly buried it beneath the annoyance she'd let surge forward.

Since then, she has shown her freckles loud and proud.

She had a redhead's skin, but her hair was more of a strawberry blonde than red, her eyes like melted toffee, as her mum always said.

Siobhan had asked, when she was little, why she looked so unlike her mum, who was short and plump, with eyes such a brilliant blue that people frequently commented on them.

'It must come from your dad's side. They say redheads run through the male side of the family.'

Only she wasn't a redhead. Not technically. And in any case, who was her dad?

'Just a passing ship, I'm afraid. I don't even know his name, or how to contact him.'

Of course, her mum had never told her that until she was much older.

Did she really not know who he was?

Or, had she lied?

6

FORTY-FIVE YEARS EARLIER – 1979 – GRACE

For my sixteenth birthday, I wanted a little party. Not much, just some of the girls from school. None of the boys. They were at that awful stage. Too young to realise what complete idiots they were being and too big to put in their place.

My skin is dull and greasy and I've those permanent little whiteheads in the creases of my nose and chin. Some of the girls say to pop them, and others say if you do, the poison goes back into your skin, and you just get more.

I pop them because I can't be like Karen who seems to grow them until they're so enormous they burst, throwing out horrible white pus and blood. It's disgusting, but she claims it's far better for her skin.

I don't agree. I find it revolting.

Maybe if Mum gave me something more than soap and water, my skin wouldn't be so bad. Oh, she makes sure I have the basics. Soap, water – although not always hot. I hate the smell of the carbolic soap she snaffles from work. After I use it, my skin feels like it's being stretched over my cheekbones. Sort of squeaky clean but dry so if I pull a face, it feels like it might crack. Until around lunchtime when it gets all oily again, especially in the heat.

When Mum's at work, I slip into her room and sneak a tiny amount of Pond's Cold Cream. I can't take much as I'm sure she'll notice and beat the living crap out of me, but if I smooth my finger across the same pattern in the cream as her finger made then it's okay until she comes to the end of the jar, and then I have to wait for her to buy a new one, tolerating my dry, parched skin in between times.

She buys the cheapest shampoo on the market, and I have to tug a comb through my thick hair while it's still wet. Or maybe she steals that too as they provide it for some of their workers because of the type of place she works in. Obviously, they've never caught her stealing.

Unlike the asylum, which dismissed her when they caught her with her bag full of residents' toiletries and a small amount of cash. Of course, she never told me that but one of the girls at school let me know, telling me how lucky I was that it was her dad who caught my mum, otherwise she could have ended up in prison. I think she was under the impression I should be grateful.

School uniform, although it's second hand, cheap shoes she sometimes manages to pick up from one of the charity shops. She's good at buffing them up, I'll give her that. Apparently, she'd had to polish her dad's and brother's shoes every Sunday when she was younger. She only did them once for me each time she brought home a new pair. The latest ones are too big and I have to jam toilet paper in the toes so they don't slip off.

She doesn't care. She says I'll grow into them. I'm not about to grow any more. Well, I hope not in any case, although I'd love to be a little taller. According to my biology lessons, I'm pretty much fully grown height wise but the chances are I'll plump out, and what sixteen-year-old wants to do that, hey? Especially when they're already curvy.

The bras she gives me are ill-fitting too. She never measures me, merely gives me her old bras. When I was twelve, they fit, although mostly they were inappropriate for a twelve-year-old, if you get my drift. Horrible, thin material and totally see-through. Not only that, but if I didn't wear my burgundy jumper on top, my nipples could be seen so clearly through my thinning dingy white school uniform shirt, something the boys found an absolute hoot.

We are not the same size.

To give Mum her due, she's short, like me, but instead of the voluptuous curves I have, she's trim, with pert breasts that looked pretty good in those pointed Wonderbras.

Mine do not. They spill over the top and wobble like the sickly blancmange we have for pudding at school. The boys do that stupid nudging and sniggering, especially in the summer when we no longer have to wear ties and we open the top two buttons on our shirts.

Some of the girls let it all out there. Big and brazen in their pure white bras that proudly take them up a whole size, flaunting themselves with the third button on their shirts undone. Me, not so much. I don't want that kind of attention. I've never wanted it. Not since I discovered how much Mum's various boyfriends lech over me.

It's gross.

'Mum.'

She looks at me over her shoulder as she slips a sandwich into her bag for her lunch. I'm lucky, I have really good lunches at school and a bottle of milk every afternoon.

She works full time with her new job and she's on a shift rota, which means sometimes she works days. I asked what she actually does in there, but she simply shrugs.

'Everything no one else wants to do.'

I think she's a cleaner in a factory. It's a rubber company. Apparently makes the rubber extrusion that goes around windscreens in cars and doors to freezer lorries. She always stinks when she comes home. Sort of a bitter smell of hot rubber.

She's been quite well off lately as some 'fat git', she calls him, has started paying her attention. He's the finance director. She comes home with lavish boxes of chocolates and the odd half-empty bottle of wine, the rest of which I can only assume she consumed with him in some seedy hotel. She hints at that. Not seedy, but she'll talk about this hotel and that.

I'm hoping she doesn't bring him home, although I suspect she won't as it sounds like this one is married. There've been a couple of married men, but mostly divorced or widowed. I think she still holds out hope that one of them will marry her and whisk her away from this sad life she leads. Whisk her away from me so she can deny she ever gave birth to me.

I would never feel like that about a baby of mine. Never make them feel the way she does with me. As though I'm not wanted. I know I'm not wanted.

It was only two years ago I found out her age. When she celebrated her thirtieth birthday with some loser or another who bought her a cake. Thirty! I was fourteen, then. I thought at first she was having them on. Thirty! Jeez. That made her sixteen when she had me. She was my age now when she gave birth. That doesn't bear thinking about. I can think of nothing worse than having a baby to look after. No wonder she can't stand me. I've cramped her style all my life.

She thinks this latest guy is going to give her a chance in the accounts department. She says she's good with numbers. She certainly knows how to fiddle any kind of cash system, not to mention her benefits. I know she claims them.

'Mum, can I have some friends around?'

'No.'

She never even gives the question a moment to sink in. Her mouth just spews out the word. It frequently does. 'No.' It's an automatic response to every single request I have.

'It's my birthday, though.'

She narrows her eyes.

I don't normally have any comeback to her automated response. Not these days. Not since I was about eleven years old and learned to keep my mouth shut.

My voice is soft, coaxing, when I try again. 'I'm sixteen. Sixteen is special.'

Her lips compress. 'Sixteen, huh? When I was sixteen, I was pregnant with you. You weren't entirely legal.'

It wasn't me who wasn't entirely legal, but my mum. Evidently, she'd had sex before the legal age of consent, which is sixteen in the UK.

I'm not sure I ever want sex. It's always seemed so sleazy to me. I would like a baby. Love a baby. But just not yet. I'd hate to think it would be as unloved as me.

Her brow knits into a tight frown. She's not got wrinkles, more lines of discontent etched into her face. Her gaze cruises over me. Assessing.

'Sixteen. We'd better make sure you have a job lined up for when you finish school. I can't afford to keep you. You can stay as long as it takes you to stand on your own two feet, find a flat, and get a job.'

I goggle at her. Panic slides its cold knife into my stomach. She's got to be kidding.

Her face is deadpan.

My mum has never joked about anything like that in my life.

She's serious. Just like she was when I was twelve and she decided to put me on the pill.

I don't take it. She insisted. Took me to the doctor and everything. Said she never wanted me to be burdened with a baby like she was. It made me feel funny though when I took it. I don't know how to describe it, but I could have bashed my head against the nearest wall. I didn't tell anyone. I just stopped taking it. She doesn't know. Never asks.

I'm hardly in danger of getting pregnant, though. I've never had sex. Never want to.

'But I want to stay on at school. Do my A levels.' I'm actually really good. I'm in the top set at school. They call it the 'grammar stream'. I work hard. I have potential. That's what my teachers always tell me.

Mum wouldn't know. She never comes to parents' evening. Somehow, she always manages to wriggle out of it.

I can see me fighting my way out of this shithole. Or at least I could, if only I was given the opportunity.

She leans back against the sink in front of grubby windows so she's just a silhouette. 'Do you think I had that chance? Do you?'

I don't understand her logic. Surely, if she was never given a chance, she'd want her child to have the chances she didn't. Isn't that the way it's supposed to work?

Not with her, apparently.

Her life was shit, so she's going to make sure mine is too.

I wriggle my feet into my oversize shoes, hoping I won't get blisters from the rub as she slings her bag onto her shoulder and makes for the door.

'Perhaps I could go to college instead. Do a typing course?' It's more of a pathetic wheedling question than a positive stance. 'I could work in the evenings to help out.'

She swings back and gapes at me, her mouth drops open. 'Are

you shitting me? You, a typist? You'll be lucky if you get a job cleaning out toilets. That's what I've had to do because of you.'

'Well, I'm not so stupid as to get pregnant.' The words tumble unchecked out of my mouth.

I never even see the slap coming until my head reels and my cheek stings.

I step back, my hand going up to skin that burns but for once I'm not abashed. She's done this one time too many.

Fury tightens my throat and I step forward, giving her a hard shove so her skinny shoulder blades crunch against the closed front door. If it had been open, she would have fallen straight through, her skinny arse hitting the hard concrete of the floor outside. That would have brought a satisfaction even stronger than the one I feel now for sticking up for myself.

I pull myself up to my tallest and glare into eyes that have a streak of terror in them. I point my forefinger right at the end of her nose as I shove my face in hers.

'Don't you ever, ever raise a hand to me again, or I'll bash you until you can't stand.' I don't know where this fury has been residing, but it bursts out now. Unleashed, it is powerful.

Grabbing her by her bony shoulders, I roll her out of the way and haul open the door, stepping out into the early-morning sunshine ahead of her.

I stride along the open walkway, passing the other closed doors in our tenement flats. I almost skip down the concrete steps, a smile plastered on my face, even when I see crazy James huddled in the corner, a grey woollen blanket pulled around him against the chill of the wind whipping up the stairwell. He doesn't need to be there. He has a perfectly good one-bedroom flat on the floor above ours. He chooses to be there.

I dip my hand into my school bag and whip out an apple I'd slipped in there at lunch the day before and half a bar of Fry's

Chocolate Cream one of the girls had shared with me that I'd forgotten about until now. I generously gift them to him and offer up a smile.

James has loitered here for as long as I can remember.

His rheumy eyes meet mine and he breaks into a crooked smile. His brown cracked teeth lean haphazardly against each other, and I back off, not wanting to catch a waft of his alcohol-fumed breath.

'Ta.'

My smile stays in place. Some stranger has probably handed him a tenner thinking they were being kind. It only feeds his habit. Instead of buying food and clothes it will have gone on alcohol.

I don't think he's as old as he looks. Possibly he's only in his thirties, maybe early forties. Rumour has it he served in the British army. He was only a kid when he was posted out to Yemen. Some strange land I've never heard of, only on the news.

When he returned, they say he was a changed man, exhibiting symptoms such as shaking, screaming, something they call night terrors, and confusion. They say he has 'shell shock'. I say he'd be better off without the booze. Maybe his tremors would stop and he could claw his way out of the nightmares.

His family were well-known toffs in the area, but as the story goes, he couldn't go back to that life and chose instead to sit in the tenement hallways, despite his family managing to get a flat for him.

I remember when he first arrived a few years ago. He didn't look so bad. Clean shaven; crooked but clean teeth. Hair short and newly washed.

Now it hangs in greasy straggles around his shoulders, not so much framing his face as hiding it, until he does a strange head jerk and they momentarily curtain open.

Rheumy though his eyes are, they narrow as they focus on my cheek that now throbs like a bitch.

His lips turn down, but he says nothing, probably deeming it not to be any of his business. After all, families in the tenement blocks never want anyone to interfere in their lives. No matter how bad they are.

Mine is bad enough.

His is worse.

7

PRESENT DAY – SUNDAY, 30 JUNE 2024, 11.25 P.M. – SIOBHAN

Siobhan leaned forward in the high-backed reading chair her mum normally sat in and rested her elbows on her knees as she dug slim fingers deep into her scalp and rocked.

'Oh God.' What was she supposed to do without her mum?

They were so close. They adored each other.

She squeezed her eyes tightly closed. She might be jumping the gun; after all, they needed to wait for the full scan results before making decisions, but her heart felt as though it had been wrenched from her chest.

The pallor of her mum's normally healthy-looking skin made her look as though she'd already passed to the other side. Chalky white and waxen.

Her mum. She wasn't used to seeing her so fragile. All her life, she'd been vital, healthy, dependable. Now she'd taken on all the signs of an empty husk, her eyes sunken deep into their sockets.

Siobhan had made the mistake of Googling bone cancer, and the odds were not good. In fact, they were diabolical. The average survival rate was two to three years. At best.

She had no idea how advanced it was until they got the

complete results, but nothing about this situation was hopeful. Siobhan needed to make contingency plans. Things she had to put in place so she could look after her mum. Make her comfortable.

She'd always been organised, focused. This was something so far out of her capabilities, though, she floundered like a drowning woman.

The crushing weight on her chest seemed to have permanently deprived her of oxygen so each breath she took was laboured and painful.

Her mum.

Siobhan dropped her hands from her face and stared straight ahead. The dark shadow of Beau, their faithful black Labrador, slipped from his bed in the corner of the room, separating himself from the shadows where three of their cats shared his bed with him. He ambled over, offering her comfort in the form of a cold, wet nose in her neck.

In a natural move, Siobhan wrapped her arm around his shoulders and nuzzled her face into the softness of his silken ear.

'Mum,' she whispered into his fur as she squeezed her eyes shut against tears that threatened.

Only, her mum had told her she wasn't her real mum. That she'd been unable to have children of her own.

Siobhan frowned as she stroked Beau's wide forehead while her mind raced, chasing away the tears.

The nurse had said her mum was suffering from post-operative delirium.

Siobhan should believe the woman, shouldn't she? After all, she was knowledgeable. More qualified than Siobhan to assess these matters.

So why was there such a niggle of doubt in Siobhan's mind?

It hadn't sounded delusional. Her mum's voice had been stronger than it had since the fall. Full of conviction. Powerful.

Siobhan cast her memory back, searching for something, anything that would give a clue, verification.

There had never been any hint she was adopted. That she wasn't her mum's natural daughter. Not that it would have made any difference if she'd had that knowledge. Would it? She'd have still loved her as much as she did. Wouldn't she?

Her mum adored her. They had a beautiful relationship. Better than most of her friends had with their mothers. Even during those rebellious teenage years, Siobhan and her mum had remained close. The few arguments they might have had were so brief and unimportant that she didn't even have any clear memory of them. Certainly, her mum had never even raised a hand to her.

Siobhan smiled as memories seeped in. Her mum had always been a quiet, private person, but she happily allowed Siobhan's occasional friends around to the house. Although now she thought about it, she could never remember her mum fraternising with the other mothers. She'd always claimed she was too busy.

Siobhan braced her hands on the chair arms and pushed to her feet, wandering across the room with Beau shadowing her footsteps. She headed to the small drinks cabinet in the corner of the room with its mismatched crystal glasses her mum always picked up in charity shops.

She reached for a bottle of wine from the wooden wine rack, also acquired from a local charity shop, then dropped her hand.

Much as she desperately wanted a glass of wine, she didn't dare. What if the hospital called her? What if her mum took a turn for the worse and Siobhan needed to get there in a hurry?

Instead, she made her way into the kitchen and reached for the tub of hot chocolate. She didn't need coffee to keep her awake. She needed something to relax her. It wasn't exactly a substitute for the alcohol she craved, but it might help her to sleep for a few hours before she made her way back to the hospital first thing in the morning.

There was nothing she could do for her mum tonight. The woman was completely drugged up. Her defences down, had she revealed a secret, or was she, as the nurse claimed, delusional?

Why would her mum hide information about her heritage from her?

Even in the worst delirium, would she really imagine that she had no children? More disturbing, that she had always been incapable of having children. It seemed a strong opinion, one that surely would not sit well with a woman who had given birth.

Siobhan stirred the hot chocolate before picking it up and moving back into the living room. Narrowing her eyes, she scanned the room. Where did her mum keep important documentation?

Guilty unease slipped like the sharp point of a knife under skin at the thought of even questioning her mum's word. But she did. She couldn't help it. The seed of doubt had been sown.

Siobhan had never needed to look for any documents in the past.

She'd got her national insurance number when she was sixteen and worked part-time as a waitress while she was at sixth form college, and her driving licence a year later when she started driving lessons.

They'd never been abroad, so there'd never been a call for a passport.

She never considered anything odd about that, but now she was second-guessing herself. Or, more accurately, her mum.

They'd moved a number of times when Siobhan was younger, in part because of her mum chasing jobs. She was a bright woman, brighter than the positions she held down. Every time she was offered a promotion they seemed to move again. She didn't like the limelight, she claimed. Despite some of the lowly jobs her mum had carried out, Siobhan never went without, never felt deprived. Rolling these memories through her mind, Siobhan saw things in a slightly different light. One she wasn't sure she was keen on.

Her mum was never one for clutter. Minimalist, if anything. Surely, though, she had important papers. Birth certificates and the like.

Siobhan could never remember a time when she'd needed any certificates. Her mum had opened a bank account for her when she was a child. She still had the same one, savings being deposited every month from her job. Money she saved as she didn't have to pay rent or a mortgage.

Cradling the mug in her hand, Siobhan lowered herself cross-legged down onto a cushion she dumped on the floor and then tugged open the bottom drawer of the antique sideboard with one hand.

There weren't that many photographs of Siobhan as a baby, she already knew that. Then again, three decades ago, did people take as many photographs as they did these days? Certainly not. There were no selfies then. They didn't exist. Not in the same context, in any case.

She placed her mug on the floor beside her and eased out one of the shoeboxes her mum kept full of old papers and photographs. The lid was faded, and the cardboard had lost much of its stiffness.

Beau grumbled as he stretched out next to her, objecting to the late night, no doubt. He probably just wanted her to go up to bed so he could sleep too.

Siobhan slipped the lid off the box and placed it beside her as she started to take out photographs and paperwork. A short stack of her mum's payslips going back a number of years. Then they stopped around ten years ago. Did she dispose of them after ten years? Had she always done that?

Studying them closely as though there was a clue in her mum's past work history, Siobhan reached for her drink and took a sip.

She set the pile to one side. There was nothing of great interest there.

She wasn't truly sure what she was searching for, except the miracle of a birth certificate which would verify that she was indeed her mother's daughter.

Siobhan blew out a breath and pushed hair back from her forehead that had begun to stick. She wasn't sure if hot chocolate was the right choice in this weather, or if guilt had the cold sweat setting in. The urge to look over her shoulder to check her mum wasn't there tugged at her.

Dragging the rest of the paperwork out of the shoebox, Siobhan shuffled through it, riffling past each neat stack, some tied together with ribbon, others elastic bands that had perished and broke as she handled them.

Nothing. Nothing out of the ordinary.

She stretched, bowing her back until it cricked and caught sight of the old-fashioned wall clock that would probably be classed as retro these days.

'Ugh. Almost two o'clock.'

She rolled to her hands and knees on the floor and gave Beau's satin belly a gentle rub before she pushed to her feet and walked stiff-ankled to the door.

'I must be getting old.' She stretched out her back and grunted, as that stray thought catapulted her mind to the frail woman in a hospital bed. Alone. In pain. Dying.

She surveyed the room, her gaze falling on the black Labrador, who raised his head, his soft brown eyes meeting hers. She rested her hand on the light switch as a sob caught in her throat. 'What will we do if anything happens to her, lad?'

She turned out the light and climbed the stairs, aware that his shadow had slipped up behind her. Glad of the comfort of Beau tonight, she didn't send him back down to his own bed.

8

PRESENT DAY – MONDAY, 1 JULY 2024, 6.15 A.M. – SIOBHAN

Eyes heavy with sleep, Siobhan could barely persuade herself to roll out of bed, but she needed to tend to all the animals before she returned to the hospital.

She glanced at the time. Six-fifteen. Was that too early to telephone and check on her mum? Siobhan had not left her mum with a mobile phone. She'd been too doped up and confused anyway. Siobhan had put it on charge downstairs and would take it with her when she visited.

She debated whether to ring, or simply get herself ready and go in. After all, the ward nurse had said they would let her know the moment there was a change either way. Good or bad, she read that to mean.

Her heart tripped over itself, fluttering in uneven beats, and Siobhan raised her hand to her chest, willing it to slow. Her hand curled into a fist as she leaned against the door jamb. She wasn't broken. Not yet. But there was a small fissure opening up inside that threatened to swallow her.

Her limbs were heavy as she dragged herself downstairs, Beau not so much by her side, more nudging his cold, wet nose into the back of her knee to shuffle her along in a silent encouragement to feed him.

She snatched up the kettle and filled it. With a little stab of guilt, she realised she had no reason to feel so physically, mentally, emotionally wretched. It was her mum, not her, who was lying in agony in a hospital bed.

She never should have stayed up so late.

9

FORTY-FIVE YEARS EARLIER – 1979 – GRACE

It's taken me three weeks to realise Mum isn't coming back. I don't know where the hell she's gone, but there's a printed notice from the council to vacate by the end of today sellotaped to the door of our flat.

She's gone AWOL before, but never for so long. Sometimes she slinks off to some guy's place for a couple of nights, leaving me alone. She's done that since I was about ten, maybe younger.

This is different.

There's no food left. No money. I have nothing except the dinners I get at school. They are good. Nutritious, better than Mum has ever made me, and I make damned sure I eat my fill of the food some kids call stodge, slipping extras into my bag if I can, especially when they have a bowl of fruit at the end of the serving counter. No one ever wants it, so I stock up. Fresh fruit only happens once a week, but I also manage to finagle bread rolls sometimes so I have something for my tea, even if they're a bit stale. I've taken to keeping a paper bag inside my school bag for just such a steal. Karen doesn't like milk – she says it's bad for her skin – so she always hands hers over to me, which I put in my bag and take home.

Even the school meals are going to stop as the summer holidays approach. What will I do then if she doesn't come back?

A cold slide of panic grips me for a moment as I push the key in the door and then turn it. I can tell straight away by the odd silence that the electric has been cut off. There's no low-level buzz that I normally take for granted as background white noise.

The place has a sinister chill despite the weather turning from mild to warm. The inside of the flat is never hot, which is a godsend in the summer and hellish in the winter.

We have an electric meter, and I don't have any more coins to feed into it. Mum kept a supply just inside the meter cupboard, but I used the last up two nights ago.

I push the door closed behind me and lean on it for a long moment.

Where the hell is she?

I've not seen her since the day I pushed her.

It took me two days to realise that feeling of superiority had gained me nothing. Now she believes I've become more confident in my own skin, she's taken off. I never got my sixteenth birthday party, nor even a card from her. What a way to treat your child.

I would never be so horrible. Any child of mine will be adored. Treated like the precious gift they are.

Pauline McCormick is so lucky. I wish I'd been born into her family. They're kind. She's kind. Not a sickly, put-on sort of kindness that Mum displays if by some miracle one of the teachers manages to catch up with her, but something that comes from the soul.

I sit next to Pauline in both English and Maths. Whenever I need a new pencil or pen, she simply slides one of hers across the desk to me without a word. I'm not sure if we're best friends as she is very popular, but she's nice to me. There's an element of awareness of my situation that she doesn't make a fuss about.

She'd noticed the bright red handprint on my face a few weeks ago, but said nothing; instead, she pushed half her chocolate bar into my hand and smiled at me as though that would make my world better. It does. She often slips over a couple of Spangles that she bought from the tuck-shop with pocket money. Pocket money doesn't exist in my world.

Pauline has the best world. A loving world. She's tall. Taller than most in our class, and has a willowy grace, like she grew into her limbs with an elegant effortlessness that the rest of us have failed to achieve.

When I grow up, that's the kind of world I want to live in. Where no one bullies you, ignores you, abandons you.

That's what I want. A family.

One day, when I have one, I'm going to keep them close, treat them right. My family will be like Pauline McCormick's. You don't need money for that. Simply a heart full of love, which I have. I'm bursting with it. Yet I have no one to lavish it upon.

I dump my school bag on the kitchen counter and look around the flat, not quite sure what I'm seeing.

Mum has been here.

She's taken everything. There wasn't much, but what there was, she's taken.

The two-seater sofa and single armchair. The neat round wooden kitchen table with two mismatched dining chairs. The small TV and vintage record player, our single vase that I've been putting a few daffodils in during the spring, that I pick from around the edge of the common when no one is watching.

She's whipped the crocheted blankets I've made at school in my home economics lessons, even the crochet hook I'd borrowed and should give back has gone. She doesn't need it. I suspect it was simple spite. Somehow retaliating against my bid for a better life.

I feel as though I'm drowning as I step into her bedroom. My breath shortens as I snatch it in and it wedges in my chest.

Empty. Completely empty.

How the hell did she manage this? She must have persuaded her latest boyfriend to borrow a van and enlist help lugging the lot down the tenement block. I wonder briefly if that rich guy has arranged it. Then again, if she still has her rich guy, wouldn't he simply supply her with new furniture?

I fling open our shared wardrobe, which she probably would have taken too except it's just a door into a recess in the wall.

One full set of my school uniform hangs there like an insult as I was the one who washed, dried and ironed them, then hung them neatly inside. The rest of my clothes have gone. Probably because she can make them fit her, even if she has to alter them.

Tears prick at the back of my eyes and a hot rush of shame floods over me.

What will people think? I've been deserted by my own bloody mother.

I let out a soft sob, trying desperately to hold back the tears, but they rush in.

I swipe them from my cheeks as I walk into the bathroom to grab some toilet paper so I can blow my nose.

She's even taken that. The bitch! There hadn't been much on the roll so I know without a doubt she's done that through malice.

The only thing she has left, other than my uniform, is my toothbrush.

Generous of her. Thoughtful.

I look again at the pink toothbrush lying across the sink and decide to leave it there. She probably scrubbed the loo with it before leaving it.

I go back and tug my uniform from the hanger. Probably the only reason she left it was in case the school came after her. Then they'd know she left me.

I blow out a breath as I roll my uniform up and push it into the top of my school bag, leaving it bulging out the top. By the time I use it, it will probably be wrinkled again, but I no longer have an iron.

Panic tightens my throat.

What am I supposed to do?

It's Friday. None of the teachers will be at school. In any case, do I dare tell any of them? They might throw me out and I'm right in the middle of my exams.

My thoughts turn to that notice on the outside of the flat door.

She knew!

Of course she knew.

All the time, I knew she was sneaking in and out of the flat. She'd left unwashed coffee cups and plates in the sink, giving me a false sense of security. Believing she would return. All along, she knew she was going. She'd probably seen that notice a couple of weeks ago and hidden it so she could make her plans without my knowledge. So I couldn't do anything. Follow her. Beg her not to leave me.

But she left. In the worst possible scenario, she's left me. Abandoned me.

Evil bitch from hell!

What loving parent would ever do that?

Only she's not a loving parent. Never has been. She's only ever looked after herself.

And now, I have to look after myself.

I make for the door and swing it open, leaving it wide for all the world to see that we've gone. 'Vacated.'

I fly down the stairwell with no thought in my mind as to where I can go, what I'm supposed to do.

Crazy James raises his head. His eyes are clearer today. Astute. That blue is piercing.

He shakes his hand free of his blanket and offers something to me.

I reach out and he presses a key into the soft flesh of the palm of my hand.

'Four-two-eight.'

I send him a quizzical frown. 'What's this for?'

James hunches his body beneath the blanket, only cold because he's sitting on icy concrete and not moving around, the silly fool. I've told him about that before, even brought him a cushion to stick under his lazy arse so he doesn't get haemorrhoids, but he lost it somehow.

He stabs his thumb skywards. 'I don't use it. You might as well.'

'Your flat?' I stare at the silver key in my hand. 'You want me to have your flat?'

He gives a curt nod, his voice rasping like a heel scraping gravel. 'I've no need of it. Help yourself.' He chin-jerks at the key I'm still holding out. 'That's the only key. You won't be disturbed.'

I suck air in through my teeth, undecided. I know James's place is going to be a complete hole and I'll have to scrub it thoroughly, but at least it's somewhere. For now. For tonight.

I curl my fingers around the key and return the nod, almost overwhelmed with gratitude. I haul back on the tears. He doesn't like me to be too demonstrative. It makes him uncomfortable.

'Why?' The words pop out of my mouth as I stare at the sum total of his belongings in a backpack and three carrier bags, and I want to bite my tongue for sounding so ungrateful. Don't look a gift horse in the mouth, as the saying goes, but truthfully, I just want to know.

His lips crook up at one side as he passes an assessing glance over me from head to toe. 'Because you're the most thoughtful one here, and I see something in you. A potential. Go on now, bugger off and let me be.' He hunkers back underneath his blanket and shuts his eyes, closing me out.

As I turn my back and walk away, it occurs to me that he's so well-spoken.

What evil has he witnessed to bring him to this?

10

FORTY-ONE YEARS EARLIER – 1983 – GRACE

James raises his head and smiles at me as I pass him on the stairwell. His voice is a low grumble that I notice has become quieter over the last year or so.

'New hair?'

I raise my hand and touch hair that's stiff enough to break if anyone so much as pats it. It was incredible when I came out of the hairdressers yesterday, but I'm not sure I've got it right. It's supposed to be a feathered Farrah-flip, but when I tried to tease it into shape this morning, it was more of a Flipping-flop.

'Thanks. I have an interview for a new job...' I glance at my watch. 'Ten-thirty this morning. I'm a little early.' I hunker down next to him, placing a mug of steaming black coffee by his side and a paper bag with a bacon sandwich for his breakfast. I made them up before I left the flat.

He's got a new job himself helping out with some community project that the government have put in place. He doesn't get paid, he's on the dole and he gets fed at lunchtime. It's given him a certain amount of pride I've not seen in him before. He stands a little taller when he's not hunched in the corner. He's recently had his hair washed and although he won't have it cut, he wears it in a ponytail, scraped back to reveal a face which would be handsome but for the burn scars across his left cheek trailing down his neck to creep under his shirt collar. Scars he's always hidden behind that thick mop of hair he has.

His eyes are bright this morning, which is always a good sign that he's not been able to get hold of a cheap bottle of whisky for a while.

'What's the job?' He reaches for his coffee and cradles it between his hands, blowing the steam with a gusty breath.

Never once has he been in his own flat since I moved in. He's never asked to shower, or even go to the toilet. He's never asked for food or drinks, but since the moment I started my job at the local hypermarket pushing trolleys just a week after my mum had left, I make sure I share my food. Even in the early days when it was only an apple each and a piece of cheese. After all, an apple a day keeps the doctor away and we both seem to have benefited from it.

Without being melodramatic, he saved me.

I have no idea what would have become of me if he'd not come to my aid. If I'd not had a warm, safe shelter and the ability to keep myself clean and presentable. I consider we worked on it together. He's more of a parent to me than my mum ever was. That saying, blood is thicker than water, well, it's rubbish.

My mother deserted me, and for that I will never forgive her. I'm so hurt, I don't ever want her in my life. I've washed my hands of her, because blood isn't always thicker than water and this kind, modest man who has seen the worst of the world gave me everything he owned, not asking for anything in return. That's got to be worth something.

One of the biggest surprises was when I walked through the

door of flat four-two-eight and discovered, not a disgusting pit, as I'd imagined, but an immaculate place that appeared no one had ever lived in. James certainly hadn't. I'm not even sure he'd set foot in there. It was dusty and I had to wash the bedding before I could use it, but there was a washing machine in the flat, which was more than we'd had. We had to use the launderette on the bottom floor of the tenement flats. A place you didn't dare leave the washing and come back to later for fear that it would have disappeared. It had been my job to sit there, ever since I was strong enough to carry the laundry up and down the stairs and reach the washer stacked on top of the tumble dryer.

James's flat is better than most. I would say the carpets were relatively new and the walls had been painted, unlike ours, which had scuff-marked walls and threadbare carpets. Then again, James hadn't lived in his flat since the day he was assigned it several years ago.

What grieves me is his apparent belief that he doesn't deserve anything.

Once I was promoted to supervisor, things became so much easier. The French hypermarket, Carrefour, pays so much more than other shops. It may not be as glamorous as some of the other stores, but I don't care. It's facilitated me going to college two days a week and one evening.

I want more. There's a burning desire deep inside to do something with my life. To mean something. To achieve.

I'm not my mum, and I never want to be anything like her. The only man in my life is James, and he's more like an uncle, or even a brother. The more I look at him, the more I realise how much younger he is than I initially thought. He's more family than my mum ever was.

I know she's around. James mentions that he's seen her from

time to time, subtle and in passing, like a warning, but I keep my head down. I have a horrible feeling that if she gets wind of the fact that I'm still living in these tenements, she'll be on me, looking for me to support her. That's why James gives me the heads up.

I've got my feet under me now and the last thing I need is her.

'Secretary,' I reply to his question.

I don't mention that it says site secretary/chain boy, whatever the heck that's supposed to mean, working on the proposed M54 motorway everyone is talking about.

The skin around James's eyes crinkles as he smiles up at me, a ray of sunlight from the open stairwell above slashing across his eyes to make them a luminous blue. Without the bloodshot whites, his eyes are quite beautiful. Lush black lashes frame them to emphasise the depth of colour.

'Oh, la-de-da. Lady of the manor next.'

I grin back at him as I push to my feet, smoothing my new, plain black knee-length pencil skirt into place. I hope it's appropriate. It may be a little tight around the bum.

I wear a uniform at Carrefour. Before I was promoted, I pushed trolleys up the car park and wore a sickly yellow cotton uniform dress that we weren't allowed to wear our own clothes under, just underwear. I often wonder if it was a man who made that rule. We froze in the winter as the hypermarket was always bitterly cold, especially in the warehouse. The dirt-brown collar and sleeves of the uniform did nothing to enhance the look. Popper buttons ran all the way from mid-breastbone to knee and regularly snagged on the trolleys, ripping wide open to expose my underwear to anyone who cared to look. There were a good number of dirty old men who cared to look.

Since my promotion, my uniform is now a completely dirt-brown shapeless jacket with matching skirt, the unfashionable flare of it making all of us look shorter by several inches, and wider too.

Not that I worry about my weight. I'm on the slim side, because in general I eat very healthily, and often not quite enough.

I do a quick twirl now, for James. 'What do you think?'

'I think you'll get the job.' He stares down at my footwear. The cute black trainers I treated myself to make life more comfortable when I'm on my feet all day long.

'It's a long walk.' I tuck my hand into my bag and pull my smart little sandals halfway out. 'I'll change into these once I get there, before I go into my interview.'

He nods and then slurps at his coffee and his face scrunches up. 'You forgot the sugar.'

'It's bad for your teeth.' It was, but I had actually forgotten his sugar.

He doesn't smile. I know he cleans his teeth now because I give him a new toothbrush every few months and a tube of toothpaste when he runs out. Last time I looked, they weren't exactly a bright, sparkling white, more of a cream, but they were cleaner by far than before, which made them less crooked-looking. At least he doesn't appear to have lost any. I suspect he's taking more care now he has something to enjoy. Everything about him is just that much smarter than it was. Maybe one of these days I can persuade him to get off his arse and stop residing in the hallway. Even though that would be detrimental to my accommodation arrangements.

Every day of that first year, I thought he would ask for his flat back, or want to share it, but he never has. I have no idea who pays for it, but the tenement block is in steady decline, looking more and more like a slum, with all sorts of rubbish piling up and supermarket trolleys abandoned in the stairwells. How they get them up there is anyone's guess. I do wonder how much longer it will be before we're all evicted or re-homed. Of course, no one knows I live in James's flat for free. No one official, in any case.

Just as James does, I keep to myself. I don't have time to gossip and have coffee with any of the neighbours, not between college and work which tie up just about every hour of my week. I'm not sure I'd want to have coffee with any of them if I could. The place is never silent; everyone knows each other's business. They don't need to know mine. I only reside here. For now, until I can claw my way out.

In the meantime, I've saved as much money as I can for just such an event of being evicted. If we get re-homed, I don't know what will happen to James. The fresh new flats that are going up won't allow him to loiter in the stairwell. Everyone knows him here. No one minds. The men ignore him, the women pity him and the few teenagers who might cause hassle tend to give him a wide berth with a healthy respect for that scarring on his face. The rumours of how he came by it are rife.

I've never asked.

It's not that I'm not curious, I just feel it's too intrusive and might rock the boat of our strange relationship.

Whatever happens, though, somehow, we'll manage. I will look after him, especially once my income doubles when I get a new job. If I get this job, it will more than quadruple.

A little shiver of excitement has me breaking out in goosebumps.

I'm not sure if I read the salary correctly, but I keep re-reading the advertisement that I've cut out and now have tucked in my handbag.

'I better get going.'

'Good luck.'

I give him a swift nod, smooth my new, albeit cheap black skirt again and trot down the stone steps into the sunshine. It's going to be a long walk. I estimate about an hour. I've applied loads of deodorant as I don't want to be all hot and sweaty by the time I get there.

If I get the job, I might have to treat myself to a bike because the buses are so infrequent along this route that it just wouldn't be practical.

There's hope in my heart as I stride out, determined my life will change for the better.

It's not long before that hope is dashed.

11

FORTY-ONE YEARS EARLIER – 1983 – GRACE

'Oh, bloody hell. What have I done?'

I slip down the wall next to James. I'm sure my face is ashen as I know there's no blood left in my brain.

James lifts his head and his clear eyes pierce into mine. 'What's wrong?'

I blow out a breath as I shuffle closer to him, so my bum doesn't freeze, I edge my backside onto the small child's mattress I bought him last week, shoving aside a bag of clothing and some of the blankets he's accrued to stop him freezing to death. I know the mattress is still clean. James is still clean. It gives me a warm feeling inside knowing he's going through a good phase. It may not last, but we'll enjoy it while it does.

I lean back, the cold wall taking away some of the hot flush of embarrassment. I tuck my legs up, wrapping my arms around them and rest my chin on my knees. 'I don't know what I was thinking, James. Why did I do it?'

James shows more interest and nudges me in the ribs with his elbow. 'What did you do?' He spreads the words out like he's talking to some idiot, his patience always on a knife edge.

'I told a lie at my interview.'

I bury my face in my hands, only peering out at him after several beats of silence.

His eyes meet mine and he gives a shrug. 'So what?'

My mouth drops open. 'So what? So what? Bloody hell, James.'

'I don't see your problem. Everyone tells lies.'

'I don't. Not this kind of lie.'

'Come on. It can't be that bad. What did you say?'

'When Mr Bates said, "I assume you are over the age of twenty-five," I didn't so much lie, but I agreed.' *Twenty-five. Yes*, I'd said.

He'd peered at me over small wire-rimmed glasses perched on a nose with skin thickened by age and pitting. His eyes were small and astute, but he obviously didn't have much experience with judging women's ages.

James shrugged. 'So what?'

Was that the only reply he knew how to give?

'So. He offered me the job there and then. I don't even think he's bothered about references. He just wants someone to start work next Monday.'

'Cool.'

'No, not cool, because when he finds out I've lied to him, he's going to fire me immediately.'

'So you should have told him the truth.'

I push my hands against the ground and leap to my feet, spinning to face him. 'I know I should have.' My voice rises with the panic inside. 'I didn't know I had any chance of getting the job.'

'And now you have...'

How can he be so calm?

'I have.' Hysteria breaks free, and I fling my hands in the air like a spoilt teenager, which I am not. Not any longer. 'You're not listening to me. I don't know why I bother.'

I stomp off, turning the corner to race up the concrete steps to the next level. Tears are pricking behind my eyes. Fury at myself for lying, at James for not understanding the importance of this bloody job. My passage out of here.

As I reach halfway, I peer down so I can give him the benefit of my ire.

He's staring up at me, those laser-sharp eyes filled with amusement.

'I can help.' His voice is a soft assurance.

I stop.

I lean over the balcony rail. 'How can *you* help?' Unfairly, I give a bit of a sneer.

'Get me a bottle of whisky and I'll tell you.'

I lean away from him. I may desperately want this job, but not enough to destroy his life. 'No chance, James. Nice try.'

I watch the pull of his lips as they twist into a wry smile.

'I'll make you oxtail soup, though.' I add.

It's a bit of a weakness with him too. Not as much as whisky, but it seems to comfort him.

'Deal.'

I move back down the steps towards him, but he holds up his hand in a stop motion.

'Nah, ah. Soup first. And then we talk.'

My shoulders sag, but I swing around yet again and head on up, my feet dragging like a miserable child.

'It'll have to be quick, I have to get into work by 2 p.m. I'm on late shift.'

'You'd better hurry then. Bring your national insurance card with you, and your birth certificate.'

My mind is racing as I open the can of soup and stick it on the stove top, letting it warm through as I dash through to the bathroom, throw off my smart little skirt and neat blouse and drag on my drab work uniform.

How am I going to tell my potential new boss that I'm six years younger than he thinks? Can he withdraw his offer? It's not like I lied. Technically.

I race back into the kitchen and turn the heat down on the bubbling pan of soup.

My hands shake as I pull out a loaf of thin white bread, wipe margarine on four slices and scrape it off again. I'm not keen on margarine, but who can afford real butter? I don't even get a discount from the hypermarket I work for.

Truth be told, I hate working there and don't want it to be my future. The girls on the tills are fine, well, most of them in any case. It's the customers with their air of entitlement. Their ingratitude. Their absolute arsiness just because they never picked up a tin of cocoa with the price label on, or it fluttered off when they put the item in their trolley.

When this happens, a runner has to check the price, memorise it while being accosted by twelve more customers who want to know where the hell we keep baby formula, or baked beans, or – God forbid – haemorrhoid cream.

College tells us that soon barcodes will be on all grocery products, and that Sainsbury's already have them on certain items. Bring on that day! Although I hope not to still be there when it happens.

I layer thin ham onto the bread and push the lid down onto it. I cut it in half and shove one sandwich into a paper bag I obtained from work. I take a couple a day. No one notices. No one cares. It can hardly be classified as stealing. There are worse things. Horrible things.

Like the old men buying dirty magazines from young girls. It shouldn't be allowed. There's a horrible perversion to it and surely we should be protecting our youngsters.

I try my best. Once I was promoted to supervisor, I put Brenda Batshit, as we call her, in charge of that counter. Such a bitch!

She knows just how to keep these men in line.

I think about the job I've just accepted with a little shiver of concern. Predominantly male. In fact, I will be the only female on site.

I pour soup into a mug until it's full and then empty the remaining inch into another mug for me. I don't need much. I pick up half of my sandwich and take a huge bite and then turn to reach for my birth certificate, the only item my mum left behind, and the national insurance card I received in the post when I was sixteen, which I keep in the slim drawer next to the sink. I slip them into my handbag so I can hand them to James on the way past.

I grab another bite of my sandwich. I'm surprisingly hungry after my long walk and all the adrenaline surging through me.

How the hell am I supposed to resolve the problem I have?

I take another bite of my sandwich, slurp down the soup, sucking in air as it burns my tongue, and unscrew the advert I'd shoved into my pocket.

It doesn't actually say twenty-five in the advert, otherwise I wouldn't have applied. Perhaps I should have been truthful and pointed that out. Truth be told, I said very little at the interview, just that I had completed my qualifications at college. I never lied, just omitted to say that I had yet to receive the results.

I am confident that I passed everything, though. Perhaps I jumped the gun a little, because armed with my Private Secretaries Certificate surely I won't have any problems getting a job. Patience is what I need.

Heat creeps up my neck into my face. Patience be damned, I really, really want *this* job. This is the one that will give me an instant boost in wages, much more than the local companies can give as it's a London-based company paying London rates.

If I don't get one quickly, all my qualifications will be worth nothing without experience anyway. That's what they told me at college. *'Get a job quickly. Experience matters. You don't want your skills to deteriorate. Take anything...'*

I wouldn't care, but Mr Bates never even asked for proof of qualifications or experience.

He told me what he wanted me to do. I said I could do it.

He looked me up and down and nodded. As if I would do. I never set the world on fire, but my heart sang when he offered me the job. Truly sang.

I throw the strap of my handbag over my shoulder, shove the last of my sandwich into my mouth, swipe up the full mug of soup and snatch up the paper bag.

I need to get moving, otherwise they dock my pay if I clock in late. Even a minute over and they dock fifteen minutes.

That's another thing that occurs to me as I lock the door and walk down the stairwell, cautious not to spill the hot liquid.

I don't have a bank account. Carrefour never required it. I'm paid every Friday in cash. It comes in a sealed brown envelope with my payslip.

James holds out both hands and I pass over the soup and sandwich.

He places the brown paper bag beside him. He's definitely eating better, which is always a good sign. It means he's not drinking.

Once more he reaches out, palm upwards.

I place my national insurance card in his hand together with my folded birth certificate.

'How old do you need to be?'

'Twenty-five.'

'And you've just turned nineteen? A couple of days ago.' He tilts his head to look up at me.

My mouth falls open. How does he know? I'm momentarily flummoxed.

'Yes.' I narrow my eyes ready to ask him how he knows, but I don't want to upset this guy who is merely trying to help.

His dark eyebrow raises. 'No celebration?'

I shrug, reluctant to tell him, in case he thinks he's been left out. Not of my party, but the opportunity to drink. 'Just a few drinks after work with the girls, that's all.' The guilt slithers through me at mentioning drinks. Will it make him fall off the wagon again?

Without opening the folded birth certificate, he pins me with a look that says he totally gets what I'm thinking, his lips a straight line for a moment before they tilt at the corners. 'Date of birth?'

'Twenty-second June 1957.'

He inclines his head.

'Leave it with me.' He tucks the documents inside his top pocket and cups the mug in his hands, taking a loud slurp.

'I don't have a bank account either, and Mr Bates asked me for those details. I'll be getting paid monthly straight into the bank,' I blurt and wonder how I will make my final pay packet last me a whole month until I get paid at the end of July. 'What shall I tell him?'

'Nothing yet. You don't have to respond until he puts the offer in writing to you. Don't hand in your notice or mention it until you have it in writing. Is that clear?'

I nod.

I'd not thought of that. I'm so excited I was about to hand in my notice when I got to Carrefour, tell my boss that I'd only be there until the end of the week, so it didn't mess up their rota for them. But James is right. What if I don't get an official offer? What if Mr Bates interviews someone else and decides he prefers them?

Sometimes James's knowledge of worldly matters is so much wider than I give him credit for. Perhaps it's because a great deal of the time he is almost comatose with the amount of spirits he consumes. Right now, he's going through a good phase. Don't get me wrong. I know he's an alcoholic and I don't think there's any cure for that.

We take the good times when we can.

By the time I arrive back from my late shift, James holds out a shaking hand and I know he's put himself in harm's way to do what he has for me. By harm's way, I mean he's been exposed to whisky again. I can smell it in the stairwell. A bit like a red flag flying.

I look at what I hold in my hand. A brand-new birth certificate. Incredibly, I am now six years older than my real date of birth.

He gives me my national insurance card. It doesn't look any different. I'm not sure. I have a bank account, too.

I don't know what connections James has, or how he does these things, but it's like magic.

James says to destroy my original birth certificate.

It's difficult to, though. It's about the only thing my mum left behind. I don't want to lose sight of the real me.

I stare at the new one with the slightest change to my surname. I wonder if that was an error, or if the slight change makes it easier for me to remember when I hear the verbal version, but harder for anyone else to check. Then: 'Father – Unknown.'

That's what it stated on the original.

'Father – Unknown.' Nothing changed there, then, and I feel a small pull of disappointment, because somehow, I believed that detail might have changed.

12

PRESENT DAY – MONDAY, 1 JULY 2024 10.15 A.M. – SIOBHAN

'Father – Unknown.'

Siobhan stared at the birth certificate. Her mum's birth certificate.

Her mother had always claimed to be an orphan, given up at birth, so this made sense. Her father had been unknown.

What didn't make sense was the second birth certificate Siobhan now held in her hands. The paper yellowed and weary, a floppiness to it the other one didn't have, as though it had been looked at, handled many times.

The one with a slightly different surname.

It wasn't a big change, but it was a change. Instead of Martin with an 'i', it was Marten, with an 'e'.

Siobhan sat back on her heels, the soft pulse in her throat throbbing until she could hardly swallow.

What had her mum done?

Why did she have two birth certificates?

Was it because her name had been spelt incorrectly originally? Surely, though, if that was the case, the authorities would have revoked the first birth certificate, destroyed it, and she would only have one. Wouldn't they? She had no idea.

Did her birth grandmother use her own name, or did she use the 'unknown' father's name really and that's why she got the spelling wrong?

Siobhan blew out a breath. She leaned her back against the settee for support as she sat on the floor.

She'd been looking for her own birth certificate.

There it was, laid out on the carpet between her stretched-out legs. She smoothed her fingers over it, flattening out the deep creases where it had been folded.

As she studied it next to her mother's two, an odd sensation started. A small flutter in her chest, a quiver.

Anxiety?

Despair?

She was unused to these emotions.

There was something not quite right.

All her life she'd felt secure, loved, safe. Somewhere along the line, the axis on her world had tilted and now she was floundering. A ship lost at sea.

Siobhan picked up her mug of tea and took a sip.

The back door into the garden was wide open and the first cool breeze stroked her warm skin, giving her hope that the heatwave was waning.

She'd checked on all the animals as the soft dawn broke, fed them, changed their water stations, sat out with the chickens in their compound for a while, watching them peck seed from the palm of her hand as she held it out. Their contented squeaks and coos soothed her frantic thoughts. For a while.

Now, those thoughts scrambled around, crazy and wild.

What the hell was going on?

She glanced at the clock. Another hour and she'd return to the hospital to check on her mum. Find out what their next steps were. There was no point running around like a headless chicken. She needed to compose herself. Stay calm.

This situation was beyond her control. The one thing she could control was her own rising panic. And she would. She'd never been given to over-dramatising situations. Maybe she could attribute that to moving house so often when she was a child. It was never done in a panic, never a drama. Her mum simply announced they would be moving the following week due to work commitments, and off they went. No tears, no tantrums, no dramas.

Siobhan drew her knees up and with her big toe poked at one of the birth certificates, staring at it as though it might come alive and slither across the floor, bearing answers.

Something wasn't right. That thought swirled incessantly in her mind.

It only now occurred to her to wonder why they had moved so often in the past. Her mum had held a variety of jobs. Nothing special. Nothing that would warrant her moving every couple of years. She wasn't some senior executive who could name her own salary. Although they had never gone without.

Only when Siobhan was old enough to hold down her own job did her mum seem to settle.

Siobhan curled her legs under her and then, reaching for the certificates, rolled to all fours, much to Beau's delight as he chose that moment to bound inside. He nudged his snout under her long hair to nuzzle her neck while his tail beat out a wild tattoo against the chair opposite, the loud rhythmic thudding breaking the peaceful silence.

She afforded him a quick head rub then snatched up the papers before he trampled them.

Odd.

She held all three in her hands and squinted at them.

The texture of one of her mum's birth certificates felt different. Not just the fact that it was more crumpled and creased than the others, but the quality of the paper. It had a waxiness. And yet...

She sank back on her heels and studied the two versions of her mum's birth certificate and drew in a long, soft breath.

'What the hell...?'

The memory shot back, bright as a reel of film playing.

Concern softened the paramedic's features as she leaned over her mum.

'Do you know your date of birth, please, Mrs Martin?'

Her mum's brow furrowed with confusion and Siobhan wanted to intervene, but the paramedic's attention was fully on her mum. The second paramedic, a tall, thin man with fine blond hair and lined cheeks, as though brackets had been etched deep into parched skin either side of his mouth, wrapped a cuff around her mum's arm and watched the apparatus for the results.

The female paramedic hesitated, her pen poised above the paperwork, one eyebrow elevated in patient enquiry.

'Mrs Martin? Grace?'

*'Miss. Miss Mart-*en.*' In stark contrast, her mum's reaction was waspish and defensive but that could be attributed to the pain she was suffering. 'I've broken my hip, not my brain. I'm not stupid. I was born on 22 June 1963.' She reeled it off with haughty confidence.*

'Nineteen fifty-seven,' I whisper over the woman's green-clad body.

The paramedic dipped her head to look at what seemed to be an iPad in her hand. 'Not 1963, Miss Martin. Perhaps 1957? That would make you sixty-six, wouldn't it?' The woman beamed a broad smile. 'Only just.' She looked at her notes. 'Did you do anything special for your birthday?'

Confusion rippled over her mum's face. 'I'm not fucking sixty-six, you stupid bitch.'

She snatched her arm away, wrenching free of the thin man, and then collapsed, moaning on the ground as she clutched at her hip.

Siobhan hadn't registered the implication of what her mum said at the time, she was more concerned about her condition and delirium from the heat and pain and mortified at her language. She'd never heard her mum use those words before. She barely ever said 'bloody'. It was as though a demon leached from inside her.

Now, though.

She stared down at the two birth certificates until her eyes blurred with unshed tears. At first look, identical.

Then there was the misspelling of the surname.

And once she'd seen it, she couldn't unsee that one minute alteration on the more crinkled paper. So small and in one of the creases, she'd taken this long to realise.

Not 1957 but 1963.

That made her mum six years younger than she claimed. Until the day before yesterday. When the truth had slipped out.

Was she really only sixty, not sixty-six? How could that be?

Siobhan had always secretly thought her mum quite dynamic for her age. Good skin, healthy, much younger-looking than parents of children her own age.

Most women lied about their age, but normally the other way round. They claimed to be younger. Not older.

Why lie?

If her mum had lied, when did that lie begin? And why?

Siobhan tilted her head backwards and stared up at the ceiling.

Crazy. The whole situation was completely crazy.

She glanced at the clock, her mind whirling.

What significance did this have for her?

Never had Siobhan had any uncertainty as to her birthright, but these two revelations gave her cause to doubt.

Was she also adopted, like her mum had been? But why wouldn't her mum have told her? They'd had honest conversations about her mum's adoption.

Or had they?

Why had her mum lied?

If she wasn't her mum's daughter, then who was she?

13

THIRTY-NINE YEARS EARLIER – 1985 – GRACE

Pain sears through my abdomen, a white-hot poker, the likes of which I have never felt in my life. Tears are streaming down my face, but I have no idea what I'm supposed to do. I feel like I'm dying.

It's more painful than having sex for the first time and that was like my body was being ripped apart. Maybe it's because I'd been put off sex by those undesirable old men that would turn up on our doorstep after Mum. Maybe it's because I'd never felt desire for anyone and didn't see the attraction of having sex just for the sake of it.

Of course, Thomas changed my thoughts on that. Tall, lean, dark-haired, green-eyed Thomas. Married Thomas, as I found out three weeks after we'd started having sex. I wondered why he was so keen to come to my little abode. He claimed it was homely. Hmm, apparently not as homely as his four-bedroom, three-bathroom new build.

One of the other engineers, solid, square Geoff, with thinning hair and a weather-roughened face, absolutely devoted to his wife of forty years, happened to mention Thomas's young, beautiful wife about three weeks ago.

It was deliberate, of course. I'm not sure how deep into the relationship he thought I was, but after I called Thomas out about it, we've not seen each other since outside of work. Thomas, it turns out, is a complete arse. Everyone on site now believes I'm a loose woman. I threw myself at him. I must have done. After all, he's a happily married man.

He fails to have mentioned how he'd coaxed himself into my life, bringing me treats in the form of cake every time he visited me on Forge Junction, most probably made by his wife at the weekend, I now realise with mortification. Flowers for the measly little vase I keep on my desk, and alcohol. It was the wine that did it when he turned up on my doorstep one Friday night with a bottle in his fist.

I don't drink. I never have. Maybe because I witnessed how it destroyed James's life. Maybe because I don't like the stale smell of it on those men who would come around looking for my mum.

Whatever the reason, one glass and I was more than a loose woman. My entire body went limp and I knew then why they call it being legless. I've been out with the girls when I worked at Carrefour, but that would be a half a shandy I nursed all night until it was warm and flat.

Wine was different. Much stronger. Somehow, Thomas convinced me into bed with him. That first time, I would put it down to the drink, but thereafter I was just as keen as him. I never would have been had I known the truth.

Naïve does not begin to describe me.

I literally have no one to talk to, no one to consult. Divided into five separate sections, each controlled by a different resident engineer and ingeniously named Contracts One through to Four plus Forge Junction, the entire workforce on the M54 consists entirely of men. Except a much older woman who holds the same position as I do on Contract One, the next contract along from us, but I've only ever met her twice, once at the Christmas party. That was when I met Thomas too. He's also an engineer on Contract One, but up until recently was a frequent visitor to Forge Junction, where I work. He's rarely seen these days.

I would have called it love at first sight in my naïveté. For him, it was lust. Pure unadulterated lust. Possibly also the fact that his wife was just about to give birth and maybe was not so forthcoming on the sex front. Or that's what the guys on site whispered behind their hands once they'd got wind of the fact that I'd slept with him. Of course, I didn't know that little snippet at the time.

I, on the other hand, was like a Duracell bunny on hormones. Without anyone to talk to about my relationship, I believed full enthusiasm was the way forward. I loved him, wholeheartedly, and there was no one to consult. No one I could trust to pour my heart out to.

At least, there wasn't once James disappeared from the stairwell.

Since I left college, I've not really kept in contact with the girls from my course. I mean, how would I explain that I am – officially – six years older than they originally thought? I could hardly put myself in the position where I could be tripped up.

Thomas was incredulous when he realised I was a *twenty-five-year-old* virgin. In fact, I think that was the attraction. The challenge.

On my hands and knees now, tears streaming down my face, I crawl towards the door. If only I can open it, I can call for help. Surely someone in the tenement block will hear me.

Not James. He's been gone since the first morning after Thomas stayed. I worry that he took umbrage. Not that we have anything like that kind of relationship. That would be odd. But we look after each other. Keep a watchful eye out.

I don't know if it's connected, but I can only assume it is.

James has always been in my life, it seems.

Not now.

Not when I need him the most.

I reach up, the door handle sways in my vision, two, possibly three images as everything blurs, my hand grasping for it.

Sick scalds the back of my throat and my whole left side spasms so I collapse on the floor and curl into a foetal position. I think it's my voice screaming out James's name, but I know he's not there. I know he won't rescue me. But he's the only one I trust. The one person I know will be there for me.

Only he isn't.

It's all my fault.

Hot fluid leaks from between my thighs and I reach down. My hand comes away streaked in thick, dark blood and I retch again, this time spewing the contents of my stomach up the front door.

As I watch, as if from afar, lumps of sick dribble down the white-painted door, my mind idly twirls through obscure thoughts. Like the last time I had a period.

It's been ages. I can't even remember.

There's a warm curl of embarrassment as my whole left side spasms again. Oh my God. I'm having a late period. That's all.

I push back from the door, mortified that I've been screeching like a banshee for help when it's just a very painful, late period.

All I can think is at least it's Saturday and I don't have to go into work until Monday, so I have two days to curl up with a hot water bottle and plenty of paracetamol.

I roll over until I'm on my knees. My forehead rests on the cool tiled floor next to the splatter of sick and I lean heavily on my forearms, puffing out in short, sharp breaths to stop my head spinning. If only I can get up and reach some paracetamol it will be okay. It's really only a very bad period. A period like I've never had in my life.

I try to push up onto my hands and the movement sends my

abdomen into convulsions, so I collapse back onto the floor, curling so tight into a ball. The pain tears through me but this time I give a guttural groan. I'm consumed with the most overwhelming urge to bear down.

Sobs break from my lips.

'Grace?'

Is it my imagination, or is someone calling my name?

'Grace?'

That one word is filled with concern.

I can barely see through the tears blurring my vision, but someone is peering through the letterbox at me.

'Grace.' The voice is low and rough with urgency.

His eyes meet mine. Dark and shadowed, pain emanating from them.

'Grace. You need to let me in.'

'James.'

Who knew he'd come back?

I reach out an arm, stretching towards him, but I have no strength left and it flops back down onto the thin carpet under me.

My teeth clench, jaw-breakingly hard, and I start to shudder, spasm, cramp.

'Can you move back from the door, Grace? I need you to move back.'

I hear his voice as if from a great distance and I know that I am dying.

'Grace.' That one word is filled with pained urgency. The words echo through the hallway and bounce off the walls. I try to understand, but I can't.

The door explodes inwards and my body jerks as it hits my feet and bounces back off.

I'm aware of others behind James, but it's him I concentrate on.

'I'm bleeding.' I raise my blood-stained hand and he catches it in both of his, falling to his knees beside me. There's no longer any shame that it may just be a heavy period. It is more than that. My body clenches hard and I groan.

'Hold on, love. The ambulance is here.'

The sound of it comes faint and distant as James's face, so close to mine, fades from my vision.

'Love,' he called me.

He's never called me love before.

It must be serious.

I'm going to die.

14

THIRTY-NINE YEARS EARLIER – 1985 – GRACE

My eyes are sticky as I blink them open.

From the bottom of the bed with crisp white sheets, an old man stares at me over the top of half-moon glasses. His denim-blue eyes are hard, disapproval etched into his features. Although that could just be my imagination.

He holds a clipboard in one hand and glances down at it. His nostrils flare at the whitened edges of his long nose and his mouth tightens before he looks up.

'Ah.' He doesn't seem to be addressing me in his officious tone. 'It looks like *Miss* Martin has decided to join us at last.'

I try to shift on the narrow cot of a bed, to pull myself up, but pain lances through my left side, up under my shoulder, and I grunt.

Several younger faces stare at me with undisguised curiosity.

The man hands over the clipboard with disdain to a younger man in a white doctor's coat next to him as a nurse hovers behind.

'Jones, without your usual stuttering, articulate to the others in your pitiful group what you believe from the notes is wrong with this young woman.'

'Yes, Mr Powell.'

'Sir. You call me sir.'

Terror grabs at my throat as the realisation of where I am hits me.

I'm in hospital.

From the look on Mr Powell's face, I have been judged and left wanting.

Jones steps forward.

'Get on with it, man, I don't have all day,' the consultant hisses out.

Words stumble from the young man's lips. 'Th... th... th...'

'This! This!' Mr Powell interjects, face filled with impatient fury.

'Thhhhh, this young, young woman presented yes... yesterday with, with abdominal pains. She was, was brought in through the cas... cas... casualty depart... ment.'

A couple of the others, I can only assume student doctors, snicker like cats at a window and I wonder if it's through embarrassment for poor young Jones who can't be any older than me, or unkindness for his affliction.

His face reddens as he continues.

'On, on presentation, Miss Martin appeared initially to be having a mis... miscarriage.'

My skin flashes cold.

A miscarriage?

How can that be?

I haven't had sex since I broke up with Thomas over two months ago.

I swallow. My sex education was at best basic. I know what a period is and I know what causes pregnancy. It seems that's all I need to know. Well, perhaps how not to get pregnant would have been advantageous. Thomas said he'd take care of all of that.

I squeeze my eyes closed, trying to block out the faces, the words, the truth.

I can't even remember the last time I had a period. I don't think I've had one since Thomas and I first started making love.

Having sex.

If it was love, he would be by my side now, supporting me. Comforting me. But it isn't love and the realisation that he never gave a damn sends a sharp pain lancing through me.

Using a condom was too uncomfortable for me, too painful, so Thomas had said it would be okay. He would pull out. He did. Most of the time.

I know I should have gone to my GP, or even the Family Planning Clinic, but that's something I wanted to avoid after all the humiliation with my mum insisting I go on the pill. Despite the amount of male visitors she had, I still never had much of a clue as to what they got up to. There was a lot of laughter and grunting, which I tried to block out by putting my head under a pillow. I'm not married, not even engaged. I don't think a GP would look on me very favourably. I'm not even registered with a practice, I don't think. Not since my mum disappeared. I never saw the need.

Until now.

I swallow my tears and want to ask the question, 'Have I lost my baby?'

Jones's voice fades back in. 'On further investigation, Miss... Miss Martin evidently had something far more serious.'

I know my voice was little above a whisper, but I am sure they heard. Did they choose to ignore my question?

'Severe,' Mr Powell interjects and makes Jones's stammer even more pronounced.

'It, it, it...' He blew out a breath, started again. 'Miss Martin... On further investigation it became evident from the sudden, severe abdominal pains down her left side, dizziness, vomiting and even pains under her shoulder blades…'

'And bleeding. Vast amounts of bleeding, young Jones.' Mr Powell peered over his glasses at the young man again, his voice laced with contempt. 'That blood from the patient's uterus was possibly the biggest pointer you could have.'

Jones dipped his head and blushed an even deeper crimson.

I want to wriggle but I'm not sure I want that obnoxious man's attention on me.

It seems I earn it anyway.

'Sadly—' he scans the faces of the young, eager-to-learn student doctors in front of him '—this is the kind of hard lesson promiscuous young women have coming to them when they decide to have sex out of wedlock.'

Heat roars up my neck and floods my face. My eyes burn as I look at him. I've dealt with workmen, engineers, surveyors and directors, all male and none of whom have ever spoken to me with disrespect.

My voice when it comes out is gravelly but loud enough for the onlookers to hear.

'Are you saying, Mr Powell, that had I been married, I would not have suffered a miscarriage? That somehow my womb would have known the difference between me being married or single?'

I manage to shuffle up onto one elbow and look him in the eye. I've never been cowed in my life, I'm not about to be now, even if this man did save it. It doesn't make him God, and if it did, I'm pretty convinced God would give more empathy.

Horrified gasps come from the students and the nurse's eyes fly wide as she covers her mouth with her hand. Evidently, people never speak back to Mr Powell. Not women recovering in one of his hospital beds, in any case. I might be naïve and shy, but I'm used to speaking with men from a business angle. I've become adept at it.

Straight talking. It was very different from the way I had spoken to the women I was in charge of in the hypermarket.

Mr Powell does not gasp. He does not cover his mouth. He does not flinch. The change comes in his laser-sharp gaze as it clashes with mine.

'No, Miss Martin. What I can assure you of, though, is that your promiscuity has brought upon you the devastating fact that should you in the future decide to get married and have babies, you will not be able to. Not only have you lost one vital fallopian tube to an ectopic pregnancy from which, if it had not been for me performing life-saving laparoscopic surgery, you would have died—' he pauses and his lips twist with distaste '—but also the raging gonorrhoea you are infected with has resulted in pelvic inflammatory disease, finishing off any further hopes of fertility for you in the future.'

Now I *do* gasp at his ferocious attack on me.

I look around at my audience, none of whom will meet my eyes, except for the nurse beside Mr Powell, whose own eyes are filled with tears. Tears of sympathy, I suspect, for the cruel, harsh delivery of my future prospects.

I flop back and raise a hand to my sweat-damped forehead, and although I am broken, I'm not beaten yet.

'I'm not promiscuous,' I croak out. 'I've only ever been with one man. I loved him.' My voice warbles on the last three pathetic words.

Mr Powell's nostrils are so stretched, his mouth tight with ill-contained fury, that I wonder for one moment if he is about to fling the clipboard at me.

'That may be what you say, it's not for me to judge, young lady.'

He hands the clipboard back to Jones once more, almost making him double over as it catches the young man in the stomach, and he turns to walk away.

I find my voice again.

'But you did judge, Mr Powell.' I'm not about to address him as sir; he hasn't earned that respect in my opinion. 'What could you possibly know of my life? You *did* judge.'

There is silence as he stalks away, followed in quick succession by his panicked minions.

Everyone departs but the young nurse, blonde hair swept up into a neat bun, tucked under a smart white nursing cap.

She steps forward, huge brown eyes glistening with concern.

'I'm so sorry.' Her voice is barely a whisper. She gives a quick glance to ensure no one else can hear her. 'He's no right to speak to you like that. If Matron had been here, she would have taken him to one side and had a word.' She glances in his direction again as he punches through the swing doors at the far end of the ward, fury in every jerky move he makes.

'He's really annoyed that you had the gall to answer him back. He's used to commanding total respect.'

I make a humming noise in the back of my throat. He didn't command with respect, he commanded with an iron fist and utter terror invoked by unfairly wielding power from a godlike position no single person should be entitled to.

'It's not that I don't respect people in authority. I don't respect people who have no respect to give.'

I see the agreement in her expression as she holds her hand out, offering me a glass of water and then a small white cup with my name on.

'What's that?'

'Your medication.'

'Yes, but what?'

She glances at the side of the cup with what appears to be a list of items written in black pen and flushes. 'There're antibiotics, two different types for the infection.' She rattles the cup. 'And paracetamol for the temperature and pain.'

'So, I really do have gonorrhoea?'

She gave a swift nod. 'Would you like me to ask Sister to speak with you about it?'

'What can she say?'

'She can give you advice going forward.'

I let out a bitter laugh. 'You mean tell me not to have promiscuous, unprotected sex with strangers?'

But he wasn't a stranger. I'd thought we were in love, that we had a future together, that when he stayed over at my flat, it was to get away from his parents' house. He'd convinced me he'd moved in with them to take care of them.

She says nothing.

'It wasn't a stranger. I was in love with him.' The bastard.

Not any longer, I'm not.

She's silent and in her own way, I feel her judgement too.

I throw the concoction of tablets to the back of my throat and swiftly swallow the entire contents of the glass of water.

Tears are welling up in me again.

The irony of me judging my mum for all the men she ever 'entertained', and yet to my knowledge she was never hurt by one of them, never caught anything nasty from anyone, never fell in love.

Well, I won't fall in love again. Not that kind of love, in any case. I'll make sure of that.

It's not just self-pity that rises inside, but a roaring deafening fury at the unfairness of the whole situation because just as I hand my empty cup back to the silent nurse, Thomas strolls into the ward. In his arms, he carries a huge bouquet of flowers and wears a wide, delighted grin across his face.

For one crazed moment, I hold my breath.

And watch.

Has he come to see me? Has he heard I'm in hospital?

Hope surges until my heart threatens to explode and every thought of never falling in love again flies out the window of this airless ward.

I hitch myself upright in bed, my hand automatically going to my forehead to push back a stray lock of hair. A weak smile hovers over my lips and the idea that he may have heard of my predicament fizzles in my head.

Thomas does not see me.

He makes his way to the slight woman in the bed nearest the door and leans down to take her and the newborn baby she cradles into his gentle embrace.

A part of me dies inside.

15

PRESENT DAY – MONDAY, 1 JULY 2024, 2.15 P.M. – SIOBHAN

It seemed like there was no point to Siobhan sitting at the side of her mum's bed, simply waiting for the woman to wake up and garble a load of absolutely unintelligible words, not least all the foul language she'd never heard before from her mum.

'I fucking hate hospitals.'

'I fucking hate doctors, keep them away from me. Fuckers.'

'I want to go home. Fuck this!'

Siobhan couldn't remember her mum ever swearing. Where had it come from? She was like a different woman. Wild and aggressive. Demented. Was this truly what confusion did to a person?

How had her mum become so ill so fast?

Siobhan surged to her feet as medics in green gowns entered the room, all of them wearing face masks which had been dropped to hang around their necks.

'What's happening?'

A nurse in blue scrubs touched Siobhan on the arm. 'We're taking your mum down to theatre right now.'

'I was told they couldn't operate until...'

The nurse bustled forward as they wheeled in a second bed and prepared to transfer Siobhan's mum over. 'Apparently, they have the results of the scan, and Mr Carmichael is going to operate immediately. He's transferred her to his emergency list.' She raised her head and spoke to the other three people in scrubs who'd entered with her. 'On three. One, two, three.'

They lifted her mum, sheets and all, onto a narrower trolley bed and hustled out with maximum efficiency and minimum fuss.

The nurse remained behind.

She gave Siobhan a sympathetic smile. 'Mr Carmichael will update you as soon as possible, but for now, why don't you go home and have a rest?' She stroked her hand down Siobhan's arm and gave it a comforting squeeze. 'You're going to need all the strength you can get over the next few weeks. Your mum is going to need you, so take the opportunity while you can to prepare yourself.'

Prepare herself? For what, exactly?

Tears welled behind Siobhan's eyes. 'I don't know what to do.' She flicked her hand toward the departing group she could see waiting for the lift doors to open before wheeling her mum's trolley inside.

'Go home. That's what you should do. There is no need for you to stay here for the next few hours. She's going to be in surgery for at least two hours, as you know it's a little more complex than usual, and then in recovery probably until this evening. My advice is take this time because you will be needed.'

Siobhan opened her mouth to speak, but the nurse continued. 'We'll ring you as soon as she's out of surgery, but you probably won't need to come back here tonight.'

Siobhan fumbled with her phone and handbag, swiping up the carrier bag of clothes she'd brought for her mum that wouldn't yet be needed.

She'd take them home and find a small case on Amazon with next-day delivery, so it didn't look so tacky bringing a carrier bag in.

She glanced through the ward as she passed by. Who was she kidding? No one cared how people brought belongings in as long as they brought them.

There was nothing she could do.

Her mum's fate was in the hands of the surgeon now.

16

THIRTY-NINE YEARS EARLIER – 1985 – GRACE

I hate doctors. I know I might be tarring them all with the same brush, but he was an unfeeling bastard. A fucking bastard.

There's a certain guilty pleasure in thinking those words, even if I don't say them out loud. It's good to have them in my mind. I've never been one to swear, and the boys at work rarely do so in front of me. The resident engineer won't allow it. He's quite old-fashioned and has a daughter the same age as me. Or so he thinks. I've seen photographs and I must say, I do mature up well, especially if I use that lovely new foundation I've bought and cover those freckles again. Somehow freckles give me the appearance of looking younger.

He may seem nice, but he's invited me over to his static caravan where he lives during the week a couple of times, and there's something I'm a little wary of about the way he asks. So far, I've been able to decline.

If word reaches him though about Thomas, I wonder if he'll make it awkward for me at work. It's unlikely the boys have told him. I don't think he listens to their gossip, but if he did, would he apply more pressure on me to come and have dinner with him? Just the two of us.

I don't think so but I'm not counting on it.

I will never trust another man ever again.

No one.

Except James.

James is the one who brought me home and for the first time since I've known him, he's come into his own flat. He's given me privacy to change into my pyjamas and slip into bed before he brings me a cup of tea.

The only reason they allowed me out of hospital was because he volunteered to stay with me for the next few days and ensure my antibiotics, which I have to take for the next seven days at least, are administered properly. As though I'm incapable of doing that myself. Me, being a poor, weak female.

I've no idea whether he just said that in order to get me out of there because when he came to visit, he looked like a caged animal himself.

I cruise my gaze over the scarring on his neck and wonder how much of his body is affected by it. He is incredibly brave. Oh, I know the rumours, but I don't mean his time as a soldier, I mean entering that hospital today to bring me home. The smells, the sounds. I never want to go back. How must he feel?

'Was it bad?'

He looks at me a long moment before he replies. 'Hell on earth.' His lips lift in a crooked line as though he's not sure whether to smile or not.

I drop my gaze. I've been in a week and I don't ever want to see the inside of a hospital again.

All I want is to curl up in my own bed and sleep until I feel better.

I don't think James is so keen. It's a big responsibility. One he's not used to.

He might be uncomfortable staying indoors, a roof over his head and a sofa to lie on. If he chooses not to lie on the floor.

My faith in him is not bullet-proof, but pretty strong. He's not going to take my drugs. He's an alcoholic, not a druggie.

I think of my purse containing £23.68 and my building society book with my entire life savings. I've scrimped, every month putting £200 into that account since I opened it. With my new job and my shiny new identification, I felt the need to save in case I'm ever thrown out of the flat. I will never be without money again. That's a promise I made myself the day my mum deserted me.

I need three months' rent up front as a deposit. I have that now. I hope.

I tug the covers up under my chin and start to drift off, the tea going cold on my bedside table.

I wonder what James thinks of the changes I've made to his flat. The homeliness I have given it.

It might be self-centred of me, but a fleeting thought passes through my drugged-up mind that he may possibly want to claim it back.

It's not something I'm willing to think about right now. My eyes flutter closed, and I relax, secure in the fact that I'm home. I'm safe.

For all the damage people have caused me – the vile consultant, Thomas, my own mum – the flickering flame of hope and ambition still flutters in my chest, resisting the pressure to gutter out.

Pain arcs through my abdomen and I curl into a ball beneath my covers as a cold sweat breaks out and my teeth chatter in staccato rhythm that I can't control. Febrile convulsions the nurse had called it. When my temperature bolts upwards.

The door edges open and James slides into the room, quiet as a ghost. In his hand is a small white pot, the same as the nurse had held out to me numerous times over the past seven days while I was in hospital.

They only released me because I'd stopped convulsing.

Yet, here I am, convulsing again. I put it down to the effort it took me to get from the hospital to home in a taxi that rocked and rolled until I felt sick and dizzy, and then, supported by James, up the concrete tenement stairs because the bloody lift was out of order, yet again.

James kneels on the floor beside my bed. I think he has far too much respect to sit on the edge of the bed.

'I just read your discharge papers and you should have had your meds before you left the hospital. I think you're a couple of hours overdue.'

My teeth chatter as I reach out from under the covers with a shaky hand.

Instead of handing the pot to me, James slips his arm under my shoulders and raises me with such tenderness, as though I was precious china.

I grunt with pain as he tips the contents of the little white pot between my stiff lips and I feel several tablets slip onto my tongue.

The bitter taste has me screwing up my face so much that I don't even see the cup of now tepid tea that he offers me until it's almost pressing against my mouth.

'Drink it all, you need to keep your fluids up. If you dehydrate, you'll be back in hospital, and you don't want that.'

I wrinkle my nose but manage to stop my teeth rattling long enough to gulp down most of the tea. It's surprisingly good, especially after the weak-as-dishwater tea they served in the hospital.

'I thought the milk would be off.'

'It was. I bought fresh.'

'Thank you.'

A man of few words, he gently lowers my head back to the pillow and smooths a cool hand over my burning brow and then rests back on his heels at my bedside.

A spasm shudders through me and I grit my teeth before I can speak again.

'Everyone is going to know at work...'

Shame floods me because I know if he's read my hospital notes then he will have seen the sick note my consultant wrote, stating that I had been admitted to hospital due to ectopic pregnancy, inflammatory disease and gonorrhoea.

My eyes fill with tears. 'All those men. They're going to know I have the clap. They're going to think I'm a right tramp, and I'm not.'

I know technically this kind of medical information isn't supposed to be bandied around, but certainly when Chris Lupin had his vasectomy everyone on site knew about it. The teasing he was subjected to. Imagine when they find out I have the clap! Being the only female on site, it's going to be hell. I can just imagine the propositions I'll get, because some of them won't give a damn about getting the clap if they can have a bit on the side. Evidently, Thomas didn't care. He caught it from somewhere and passed it on.

'I might lose my job.' The words break on a soft sob. I love my job. It was the biggest break I've ever been given and there's no way I'll get another if I get sacked now. I'll be back to pushing trollies if I'm lucky.

My pain is reflected in his eyes, but James gives a slow nod. 'Leave it with me.' He runs a critical gaze over my slight body beneath the covers. I've probably lost loads of weight just in that short time in hospital. The food was good enough, but I barely had an appetite.

When his gaze settles back on mine, he gives a wry smile. 'I think you need another week off work, and appendicitis would sound better. Don't you agree?'

My attention is consumed with him, and I recall the perfect replica of my birth certificate and national insurance card.

My lips bow up in a wobbly smile to reflect his.

'Appendicitis would be perfect.'

17

PRESENT DAY – TUESDAY, 2 JULY 2024, 3.15 P.M. – SIOBHAN

Siobhan linked her fingers together tight enough to break them as she stared at the frail-looking woman in the hospital bed. Devoid of all colour, she was almost as pale as the pillow she rested her head on, barely recognisable as Siobhan's mum.

'We may just have performed a miracle,' the surgeon told her as he stripped off his protective hat and mask and dumped it in the relevant bin. 'I'm not saying your mother won't need to have further treatment, but we detected on the scan what appeared to be one large tumour formed over her hip bone, which was the cause of the breakage. On further investigation, we discovered that there doesn't appear to be any further evidence of tumours. So, on removing the affected hip, we may also have removed the cancer in its entirety.'

Heat raced over Siobhan's skin. It couldn't be. They couldn't be lucky enough for that to be the case.

'Before we get over-excited...'

But he already looked thrilled at the prospect of curing this woman.

'We believe your mother has chondrosarcoma, which is a tumour that grows either on or in the bone. Her tumour appears to have grown inside her hip. Initially, we thought it might be metastasised cancer from a tumour elsewhere, but when we discovered it was the primary, we wanted to act fast and remove it to give any cancerous cells less chance of escaping.'

He ran a long-fingered, slender hand over a face that was rapidly turning weary and sighed. Siobhan imagined he'd only just finished his operating day and was now catching up on his follow-up rounds.

'We'll give her a scan and more blood tests over the next few days when the team get back together and make a decision as to whether she'll need further treatment such as chemotherapy or radiotherapy. I think that's a step that can wait. We don't have to rush it. She needs recovery time from the operation first.'

He leaned on the doorframe and crossed his arms over his chest. 'Your mother may just have had a lucky break... literally. It does help that she's incredibly healthy for her age. I would have put her at several years younger, taking into account her physical well-being, other than the obvious broken hip. Her kidney functions are that of a much younger woman, taking into account how fast they recovered. Her bones are remarkably good other than in that affected hip. Tumours aren't caused by age, though.'

He paused.

Siobhan's face flamed even more wildly and she dropped her gaze from his.

Should she tell him that her mum was possibly several years younger than he was led to believe?

She raised her head again. 'I hope my skin is as good as my mum's when I reach her age.'

A smile stretched over his tired face to make him appear younger.

'Beautiful skin is genetic. Nothing to do with all those expensive products women apply. My wife has incredible skin. Sadly, my mother does not. We only hope that our three daughters are genetically predisposed to their mother's side of the family.'

Siobhan's mouth dropped open.

He almost shook himself as he realised how much he was revealing, probably due to exhaustion.

Siobhan's mouth hadn't dropped open so much because he'd told her his family secret, but because what he said held a truth that suddenly hit her hard. She hadn't inherited any of her mum's genetic make-up. Or certainly, it didn't appear so.

His voice faded back into her consciousness... 'We'll update you once we have further information.'

He backed out the door, leaving it open as he went. Siobhan came to her feet and followed him. She poked her head out of the doorway, looking first one way and then the next only to see nurses bustling through the wards.

She wasn't sure how long it would be until another nurse came to check her mum's obs, but as soon as she sat down in the large wing-back chair next to her bed, she delved into her handbag and plucked out the small white package that had been in her parcel box from the day before. With no time to open it as she dashed to the hospital, Siobhan had stuffed it into her bag and almost forgotten about it during the frenetic moments as her mum was wheeled back through from recovery.

With a long glance at her mum to check she was still sleeping comfortably, Siobhan coaxed open the small white box, about the size of a book, with unsteady hands.

She took her time, reading each section of the instructions on the DNA testing kit, her eyes getting bigger and bigger.

She had no idea. None.

Was it truly this easy?

You spat into this tube, sent it away and they identified you, sending the results to your email inbox?

How strange that they didn't require any proof of who you were. You didn't have to supply a birth certificate, a passport, an NI number... Nothing.

Surely anyone could send one of these away for anyone else... All provided you could persuade them to spit into a tube.

She sat back, peeled the protective layer off the small box that contained the tube to spit into and sighed.

Was she really going to do this?

She ran one finger down the length of the tube.

The feeling of disloyalty squeezed at her chest and she allowed the flap of cellophane to flop back over it.

She couldn't do it. Her actions in ordering the DNA testing kit had been born of panic and desperation. She was her mother's daughter. She knew she was. There was no need to prove it. Was there?

She drew back the cellophane once more and took out the tube to study it. Simple. She could spit into there and send it away and no one would be any the wiser. Only she would know.

A muffled sound came from the bed as her mum moved, the agonised groan became louder, more insistent.

Siobhan leapt to her feet and leaned over her mum, placing the tube on the bedsheet.

She cupped her mum's cheek in her hand.

Eyes tightly closed, her mum gagged.

Siobhan snatched up the call bell and pressed it. 'Mum, Mum! Are you okay?' She had no idea what to do. How to help her.

Panic put a stranglehold on her as a nurse opened the door and popped her head around.

'My mum!' Siobhan gave a wild wave towards her mum.

Almost tempted to tell the woman to get a move on, Siobhan held her tongue as the nurse seemed to glide across the room without any speed while her mum retched.

'I think she's going to be sick.'

The nurse took hold of her mum's wrist, again with so little haste Siobhan ground her teeth together. Couldn't she just hurry up? There was something wrong with her mum. Didn't they understand?

'Hello, Grace, are you okay?'

Of course she wasn't. Her mum let out a tortured grunt which could have been a 'no'.

'Can you do something to help her, please?' Siobhan tagged the 'please' on to stop herself from swearing at the nurse. Come on, come on. Do something!

'It's not unusual after anaesthetic. There's nothing in her stomach to sick up, in any case. She was nil by mouth for some time before her operation.' She looked at Siobhan with a reassuring smile. 'We should have had a sick bowl in here, but they probably thought she was fine when they discharged her from the recovery suite. I'll just go and get one, but there will be nothing more than saliva in her mouth.'

As she reached the door, she turned. 'I know you're anxious, but your mum is as well as can be expected. It's horrible to see your loved one in pain and distress, but the best thing for her is for you to remain calm.'

Siobhan realised in that one moment that the nurse wasn't slow. She was serene, observant. Every move she'd made had been calculated, controlled. Reassuring. She was doing her job, something she evidently carried out day in, day out. If she charged around like a headless chicken, as Siobhan initially wanted her to do, then she'd have run herself into the ground in the first two hours of her overly long shift. If the nurse panicked, how could she instil faith in the relatives?

Siobhan's mum gagged again as the nurse stepped into the hallway.

'I'll take her obs in a moment as well. I'll just grab the equipment. Don't you worry yourself, we'll be keeping a close eye on her.'

She barely heard anything beyond the word 'saliva' as the nurse slipped quietly away.

Not entirely sure what compelled her to do it, Siobhan stepped close to her mum and uncurled her fingers from around the small tube she held in her hand.

She glanced at the open doorway and heard nothing in the hall, just the distant clatter of the food trolley arriving further along. She doubted her mum would be up to any food yet, not with feeling so nauseous.

Her mum continued to swallow and swallow, her mouth evidently full of spit.

Without hesitation, Siobhan clawed the lid from the tube and thrust it towards her mum. 'Here you go.' She held it carefully under her mum's mouth, her fingers shaking slightly as she cast a guilty look over her shoulder. 'Spit in here, Grace.' She deliberately didn't call her 'Mum' in case she threw another tantrum in her confusion. She simply wanted to get this done as quickly as possible.

Her mum obeyed. Compliant. Obedient. So different from the day before as she leaned her head weakly to one side and dribbled spit from lips that barely opened.

Siobhan's own stomach protested as she tilted the tube away from her so saliva drizzled down the inside of it to pool in a sticky glut in the bottom. The instructions had said not to brush your teeth beforehand. Certainly, her mum had not done that, for a couple of days, Siobhan hazarded a guess. She would help her once her mum had stopped retching.

She'd also get the flannel out of the small bag she'd brought along and give her mum a good wash. Her mum was a proud woman. If she was in her right mind, she'd hate to think that she was sweaty and unkempt.

As her mum spasmed once more, Siobhan whipped her hand away because, despite the nurse's reassurances, she wasn't entirely sure her mum wouldn't spew up on her.

Wrinkling her nose, Siobhan screwed the lid back on the tube and tucked it into her pocket, turning just as the nurse slipped back into the room with monitors and equipment on wheels trundling behind her.

Her heart beat hard enough to send her dizzy.

Guilt riddled her. What had she done? It felt so wrong, and yet instinct had taken over before she could stop herself.

The nurse shot her a wide smile as she handed over the cardboard bowl. 'Just hold that under your mum's chin while I set this up if you don't mind.' She smiled again. 'Sorry, we're a little short-handed today. We've had several off with Covid this week, there seems to be another surge of it. Technically, we can still come in, but this is such a high-risk ward, we prefer not to if we are ill.'

She gave a small cough and Siobhan wondered whether she was also symptomatic or if it was simply the thought of Covid, or even in response to her mum starting to choke again.

'Here you go.' Siobhan slid the bowl under her mum's chin as instructed.

'I don't want it. Take it away.' Her mum slapped a loose hand at the bowl.

Siobhan shot a doubtful look at the nurse, who shrugged.

'She probably doesn't need it.'

The woman's calmness struck her as impressive. Obviously experienced, this to her wasn't a high-priority situation. Her patient was in no danger. Siobhan regretted her earlier judgement and the desire to scream at the woman to get a move on. There was no need. She was in control.

As the nurse strapped a cuff around her mum's forearm, she glanced at Siobhan.

'Why don't you sit down? You're looking a little peaky yourself. There's a cup of water there for your mum, but she has no need of it yet. I'll get a fresh one for her in a minute. You take some small sips.' She gave a quick smile. 'I could do without you fainting on me.'

Without protest, Siobhan reached for the plastic cup of water and sank into the chair beside the bed, on the opposite side to the nurse. She took a sip and tipped her head back, her racing heart refusing to slow down, her head spinning. Was that what guilt did to you?

'I maybe haven't drunk enough water. Thank you.'

'Ah, it's easy enough to dehydrate in this weather. We'll be keeping a close eye on your mum to make sure she drinks enough, but there's not much point until she stops heaving. In the meanwhile, she's still hooked up to her drip.'

Siobhan closed her eyes. She wasn't sure if it was dehydration or the rush of adrenaline at almost getting caught.

What the hell had she done?

By her actions, she'd already turned the corner and was heading down the wrong road.

Guilt warred with curiosity and the curiosity won out.

She had her mum's DNA sample in her pocket.

Why waste it?

Besides the raging disloyalty, Siobhan felt the pull of needing to know the truth. To find the answer to a question only she was asking.

Why would her mum make such a peculiar statement? Surely, even confused, no one would ever deny the existence of their offspring.

Siobhan rolled her head to one side to watch the nurse

performing her duties, but black spots exploded behind her eyes like mini fireworks. Her limbs went weak and she let out a small moan.

The nurse trailed an assessing look over her while she finished with her mum, and the cold sweat of conscience clawed its way up Siobhan's neck and into her face. Clammy cheeks heated up, but she hadn't the energy to raise her hand and wipe the sweat away.

The nurse made her way around the bed and circled Siobhan's wrist with ice-cold fingers.

Siobhan drew in a breath. Held it.

'Breathe. Nice and slow.' The nurse checked a small clock, and she pressed fingers into Siobhan's pulse. 'You're having a little panic attack. Your pulse is a bit high. Just stay there.'

Siobhan imagined the tube burning a hole in her pocket and dropping at the nurse's feet.

'Slow and steady.' The nurse clipped something onto Siobhan's middle finger and then perched her bottom on the bed so she was facing her. She reached out and took Siobhan's mum's hand into hers. 'You all right, Grace?' She gave it a light squeeze and Siobhan moved her head so she could watch her mum.

'Looks like your daughter is just having a little panic, no need to worry.'

'Shh...' Her mum's voice was a husky whisper. 'Siobhan...'

Siobhan's heart sang as tears sprang to her eyes. Her mum recognised her. She knew who she was.

She offered up a wobbly smile as her vision blurred. 'She knows me. She knows who I am.'

The nurse's brow twitched in confusion for a split second before smoothing out.

Siobhan kept her attention on her mum as she explained. 'After her accident, she didn't recognise me.' She stared at her mum. 'You said I wasn't your daughter, Mum, that you couldn't have children.'

There was a slight tightening of her mum's mouth, nothing so obvious that anyone not looking closely would notice, and the nurse's attention was currently on Siobhan.

Siobhan wanted to hear the denial from her mum's lips, but she remained silent, closing her eyes instead so she broke contact.

'The other nurse said she had post-operative confusion.'

'Delirium,' the nurse corrected as she took the clip from Siobhan's finger. 'Your pulse rate is a bit high, but it's not surprising under the circumstances. Make sure you look after yourself. Keep well hydrated.'

She pushed herself away from the bed and started to tidy the equipment. 'I'm going to leave this in here. We'll be checking your mum regularly, so don't worry.'

'Can I give her a bit of a wash?'

The nurse's brows rose as her eyes widened. 'Your mum had a full bed bath first thing this morning when we came on shift. We do it ourselves as part of our infection control as she's still quite poorly and the effects of the anaesthetic are still in her system. But your mum managed to wash her face and neck herself, didn't you, Grace?'

Her mum nodded, eyes dull in their deep sockets, studying Siobhan as though she wasn't quite sure she knew who she was. Perhaps the confusion came and went.

Siobhan smiled, hoping that it looked reassuring. 'That's nice, Mum. I brought you a toothbrush and toothpaste.'

Her mum's brow crinkled. 'You already did my teeth, you made me spit out.' Her tone was slightly accusatory, as though she suspected Siobhan had done something wrong. Guilt surged to the surface until Siobhan's skin tingled.

She'd never told her mum a lie, not in her memory at least, not even a white lie. They had a wonderful relationship.

Her mum had always respected her wishes, her need for privacy from time to time, and expected the same in return. It had worked, which was why they were both so close.

Which was why the guilt gnawed at her now.

Siobhan met the nurse's eyes and gave an imperceptible shrug and a quick raise of one eyebrow as though she had no idea what her mum was talking about and the heat of deceit rose again.

The nurse turned to her mum and leaned over her. 'No worries, Grace, I think your daughter was just trying to help you while you were having a little coughing fit. We thought you were going to be sick.'

'I am sick. Sick of this. When can I go home?'

She'd lost her earlier aggression and her pitiful plea tugged at Siobhan's heart.

'Not today, Grace.' The nurse leaned in. 'Are you in pain? You're allowed some medication now, if you want.'

'I hate hospitals.'

To Siobhan's knowledge, her mum had never been in hospital, except possibly to give birth to her. If indeed that was the case.

'I know.' The nurse smiled as she bustled to the door. 'Me, too.' She gave a quick wink and pulled the door open. 'I'll be back in a minute with some painkillers, there's no need for you to suffer unnecessarily.'

When Siobhan turned back to her mum, the other woman stared at her with narrowed eyes. 'What did you do?'

Siobhan's breath stuttered in her throat at the astute accusation in her mum's gaze.

'Nothing, Mum.'

Silence hovered in the room. Her mum gave a slight head tilt. She pressed her lips together in a straight line of disappointment. Siobhan's heartbeat throbbed in her ears.

Her mum licked her lips and one dry word crackled from them.

'Liar.'

18

THIRTY-FIVE YEARS EARLIER – 1989 – GRACE

If there's one thing I cannot stand, it's a liar. My mum was a liar. It was constant. I'm not sure there was a single thing that came out of that woman's mouth that wasn't a whopping great lie.

At one point, she told me my dad was a famous actor, played a major role in a series of spy films. Not Bond, but one of those. I almost died of embarrassment after writing to the actor declaring he was my long-lost dad. She cackled with laughter at that one. I never received a reply from him. I assume he was in receipt of regular declarations of his parentage in amongst those of undying love for him.

Then there was Thomas. His lies were damaging beyond belief. Lies I will never recover from.

I never lie.

Not unless it's absolutely necessary, so don't judge me.

Technically, I never lied. I just accepted forged documents from James and used them to my advantage. It's not a lie. It never came out of my mouth. Well, on the one occasion when I told Mr Bates I was older than I was. That was an exception. Maybe too, I pre-empted the results of my qualifications, but that's a moot point as I did pass everything with distinction. Well, everything except office practice, which I scraped a pass. And the A levels I took at night school. They weren't so hot.

And once again, when I wanted to get away from the construction industry and into something a little more sophisticated. It was a white lie. Sort of. A tiny one. The kind any up-and-coming young woman would use to get out of where she was and move on.

When they asked if I could use a computer, I nodded. After all, I could type. Technically, I thought an electronic typewriter would classify as the same thing. It turned out to be nothing like a computer, but everyone else was in the same boat, apart from Mary, the managing director's personal assistant who was more than willing to share her knowledge. I think it may have been more that she wanted to show superiority. But it worked for me.

I realised how quick I am to learn anything IT-based.

I was promoted from secretary to the fleet manager to PA to the commercial director, all within three years. My life changed once more. I commanded respect. I worked with women of all ages and backgrounds in a bustling, happy atmosphere and I no longer had to trudge through mud in wellington boots on a construction site.

No. I went up in the world. One big leap, right into stiletto heels and smart suits.

That was then. And I'm here now.

My first day at yet another new job and my nerves are jittering. I know this is natural. I do it every time I start a new job.

James is the only one I ever confide in. I have lost faith in human nature. From a mother who cared about no one but herself, to a man who deceived me, colleagues who let me down, bosses who undermined me, and a hospital consultant who belittled me.

One of the main reasons I wanted to leave my construction site job is because I was treated so unfairly and there was nothing in the world I could do about it, no action I could take. With being a

PA, I wasn't a member of a union like all of the construction workers. So, when Mr Bates decided in his wisdom that my sick leave had actually been annual leave, I didn't have a leg to stand on, metaphorically speaking. I had handed in my sick notes. They were ignored. When the big boss speaks, no one is going to listen to you. No one is going to challenge them. Their word is law and no matter the murmurings of equality in the air, it doesn't happen for young single women in an all-male environment. I'd never encountered a problem with Mr Bates before because I always kept my head down and worked hard, but I had witnessed him being a bit of a stickler when it came to saving money.

So, it was put up or shut up.

I shut up.

For a number of years.

When I made my move, it was in my time, to the next place. It gave me a leg up to the right place.

I really do hope this is the right place.

Oh, I didn't mind my previous employment, but I'm not a natural gossip, and gossip was rife there. The more you keep your personal life to yourself, the more people want to pry into it.

Which is why I applied for this job. I'm exactly the right age, experience and knowledge under my belt and qualifications in abundance. Thanks to James's ex-military friend making a couple of small adjustments to my grades. It wasn't so difficult to make a D into an A. Not for a man with his skill set. It wasn't a terrible dishonesty, and it just gave me that leg up when I needed it.

Things seem to be going in the right direction for me recently. I'm no longer in the tenement flats, which were recently demolished, but I now have a two-bedroom semi-detached house that despite my buying it for £16,500 is now worth in the region of £42,000. I stretched to my limit to buy it, but luckily for me, it was just before the boom and thanks to living rent-free in James's flat for a number of years, I had saved more than enough for a deposit and basic furniture, instead of the rent that I thought I was about to commit to.

In all fairness to Mary, the managing director's PA, it was her superior look of disdain when she discovered I was 'throwing my money away' on renting accommodation instead of buying it that inspired me to consider purchasing a house.

I have a small car. A little Ford Fiesta. It's a few years old, but I love the bright red colour. I think that's why I got it for a good price. That and the fact that James meandered in while I was spluttering my way through the negotiation as they asked if my husband would like to check it over first.

He declared he was my dad, although goodness knows he's not old enough. Then again, neither was my mum. He was having one of his good days, despite refusing to live indoors during the summer and, once I bought my house, he slinked off to find another dump to live in. A stairwell or a hallway.

Occasionally, I search for James if I've not seen him for a while, and find him the worse for wear, slumped over in an alleyway, or curled in the foetal position in a shop doorway. On the whole, though, he seems to have fared better and is living on and off at some sort of homeless facility which is trying its best to get the residents onto programmes to assist them in their fight against alcoholism, and lately many of them are now on drugs.

Thankfully, James still hasn't succumbed to those.

For weeks he seems fine. Several times he's got himself a job. A bricklayer, a landscape gardener, a labourer. All these manual labour jobs which denigrate his intellectual abilities. Because James is massively intelligent.

It's sad that whatever destroyed him in the army has never been put to one side, and every so often it raises its ugly head and destroys him all over again.

When he re-surfaces, I'm here for him.

Just as he is always here for me when I need him.

Currently, neither of us seems to need each other, although I could have done with a pep talk last night from him regarding my latest venture.

Justin Schneider, adventurer and entrepreneur, has chosen me to be his next personal assistant. My one misgiving – and it is a big one – is that he chose me without personally interviewing me. I have neither met him nor spoken with him on the telephone.

Apparently, he was climbing Uhuru when his most recent PA took off without notice and left him high and dry. I had to look it up in an encyclopaedia. Uhuru is the highest of three peaks on Mount Kilimanjaro, which is in Tanzania, Africa.

I'm a little bit in awe if the truth be told.

In his mid-thirties, Justin was on his honeymoon when he received the notification of his PA's desertion. According to the agency that managed to place her elsewhere, she'd burnt out after single-handedly organising his wedding.

Reluctant to cut his honeymoon short, he had left instructions for the agency I was registered with to obtain a replacement with immediate effect.

The agency believed I was the right person for the job. Right age, right experience and perfect attitude. My one shortfall, according to them, is precisely that... I am short. All his previous PAs have been of a certain height. Known for their willowy elegance.

I am not willowy, nor exactly elegant.

I don't think so in any case. I am short, on the curvy side – some would say well-rounded – and pretty. But nothing to write home about.

Apparently looks are important, though, for this position. Presentation is all.

Not only will I be his PA, but also his social secretary. In this case, that doesn't mean simply making his social appointments, but frequently attending functions with him.

I check in the mirror.

I've invested in a new hairstyle, which isn't exactly me. Instead of the Farrah Fawcett flip, I've now gone sleek and smooth. It looks flat to me, but I've pulled the sides back and clipped it in a beautiful black velvet bow.

My black suit was an extortionate price, but I felt it necessary to look the part, especially on the first day, and my first meeting with my new employer. The Windsmoor suit will look, even to the keenest of eyes, expensive and, dare I use the word, elegant with its impeccably tailored pencil skirt with a smart kick pleat, and matching neat little jacket that pinches in at the waist and has a sharply creased peplum at the back.

The three-inch court shoes that I exchange for the flats I wore to drive in may kill me, but I'm trying to make myself taller. I've worn heels for the past few years, but rarely quite this high. A little bit of pain won't kill me.

I don't want to lose my job on my first day because I don't meet the height requirements. Anyone would think I was applying for the police force.

I don't care, I really want this job, after all, I have left a very good position for this one. I don't want to lose it before I even begin.

I have every confidence my shorthand and typing skills are honed.

My last boss dictated like a demon. He'd dictate for an hour until my hand almost fell off.

Fifteen minutes early, I park my car and step out, slamming the door as I know the catch doesn't always work. I hitch my handbag onto my shoulder and tug my jacket into place while straightening my shoulders.

I take a moment to assess the immense edifice of Justin Schneider's home, where the headquarters of his business is also registered.

My mouth drops open, but I quickly close it, conscious that someone may be watching my arrival from one of the dozens of windows overlooking the circular driveway where I have just pulled up.

There are no other cars but mine and I wonder if I have made a mistake.

I mount the stone steps up to the imposing thick oak front door and pause for a moment. What the hell am I supposed to do? I can't see a doorbell. Am I supposed to use the brass knocker which is bigger than my fist?

I raise my hand and the door opens.

Not a strained creak – my imagination tugs me down the path of all horror movies – but silent. The only saving grace is the fact that it's just after 8 a.m. on a bright sunny day and not a misty dusk.

I rein in my imagination as a tall bald-headed man wearing what appears to be an evening suit opens the door. He stands silent for a moment, sharp eyes assessing me, his arms crossed over a broad chest, like he's watched too much James Bond.

This surely is not my employer. I know we don't get a physical description but I'm pretty sure when I scoured the newspapers for information on him, Justin Schneider had hair and cut a pretty good form in his khakis. A bit like Indiana Jones.

I must be at the wrong address.

I open my mouth to speak, and I am halted as one brow raises. I would call it an eyebrow, but there is no defining hair. Like his head, it is smooth and bald. Possibly he has alopecia.

I close my mouth again.

'Miss Martin?'

My breath rushes out to accompany my one-word answer. 'Yes.'

Disappointment flickers across his face and I feel I have fallen at the first fence.

'I imagine the agency did not give you a map to follow.'

I think of the engagement letter folded up in the bottom of my handbag. On the back were the instructions on how to get to the place, but I'd used my own map in the car. It wasn't exactly rocket science to locate the place... or was it?

I shake my head, my distaste for lies overridden by my desperate desire not to lose this job before I've even started.

I give an apologetic smile. 'Perhaps it got lost in the post.'

He knows I'm lying, I can tell by the almost imperceptible tightening of his lips.

He nods in the direction of my car. 'Does this look like a car salesroom?'

I don't quite understand what he's getting at. Mine is the only car there.

And then the penny drops.

Mine is the only car there.

'Oh. Sorry. Sorry.' I stumble headlong into apologies, only to be cut off.

'If you had looked at the map the agency sent you, you would have been directed to a separate entrance to Crest Park. If you imagine you are welcome in Mr Schneider's private accommodations—' he gives a disdainful flick of his fingers in the direction of the glorious Hall behind him '—then you are sadly mistaken.'

I'm tempted to apologise again but clamp my mouth shut as he thrusts out a folded piece of paper.

'I suggest, young lady, you get back in your car and make haste, before you are late for work on your first day. A sackable offence, I believe.'

My fingers shake as I take the paper from him, dropping it so it flutters down the stone steps as the breeze takes it away.

I chase after it, turning my heel on the bottom step as I stomp on the paper, refusing to allow it to escape me. I bend over and ease the map from my stiletto and stare at the hole I have created in the middle.

When I look up, the man is gone.

I do a quick, ungainly trot back to the car, my turned ankle burning and my snug pencil skirt restricting movement.

Heat rushes into my cheeks and I almost cry.

How did I get it so wrong?

I open the dirty piece of paper across my steering wheel and study it. On closer look, the now double hole is on either side of the essential part of the map.

I'm supposed to be there for 8.30 a.m. It's already 8.15 a.m. I don't even pause to change back into my flat shoes to drive.

How long will it take? It looks like miles. Am I about to lose my job?

19

THIRTY-FIVE YEARS EARLIER – 1989 – GRACE

I trace my finger along the map from where I am currently parked, all the way along the majestic drive I have just come down which must have taken five minutes just for that, back onto the main road which loops around to the other side of the Hall. According to the little map, it's approximately eight miles, not including this long drive.

My heart bangs in my chest, and I can barely breathe as I slam my car into gear and my smooth-soled stiletto slips on the clutch and my heel catches. The car leaps forward in three lurches and in response I hit the accelerator and shoot off, leaving gravel spitting up on the semi-circle of the driveway, almost taking out an ancient walled fountain in the middle as I quickly correct my steering.

I floor the accelerator and speed along the straight, single-track driveway, able to see almost to the horizon. At least there is no one coming towards me.

I glance in my mirror as dust clouds up behind me so Crest Park is swallowed up.

As I reach the end, I slam on my brakes and the car does a little fishtail that takes me by surprise. A squeak comes from my lips as the car rocks from side to side and just about stops before reaching the carriageway ahead of me as a tractor with a fully laden trailer trundles past.

Fate has thrown me a curveball.

Sweat pools at the base of my throat and my back is cold and sticky until my flesh turns to goosebumps. I shuffle forward in my seat, so the sweat doesn't soak into my smart white camisole top, and wind down my window. Choking on the putrid smell of manure the trailer in front of me is hauling, I quickly wind the window back up again, but the stench is now trapped in the car with me.

Tears spring to my eyes and I hold my breath, hoping to hell I'm not going to arrive late, with make-up running down my face.

I smack the palm of my hand on my leather steering wheel and grit my teeth. I will not cry.

I poke the nose of my car out from behind the trailer to get a better look at the road ahead, but it's not straight.

A car speeds at me from the opposite direction and I fall back against the driving seat. My fresh new suit soaks up my sweat and I contemplate whether this job is worth my life.

I'm going to be late.

I accept that.

What I can't accept is that I'm going to lose this job before I even start it.

I see a gap and floor the accelerator once more. My car speeds past the tractor just as I see the right turning up ahead. I spin the steering wheel and pull on my handbrake at the same time, doing the most incredible handbrake turn.

Admittedly, there were a few things I learnt working with an all-male workforce, and driving recklessly across site in a long-wheel-based Land Rover was one of them. Although much heavier than my little car, which swings a little wildly for a moment before I power it down another long driveway and into a car park, where apparently all the employees park. If only I had read my instructions a little more clearly instead of being focused more on my appearance. Hardly an endorsement for 'pays attention to detail', one of the essential key features of the job description.

As I fling open my car door and leap out, heading straight for an almost identical set of stairs up to the oak door, a tall man steps out, I assume to greet me.

Dressed in a dinner suit, the very same man towers there. With a bald head and bald eyebrows, one of which twitches with a kind of wicked amusement, I swear there's a smile hovering on his lips as I run up the steps on the balls of my toes, so my stilettos don't catch. My ankle burns like a bitch.

'Miss Martin, I presume.' He makes a point of looking at his watch for a long moment and then back at me. 'Cutting it a bit fine, aren't you? I trust you had a good journey.' He sniffs and I wonder if he can smell the scent of manure that had encased my car.

I open my mouth but I can only gasp in a breath as I pull up in front of him. I have to tilt my head way back to look up at him.

'I'm sorry, I...'

He raises a hand to stop me mid-flow.

'Let's not keep Mr Schneider waiting, shall we?'

I stutter, unsure how the man had steamed through from the other side of the immense Hall without breaking into a sweat, like I had myself.

I break out into a trot of tiny steps as I attempt to keep up with his long strides, my skirt inhibiting the length of my own stride and my heels skidding on the slippery waxed surface of the enormous hall we charge along.

A cool waft of welcome air greets me as we make our way through the rabbit warren of corridors, which become cooler and darker each turn we take until we arrive at yet another huge, wooden door. A beautiful, unattended antique desk is angled outside as though a gatekeeper should be sitting there and I realise that gatekeeper is about to be me.

The man raps on the wooden door with the bare knuckles of one meaty fist, and we wait. I never hear an answer before he opens it, but evidently, he must have.

This door does creak, and I almost back away before common sense tells me I'm quite safe. I must be safe.

Although nobody knows I'm here but the agency, and would they even miss me? I didn't tell James the nitty-gritty details of exactly where I was going either.

My heart is pounding so hard I have no other sound in my ears but the quick rush of water. I'm so lightheaded, I wonder briefly if I'm about to faint.

As the man who brought me here steps to one side and makes an exaggerated fanfare of showing me in by stretching his arm wide, another man rises from behind a huge, glossy wooden desk, at a guess, walnut.

'Hello.' He strides across the wide room towards me. 'How good of you to step in at so little notice.' He encases my sweaty hand in his large, cool one and a broad grin stretches across his face, causing deep brackets to form either side of his beautiful mouth.

I am already breathless, but the sight of him sucks every morsel of oxygen from my lungs.

He is, quite frankly, movie-star handsome. Thick blond hair flops across his forehead to tickle at long black eyelashes that fringe blue eyes as deep as the ocean.

I know I should correct him, but I stare at him, gormless and open-mouthed.

The loud click of the door closing shakes me out of my daze as Mr Schneider releases my hand. 'Come in, Faith, come in.' He turns his back, heading for his desk.

'Grace.' My voice comes out a hoarse whisper.

He whips around and stares at me as though he wasn't expecting an answer. 'I beg your pardon?'

I let out a small cough. 'My name is Grace.'

'Hmm, unusual. Old-fashioned. As in Grace Jones?'

The singer was making a name for herself for more than just her singing.

'That's right.'

'Ah. Does that make you a slave to the rhythm?'

My nerves are jangling, and it takes me a moment to grasp his meaning. All too late, I let out a feeble laugh. I seem to have killed the conversation.

'Take a seat, Grace.'

'Thank you.' I edge onto the leather chair in front of his desk so that when he sits down, I am face-to-face with him.

He has to be the most beautiful man I have ever seen. For once in my life, I am overwhelmed by someone's looks. I've never considered myself shallow, but everything about this man exudes a certain presence. A confidence in his power.

'Would you like a drink? Coffee, tea?'

I shake my head and then think better of it. 'Water, please.'

He gets back to his feet and makes his way to a small table where he pours black coffee from a percolator into a fine bone china cup and places it onto a saucer. I recognise the make, sure I've seen it in the newspaper under collectables.

I love reading the newspapers, and certain magazines. There's so much information in there that proves useful. Little snippets that can be used to show knowledge.

He hands me a crystal glass he's filled with water from a matching jug.

He places his own cup and saucer down and makes himself

comfortable, resting his hands, fingers linked on the leather blotter in front of him.

'Grace.' He pauses to make sure I'm not about to correct him. 'Thank you for coming here today. I really appreciate you filling in until we can find someone suitable for the position.'

My heart drops. I am stunned.

All the effort of getting here today has my head reeling. I haven't given up my job, my livelihood for a temping position. This is supposed to be permanent. I've signed a contract, and I know for damned certain it was permanent, not temporary. I'm not stupid, but I am silent.

'Obviously, I won't expect you to carry out the full extent of duties while you are here.' He runs a critical eye over me as though he has judged and found me wanting. I've seen that look before.

I raise the glass I'm cradling and a little of the water sloshes onto my perfect skirt that I paid a fortune for as an investment in this job. I take a gulp and place the glass down in front of me. My fingers shake and when I pull them away, they cling to the glass, so it slides towards me precariously, threatening to fall off the edge of the desk.

He pauses, watching, and then slides a crystal coaster towards me as though I committed a sin by putting the glass on his precious desk, instead of keeping it held in my hand where he'd put it.

I take a deep breath.

'Mr Schneider.' I cough again. 'I must admit to being somewhat confused. I have just given up a perfectly acceptable job, a good job...' Fear actually grasps at my insides. I have just given up a brilliant job for this. Something that amounts to no more than a temping contract. I swallow. It has to be said because I can't walk straight back into another job, not one of this stature, nor return to my previous one. They've already replaced me with little courtesy as, apparently, I had let them down by leaving at such a time. Was there ever a good time?

'I was given the impression by the agency that this was a full-time, permanent contract.'

His face freezes. Those beautiful blue eyes are as cold as ice. They skim over me, cool and assessing. 'No.'

'Sorry?'

'No, you will not do. I did not commit to a permanent contract. I would not. Not without interviewing you personally. I've told them to have interviews lined up. In the meantime, I have been led to believe you've agreed to cover for a fortnight.'

'A fortnight?' My voice pitches upwards. Adrenaline from the wild rush around the Hall has seeped from my limbs to leave me weak and helpless as a kitten. 'I... I gave up my job.'

'More fool you.'

'No.' Anger pierces through the numbness. I shake my head and meet his eyes dead on. 'No, Mr Schneider—' I enunciate my words slow and clear '—I am nobody's fool. I would not have given in my notice for a two-week temporary assignment.'

One eyebrow raises as he stares back at me.

'I suggest you speak with your *temping* agency.'

I place my hands on the desk and push to my feet. I give a curt nod. 'I will do that. Right now, I won't waste any more of either of our time.' I nod and move to turn away.

I see a leap of something in his eyes as I turn. Is it admiration?

'Wait. Wait just a moment.'

I stand, pulling myself up to my straightest, and say nothing while I wait for him to peruse me all over again. I am insulted. This is not a cattle market.

'It's not my looks you are employing me for, but my skills, which are impeccable.'

A rueful smile curves his lips. 'I've never had a problem

recruiting women of a certain... shall we say, presentation. It's important when I'm entertaining as my wife doesn't like to participate in that side of our relationship. She is, for want of a better word, a bit of a recluse.'

'And so you take tall, attractive women along, to what end? Are they a replacement for your wife?'

He considers me for a moment, insult hovering on his face. 'No, Miss Martin.' I notice he has dropped my first name in preference to using my surname. 'I am not unfaithful to my new wife.'

I hadn't meant that he was unfaithful, but I am no longer in the mood or position to back down from what I said. I'm not about to grovel or apologise.

'I cherish her. But I consider in my position that there is a certain expectation when I attend functions. People in my circle—' he cruises his gaze back over me again, excluding me from that inner circle '—have standards.' He flicks elegant, manicured fingers towards me. 'They expect the whole package, and I have always provided that.'

I snort. 'And how has that worked out for you, so far?'

I expect surprise. What I don't expect is a quick bark of laughter.

He throws back his head and reveals perfectly straight white teeth.

'Not very well, lately,' he admits.

'No. Indeed.' I cross my arms over my chest. I have nothing to lose because quite honestly, the moment I met his manservant, I knew I would never fit into their world the way they would want me to.

'Mr Schneider, in the past five years, you have managed to lose six PAs.' I know this as it was one of the juicy morsels the woman at the agency let slip. 'That's averaging one every ten months. It's hardly a stellar record. In my opinion, you cannot have gained any loyalty in that time and how can there be any continuity?'

A ghost of a smile whispers over his lips. And yes, I think there is a growing admiration lurking beyond his assessment. 'So, why do you want the job?'

This is where I'm going to have to come clean. 'Because I think I am far better than any of your previous PAs, and if I'm not, I will have had ten months' experience at a very executive level and will be snapped up in no time at all, having held on to my position here.'

'But you don't have a position here.' He looks at me over the rim of his teacup as he takes a sip of the black coffee.

'I have a permanent contract, not a temporary one.'

'So, sue me.' He shrugs as he places the cup down again, every movement slow and deliberate.

I press my lips together. This is a game to him. There's no way on God's earth I could win against him in a court of law.

I unloop the strap of my handbag from the back of the chair and slip it over my shoulder. 'Good luck, Mr Schneider.'

I turn on my very thin heel and head for the door.

Just as I reach out for the thick brass doorknob, Mr Schneider calls out.

'Okay, Grace.'

I stop with my back to him.

I bite back on the sharp sting of tears that threatens. I've been through worse. This humiliation is just another step to make me stronger.

'I'll give you two weeks to prove yourself.'

I make a slow turn and study him from across the room. 'That would still be a temping contract, Mr Schneider. Long enough for you to source another executive personal assistant.' I shake my head. Really, I should take him up on it; I will need a job and money, and temping contracts pay peanuts. 'No deal.'

The words slip out before my mind has persuaded my mouth to keep quiet. That's the problem with me sometimes, I can't help but speak out. Against injustices.

He leans back in his chair, his big frame pushing so it rocks. His eyes narrow in contemplation.

'I think you may be more intelligent than you are given credit for.' His waspishness simply serves to make me even more determined.

I tilt my head. 'I think if you check with the agency, I am very highly sought after, and I come with impeccable references.' Well, if I didn't, I could always get James to sort that situation out. 'If you think you can just click your fingers and find someone with my experience, talents and abilities, then you're *not* as intelligent as they give you credit for.'

This time choked laughter comes from him and his eyes gleam with amusement, turning his good looks into something beautiful.

He seems to be enjoying this. Is it all a game to him?

He takes a moment and the smile slides from his face again. 'What would you suggest we do about this situation?'

I could tell him that we should revert to the original agreement, but I sense that would cause an impasse. I also don't believe it's about the money for him. But it is to me.

I wander back towards his desk, my heels tap-tapping on the wooden floorboards, my feet already killing me.

'Give me four months without interviewing or engaging anyone else.' That should give me more than enough time for job searching again. 'I will sort out your life, both work and home, during that time and have things running smoothly. After that, should you wish me to go, I will leave without causing any waves.'

'You sound confident that I won't want you to leave.'

'So confident that if you want me to stay, you'll give me a 30 per cent pay rise.'

Satisfied at the flash of astonishment, I stop walking as I reach his desk and look down into those pure blue eyes. Magnetised by the pull of them.

It's his turn to cross his arms over a wide chest.

'Taper reckons you'd be an asset to my Formula One team. He says you cleared the drive in record time in that rusty little car of yours.'

I try to hide my surprise that the manservant had watched my race around to the other side of the park. Also, that he had not made direct mention himself, although he had seemed a man of few words.

I say nothing.

I'm not sure if I am supposed to respond.

He picks up a pen from his blotter and taps it end on end. A Montblanc, I see, and the colour he uses is green. I hold my breath as his gaze holds mine.

'Very well, Grace. It's a deal.'

I nod, my emotions raging between wanting to celebrate that I've managed to cling on to this job and a crawling doubt that I've bitten off more than I can chew.

20

PRESENT DAY – WEDNESDAY, 3 JULY 2024, 8.15 A.M. – SIOBHAN

The moment she'd packaged up her mum's DNA sample pot and posted it, Siobhan had immediately sent for a second one for herself, not allowing her nerves and misgivings to get the better of her. Once it arrived she barely gave it a second thought before she spat into the vial and sent it off, too. Only afterwards did the doubts set in.

She needed to bump her guilt to one side and look at it from a different perspective. That of proving Grace was her biological mother and that it was pure delirium that had caused her to make that comment.

A remark that continued to gnaw at Siobhan, casting doubt that refused to be doused.

She could wait until her mum felt better, until she was of sound mind, and ask her, but what would that achieve? Her mum would most likely deny it. Then Siobhan was in the situation where trust was eroded between them and she'd be obliged to lie to her mum by going behind her back. It was a vicious circle. One she didn't want to think too deeply about.

This way, there was no edge to the enquiry. It was merely a check. One her mum need never know about.

Her mum was due out of hospital that day, probably late afternoon they'd advised, having spent five days there. It seemed nothing for such a huge operation, but the nurses assured Siobhan that under normal circumstances, her mum would have been out two days earlier.

Two to three days to recover from a hip operation before being sent home. That barely allowed any time at all for recovery from anaesthetic, which stays in the body for several days, never mind a major operation. Apparently, it was better to get patients up and walking as soon as possible to avoid any kind of blood clots forming or fluid gathering around the operation site.

Her mum was fit and healthy, they assured her.

How could that be? She had bone cancer, didn't she? That's what they'd told her when her mum was first admitted.

A little tremble of horror rode through her as the insistent picture of her mum rose again in her mind's eye. She loved her, there was no question of that. She simply couldn't envisage her life without her wonderful, vibrant mum. Hopefully, she didn't have to.

Now they seemed to have back-pedalled on their diagnosis. Yes, there'd been a tumour growing inside her mum's hip, the part they had removed and replaced entirely. There appeared no further evidence of bone cancer. Her mum's bloods had come back clear, although bordering on anaemic, for which they had given her a blood transfusion while she was undergoing her operation, and the full-body MRI scan they put her through showed nothing suspicious. That tumour was the primary and there were no other secondaries.

That didn't mean she was clear and free. It wasn't the end of it – this could only be the start of their journey together down this road – but at least it gave them hope, something to cling to. And Siobhan needed that reassurance. Within the blink of an eye, their roles had reversed and she was now the adult. More than that, she would be her mum's carer until she was mobile and fit again.

Siobhan took a gulp of her hot coffee, enough to make her eyes water as heat burned all the way down her throat. She came to her feet and stared out of the window into the field. She'd walked Beau at 5.30 a.m. as heat and worry had combined to give her a disturbed night.

The walk had done them both the world of good and now Beau stretched out on the cool tiled floor of the old farmhouse kitchen, his thick fur still damp from the swim he'd had in the river.

She looked on at his inert body, a smile curving her lips. She should have jumped in the water with him, perhaps she'd be as chilled.

She considered the day ahead of her. She'd take a trip into the office and catch up with everyone before she picked her mum up after lunch. She let out a sigh, confident she was fully prepared for her mum's arrival. Fresh bedding on both their beds, upstairs carpets vacuumed, downstairs floors mopped, both bathrooms scrubbed until they gleamed. It wouldn't last, not in an old farmhouse in the summer months. A little quiver of anticipation spiked through her and she allowed herself a smile. Her mum was coming home. It didn't matter that dust motes already danced in rays of sunshine slanting through the panelled windows she'd had cleaned two days before by Chris, the local window cleaner.

Just having that task done had made such a difference, but the moment the local farmer decided to plough one of the fields, or harvest, the windows would once again be thick with dust and when he spread chicken manure, the stench would fill the house for days.

Siobhan circled around, contemplating the huge, old kitchen

which slid into a dining room on one side and a conservatory on the other.

Perhaps she would get a cleaner in for a while. There was bound to be someone in the village who wanted to earn an extra few pounds to come in once or twice a week. She should have put an advert in the village post office, but she hesitated. Her mum possibly wouldn't want that. She liked her privacy.

They normally shared the task of cleaning. Once a week on a Sunday morning, they would don their rubber gloves and scrub the place top to bottom. It would take them a few hours, but there was always a sense of satisfaction once their house was gleaming.

They weren't untidy people. In fact, her mum had instilled in Siobhan an almost neat freak personality. She wasn't OCD, a term that was used all too often to describe fussy people, rather than neat people. If something was out of place, she wasn't compelled to put it in the correct place, it didn't annoy her. But she was a minimalist. She didn't collect ornaments, nor hoard magazines. Siobhan was like her mum. Grace had few possessions since they'd moved so much in Siobhan's early years.

Siobhan let out a soft snort as she dried the side plate she'd used and just washed. She placed the plate on a shelf, just so, and looped the tea towel over a hook on the inside of one of the cupboards so it couldn't be seen. Just like her mum would.

Her heart warmed.

Wasn't that proof enough she was her mother's daughter?

Or was that nature versus nurture?

Her mum's computer gave a sharp ping to signal incoming emails and Siobhan shook herself from her reverie and dashed back to the kitchen table. She bumped her mug on the surface and sat, pulling the chair up close as she opened her mum's laptop with shaking fingers and tapped in the password.

With some urgency, she scrolled down the long list of spam

downloading, until she spotted what she was looking for. That elusive email she'd looked for each day.

Her heart skittered as she recognised the sender's email address.

This was it.

She opened it.

She read the instructions.

Now what she needed to do was pretend she was her mum, giving her daughter permission to deal with the account, transfer it to her own email address in order to make sure her mum didn't see anything to do with it.

Her stomach churned as Siobhan carried out the transaction. It was so disloyal. Her breath backed up in lungs burning with remorse while she waited for the email to ping through to her own laptop with a link for her to sign in.

As it did, she sighed, shame washing through her in waves of self-recrimination which she steadfastly overruled. It had to be done. On top of everything else that had happened, the stress was turning her into some kind of obsessive idiot.

Her fingers hovered over the keyboard. Could she do this?

Yes, she could.

She sent a confirmation and then deleted everything from her mum's laptop that related to the DNA site so her mum would never know.

Never one to underestimate her mum's abilities, she also clicked through to the laptop history and deleted everything that might bear any relationship to DNA testing and hoped that no pop-up adverts came up on her mum's laptop.

She'd carried out the research on her own computer, but that didn't mean to say something wouldn't flag up with the way algorithms worked. She wasn't a conspiracy theorist, but there had been times when she'd had a conversation with one of her colleagues at work then found an advert relating to that very subject pop up on her laptop the following day. Maybe not a conspiracy, but she also didn't believe in coincidences.

Also, her mum was an intelligent woman.

Siobhan never understood why her mum didn't do something more ambitious with her work life. She was intellectual. The rapid progress of the internet and computers had never phased her. And yet she chose to live a simple life. A hermit's life.

Why would that be? It had never occurred to her before. She'd not once questioned her mum's decisions.

Conspiracy theorist she may not be but now she had evidence of her mum's transgression regarding her birth certificate, Siobhan's mind reeled with the possibilities of what her mum had done.

She could ask her outright, but the woman wasn't in a fit state and Siobhan didn't want to upset her. Didn't want to cause friction when the most important thing in their lives was her health and recovery. Whatever the outcome, Siobhan wouldn't love her mum any less. Would she?

She leaned back in her seat as the next email came through on her own laptop. This was it.

Here was the link to the DNA site.

She drew in a breath as she waited for it to load, not sure exactly what it was she expected to find. Not sure exactly what it was she wanted to find.

Proof. That was all she wanted. Quite simple, really. She wasn't trying to find her entire family tree; she'd never even given it a thought before now. All she wanted, all that was important to her, was proof.

Proof that she was her mother's daughter.

She had to be.

Didn't she?

The soft buzz of her phone had her jumping with a guilty start.

She snatched it from the table, glancing quickly at the withheld number, and tapped 'answer'.

'Hello, Siobhan Martin speaking.' Heart thundering in her chest, Siobhan came to her feet.

'Ah, yes, hello, Siobhan. Sister Stanley here, Blaire Ward, Wrexham Maelor. I'm calling about Grace Martin.' Sister Stanley's rolling Welsh tone was made for her vocation as it soothed from a distance. 'Your mum had a very good night's sleep, and we've already had her up and showered this morning. She's moving around very nicely. She's a strong lady, determined to get mobile, which is just what we want. You can collect her whenever you're ready. Doctor has already done his rounds and says she can go home straight away. We'll have the paperwork ready for you when you arrive with all the information you need to help Grace on her road to recovery.'

Shock almost made her stutter. 'Now? I can pick her up now?' She'd thought she had the whole morning to organise herself with work.

'No reason why not.'

Siobhan's heart hammered in her chest.

'I'll be there shortly.'

'There's no rush. When you're ready.'

Aware there probably was a rush, that they were in desperate need of the bed, Siobhan responded, 'No. It's okay. I'm on my way. Do I need to bring anything?'

She glanced at the soft glow of the laptop, her fingers itching to scroll through the results.

'Some fresh clothes, I think, so she can change out of our cheeky gowns. Something loose fitting, maybe even shorts in this weather, with front fastening to make it easier for Mum to get them up and down. A nice, loose T-shirt, nothing too difficult to put on. It may be her hip we've replaced but everything is an effort at first until she gets herself used to things.' All business with angel wings, Sister Stanley continued, 'I'll let her know you're on your way. We'll have a wheelchair ready to take your mum to the car.'

'I'll be there in half an hour.'

She placed her phone on the kitchen table and wiped suddenly sweaty hands down her summer lightweight dress. Torn between darting away to collect her mum and fear that her disloyalty would be discovered, Siobhan circled her gaze around the room to check that everything was in place.

Beau was still stretched out in the coolest place. The cats were most likely on the beds upstairs or flat out on a windowsill sucking in the sunshine until their fur became too hot to stroke.

Siobhan picked up her keys and reached out to close her laptop lid just as it pinged.

She froze. Looked closer at the incoming email.

Her DNA results had arrived, too.

21

THIRTY-ONE YEARS BEFORE – 1993 – GRACE

'I think she's lost her mind.'

My perfectly manicured fingers race across the keyboard and I ignore the buzz of conversation going on around my head.

I think Justin and Gordon believe that when I have my audio earphones in, I can't hear them above the dictation. I never miss a single conversation. Then again, I am paid handsomely for my discretion. And I am discreet.

Who would I tell?

Also, I trust Justin. He's a straight-shooting businessman. Ruthless on occasion, but what businessman of his standing isn't?

'Mad as a box of frogs.' I've heard Justin say this frequently, lately, about Leonora. Not to anyone but Gordon, but it does make me a little uncomfortable that he says it at all.

It's not true. At least, I don't think it's true, although she has been rather more demanding of his time since her pregnancy. Clingy.

That's understandable, isn't it?

She's forty-two and this is her first pregnancy. The money they've invested, the clinics they have visited. I believe it's put a strain on their marriage. She's desperate for this baby and rightly so. She's so emotionally invested in it.

Much as I would dearly love a baby, there are two things that I am resigned to. One, I'm not interested in a relationship of any kind with anyone. Not since Thomas. Married men are completely off the cards, and let's face it, men that would appeal to me at this age are all married, or divorced. For good reason. Secondly, and the death knell of any fancies I might have, is that I am infertile. Barren.

I have no one else to blame but myself. And Thomas. I will always blame Thomas.

I've not seen hide nor hair of him since I left the construction site. I do not want to know how his newborn baby progressed through nursery, primary and their future years in secondary school.

It does not interest me. That baby was not mine. Mine died.

I don't deny the pain of it still lingers, deep in my gut. I force myself not to look at babies, not to form any kind of attachment, because my heart cries out for one.

I don't raise my head as Justin and Gordon continue to talk, both standing next to my desk at the entrance to Justin's office. He perches on the edge of it as he so often does, his back to me. I don't know why they don't go into his office for more privacy. Then again, I think privacy has been bypassed between the three of us. Justin's personal life is as open as his business world. He doesn't hold back, not since I inveigled myself into every aspect of his life.

I have deliberately made myself indispensable. Slowly, since that first day, I have insinuated myself into everything. Justin's entire existence is controlled by everything I do for him. He hates when I take a holiday and jokes about the business falling apart every time I have a day off. Which is seldom. He won't have a temp. Not since that first holiday I took when he called me halfway through the week to beg me to get rid of her, telling me she was about to ruin him, and she kept crying.

Being cynical, Justin is exactly the type to reduce people to tears. He's an insidious bully. Had I succumbed that first day, I would not have held on to this position. There were many times in the beginning that he managed to upset me. Not once did I show it in front of him. I am stoic. My mask is in place.

It's not that he shouts, but his sarcasm can slice through even the thickest of skins.

I tune back into their conversation.

'I've told her, she's losing the plot. She needs to see someone.' He pushes off my desk and paces, running a hand back through his fine hair.

Gordon smiles. It's the indulgent smile an adult gives his child, although he can't be that much older than Justin. Maybe mid-forties. His alopecia perhaps ages him. Not so much his bald pate but his naked eyebrows. He has eyelashes but they are blond.

'Perhaps it would do her good to have some counselling.'

Subtle, supportive of Justin, but affirmation that there is something wrong with his wife.

Justin leans on the doorframe into his office, arms crossed over a chest that has broadened in the last few years since I've worked for him. He's younger than Leonora and his fortieth birthday earlier this year seems to herald the decline of his Hollywood good looks. His once lush blond hair has started to recede, the swathe of it that fell across his forehead now slicked back so as not to show how thin it has become. His face is a little puffier than it used to be, chiselled features not as well defined. Blurry at the edges. I've noticed his eyes are often bloodshot. That could be due to a distinct increase in his drinking. He likes a single malt. I place the order, keeping a spreadsheet of the varieties he's tried, which ones he prefers. Which ones not to purchase again.

This is another way I've made myself indispensable.

From minutes of meetings, to travel and soirees, from birthday parties and presents for Leonora, to holidays and car purchases, from engaging employees, business and domestic to dismissing the same. I have a hand in it all. And I am good.

From the first month I worked for him with my discovery of my predecessor's inability to file alphabetically, through to realising the vast sums of money we were being charged by a third-party supplier for the heating of Crest Park.

Justin was bowled over by the fact that I can transcribe from a dictation machine, or take shorthand verbatim, which is a dying skill. A skill he'd never actually utilised before because none of his previous PAs have been qualified to do more than type – badly – and paint their nails. Maybe I'm a little harsh here, but my point is he went more for the looks than the ability. Most of them were qualified to a certain standard, but not the standard a job like this requires, which is why they burnt out so quickly, or he moved them on.

Over the years, I have had my unvarnished finger on the button, and I have depressed it many times.

I'm not ruthless in the same way Justin is, but I do have an edge. I do not suffer fools gladly. If I find the gardener has been smoking weed behind the potting shed, or the chef has been consuming more wine than acceptable, they are gone. I give them a chance, but if they don't take an initial warning seriously and buck their ideas up, I have to let them go. No messing around. I am not averse to giving anyone the push who is not doing their job in the right manner.

I am, however, sympathetic enough to know when the chambermaid is having a hard time with her boyfriend and has a momentary lapse, or when Mrs Blackwood is struggling to climb the stairs because she needs a knee replacement. It didn't take much to arrange for that knee replacement to be carried out in a private Harley Street clinic with the account settled by Crest Park. After all, Mrs Blackwood is especially precious to Leonora, who has known her all her life.

During her convalescence, I arranged for a lift to be installed where the dumb waiter used to be. Sadly, it only gave Mrs Blackwood another two years of service to Crest Park before she took the decision to retire. Sly old fox. She certainly waited long enough for us to not be able to reclaim the cost of her knee replacement. Not that I would have approved such a thing. But she thought it.

She wasn't happy, though.

I think the whole domestic situation between her beloved Leonora and Justin took its toll. She was torn between the woman she served and the man who paid her.

I still send her a bouquet of flowers from Leonora for her birthday, a hamper for Christmas.

I feel maybe that's when Leonora's confidence went into decline.

Having lost her parents before Justin and Leonora were married, I feel she is a lonely soul and it's not surprising she's desperate for a baby. For family.

She has a sister, I'm led to believe, who lives out in Australia, or Singapore, possibly. She married a man in world banking and has rarely been seen since.

It's not my business.

At the end of the day, I am salaried staff, and I am paid to look after all aspects of Justin Schneider's life including the welfare of his wife. But I am not her friend, nor would she want me as her friend. Just as Mrs Blackwood was employed. Their relationship was a little different, but Mrs Blackwood still took off when she decided to retire, leaving poor Leonora alone again. Mrs Blackwood was not her mother. She was not her aunty. She was a housekeeper. Once the bond had been broken by distance, it was gone.

I take my instructions from Justin. He is my employer. My allegiance lies with him. Although not always my heart.

His recent disloyalty to his wife, however, makes me uneasy, no matter if it is only in a small circle of friends and Gordon.

He doesn't lower his voice, and my fingers never hesitate in their swift cruise of the keyboard. I'm a touch typist, I don't need to look at the keyboard, so I keep my gaze straight ahead as I listen.

'I told her if she doesn't pull herself together, I'll have her committed.'

My fingers do falter now in rhythm with my stuttering heart. He has to be joking. What a vile thing to say to her.

I quickly backspace and erase my error, my fingers flying now in case there's any suspicion that I may be listening in.

I am.

I edge my foot off the dictation pedal so it doesn't click, and continue to type. I drop my gaze to my screen and copy the text at the top of the page, just in case Justin looks over my shoulder to check what I'm doing. I can always plead ignorance that the tape had rewound and repeated itself. Those small technicalities are beneath his high-tech interest.

The tightness in my chest is almost painful. His poor wife. Leonora may be anxious, but certainly, she doesn't deserve this kind of betrayal from her own husband. And to discuss it in front of employees, no matter how trustworthy.

Gordon's voice is controlled. 'That's a little harsh.'

The condemnation in his voice goes unnoticed by Justin, but I pick it up in the gravel tone of Gordon's voice. Shocked, I glance up and see the tightening of his jawline. I've never witnessed a response like that to Justin. He's his butler. Gordon reserves that tone for those he considers his underlings. Myself included.

'Harsh? The woman has lost her marbles. I've had to ask Grace to stop putting her calls through to me every five minutes.'

My ears perk up at my own name. My head is bowed again now, but in my peripheral vision, I see Gordon's head turn. He stares at me, and my fingers do not stop. However, heat rushes into my cheeks, fiery and threatening.

He's caught me.

I raise my head, making my eyes a little unfocused, my lips quirking. I hope I didn't leave it too late. I remove my headphones.

'Did I hear my name?'

Justin doesn't flicker but I'm sure I saw something in Gordon's eyes.

'I was telling Gordon about Leonora being… clingy.'

I place my headset next to my keyboard while I contemplate my reply. I do not hold back in my honesty but, unlike Gordon, I temper my tone.

'She's pregnant, Justin, and concerned. This may be her last, her only chance.' I try to pitch my voice so it's not judgemental, although the words are, because actually I want to scream, *'What the hell do you think you're doing? The woman is frantic, she needs your support, not your self-centred, egotistical, bombastic, superior attitude. You should be grateful she's even carrying your baby. The child who will take over the empire you've built.'*

I smile, tilt my head. 'She's anxious.'

'She's got good reason to be anxious.' He cuts across me and I'm not entirely sure what he means.

I frown. 'Is something wrong? Would you like me to call the doctors? I can arrange an appointment.'

'No!' That one word shoots out like a small bolt from an archery bow and stops me dead.

Justin really is not in a good mood today. These are the days when I keep my head down and work.

Eighty-five per cent of the time, Justin is pleasant. Businesslike. That's how our relationship runs. He demands, I obey. We do not mix business with pleasure. When I attend his functions, it's on a professional basis. I am there to ensure everything runs smoothly. I melt into the background where no one notices me, but everyone benefits from my efficiency.

He never loses his temper with me, but once in a while, he bares his teeth. That is when I back down.

I need this job. I love this job.

Not only am I incredibly well paid, which means I have an exceedingly healthy bank balance, but my pension fund is steadily on the rise for when I decide I've had enough and want to retire.

I will not have had enough for a long time.

Who else gets to jet around the world at the drop of a hat on a private plane? Who else gets to rub shoulders with the rich, the famous, the elite?

Me.

And I want to keep it that way. I enjoy my way of life.

I catch Gordon's quiet look of disapproval. I don't think he has ever warmed to me since the day I arrived.

I fold my hands in my lap and wait, hoping that my gaze contains none of the distaste I feel for both the topic and the man.

Justin's jaw flexes and I see, once again, his younger self. The underlying power of a lion in his prime. Physically, Justin may have allowed himself to slide, but mentally he is at the top of his business game. I can't see that changing anytime soon.

'Leonora has nothing wrong, physically. The baby is fine. I think her brain has become unhinged, though. Her hormones seem to have flicked a switch in her brain.'

I will admit to her seeming so much clingier, but I do not interfere with their personal lives, and I am aware that we have no idea what goes on behind closed doors.

To my mind, Justin's relationship with Leonora has always run smoothly. He's always adored her. My time has often been consumed with finding her the perfect champagne truffles for her Christmas stocking, an incredible holiday for the two of them for their anniversary, a new car for her special birthday. Before now, I've never had cause to think there is anything wrong. Something has triggered a change of direction.

'I think she misses Mrs Blackwood.'

'I think she misses her sanity.'

I can't help compressing my lips together. I know it shows my disapproval, but really, there is no need for that. I try and disguise it with a question. 'Would you like me to see if there's anything I can do to help her?'

'Do you have a degree in psychology?'

I can see we are not going to get far on this subject. I need to find a way to call an end to the conversation.

Using my hands, I push up from my desk and come to my feet. 'Well, it's not really my business. Perhaps I can get you a coffee.'

Justin snorts. 'Watch out. Here comes the ice maiden.'

I force a thin smile. He's called me that before. Normally with pride when he introduces me to one of his peers. I don't normally take insult. He is proud of me. Proud of my organisational skills and the proficiency I have to blend into the background unnoticed when required. Proud of my apparent ability to remain calm in the face of any situation.

This, though, is barbed.

Not only is Leonora getting under his skin, but evidently, so am I.

I take in a breath and make to move past him, unable to disguise the flash of annoyance as I feel a flush of warmth wash over me again.

In a lightning move, Justin snatches at my arm, his fingers digging through the silk of my blouse to hurt me.

I draw in a horrified gasp and step back onto Gordon's foot, the whole weight of my body through that one thin stiletto. It's not my fault, he shouldn't have stepped in so close, so claustrophobically close, trapping me between the two of them.

A grunt of pain comes from behind me, and I swear I heard, 'Oh, fuck,' as I wrench my arm from Justin's grasp and swivel my heel a little deeper into Gordon's buffed-to-a-mirror Italian leather shoes.

My elbow ploughs into what I am sure used to be a toned muscular stomach that has pretty much gone to seed by the feel of it.

A whoof of breath comes out of Gordon as he doubles over.

Justin steps back and spreads his arms wide, as though I've attacked him, not the other way around. His eyes are wide with feigned innocence.

I'm not having that! It's a slippery slope once I let physical abuse go unchallenged. I will not let another soul bully me. I had enough of that from my mother.

Without another thought, I step into his space, let the ice maiden slip and glare up at him. 'Don't you ever touch me again.' I actually poke him with a perfectly manicured nail right in the middle of his 100 per cent silk tie. 'Understand?' My voice is a low threat as I snarl up at him, the way I snarled at my mum that day. 'I'm not on a high enough pay grade to be manhandled by you.' I fling an arm out to indicate Gordon, who is silent behind me. 'Or anyone.'

Wheeling around, I snatch my handbag from the back of my chair and, holding my head high, I stalk from the room, nerves quivering as my eyes fill with unshed tears that I will never give them the satisfaction of seeing.

I head straight for the ladies' bathroom and bolt the door behind me, leaning against it weakly as I go boneless.

Knees like jelly, I wipe tears from my cheeks with the back of my hand.

In all these years, I have never felt threatened by Justin or Gordon. I've always been aware of their unnerving power, the kind of strength that comes with strong egos, people who have clawed their way to the top using fair means or foul. I have witnessed them wielding their strength. Never has it been directed at me.

That experience has left me shaken. I stare back at the terrified eyes in the mirror and can't push back the image of Justin grabbing my wrist and Gordon stepping in close as though he too was about to take part in our tussle.

My wrist throbs and I lift it to my mouth, pressing my lips against the heat of the burn Justin has given me.

I have never felt in danger.

Until now.

22

PRESENT DAY – THURSDAY, 4 JULY 2024, 12.35 P.M. – SIOBHAN

Pride mingled with joy and fear and concern, all balling up inside her chest as Siobhan settled her mum on one of the dining room chairs after watching her quite ably swing her body between the crutches she'd been sent home with and then witnessing the exhaustion in her mum's expression.

'I'll get us some lunch.' She moved across the room, not willing to let her mum out of her sight. She didn't imagine she would keel over onto the floor, but it was always a possibility. The weather was incredible. So hot she could faint.

'Don't fuss, love.' Grace reached over and smoothed her fingers over the back of Siobhan's hand, giving it an affectionate squeeze. 'I'm absolutely fine.'

'Well...' She turned her hand over in her mum's and gave it a quick squeeze back. She wanted to argue with her, but it seemed cruel. She settled instead for pacifying her as she slipped her hand away and unpacked the shopping bag she'd brought in from the car. Essentials she'd grabbed from the local Co-op just around the corner from the hospital on her way there. 'Just take it easy, you're not running a marathon.'

'I know, love.' Her mum leaned her forearms on the table and slumped slightly. 'I feel exhausted. Who'd have thought having an operation would make you feel this tired? I can spend all day mucking out horses and chickens and I don't feel like this.'

Siobhan picked up one of her mum's homemade tomato and basil soups she'd got out of the freezer before she left and tipped it from the freezer bag into a small pan. Putting the heat on medium to warm it through, she lifted a fresh loaf of bread and a packet of ham from the now empty bag. 'I know it's warm, but I thought you might like soup for lunch and a sandwich. Maybe easier for you to manage.'

Her mum let out a rusty chuckle. 'You know I'm not actually an invalid. I broke my hip, not my teeth. I'm ravenous. I think I was served breakfast at about 6.30 a.m. and they only brought me porridge.'

'Oh dear. Why's that? I thought you weren't keen on porridge.'

'I'm not, but they had an unexpected patient in during the night and I think they had my breakfast.'

'Oh, how does that happen?'

Her mum shrugged. 'It doesn't matter. It may have been my mistake. Those codeine tablets send me yampy.'

Siobhan gave a half smile as she glanced at her watch. 'That reminds me, you're due more painkillers now.'

'Not until after we've eaten, or I'll be on my back. I tell you, I've never felt so weird. They send me completely off my head. Obviously, I'm not a prime candidate for being a drug addict, or an alcoholic.'

With a suddenness, her mum pressed shaking fingers against tight lips and fell silent as though a ghost of a thought disturbed her. She turned her head from her daughter, Siobhan suspected to mask her tears.

Perhaps the journey had been too much for her. Maybe she

needed to rest. She circled the table and wrapped her arms around her mum's shoulders, giving her a hug full of warmth, without squeezing too tight in case she hurt her.

'Would you like me to help you up the stairs to bed? I can bring your lunch up on a tray.'

'No, love.' Her mum's voice came out as a husky whisper, as though she was fighting back tears as she turned her head into Siobhan's shoulder and looped one arm around her waist. 'I'll have it here. It's easier to sit at the table than try and prop up in bed.'

'Okay.' Siobhan disentangled herself and gave her mum's back a brisk rub, unwilling to see the woman become distressed. 'Whatever's more comfortable.' Siobhan chose to give her mum a moment to compose herself as she backed away. She reached for the steaming pan and divided the contents equally into two separate soup bowls. She turned and placed one in front of her mum and the other in front of her empty chair and then made a neat stack of the sandwiches she'd made and placed them on a plate between the two bowls.

As she pulled in her chair, lifting it so it didn't scrape on the tiled floor, her mum picked up her soup spoon with a hand that tremored. A dart of pity squeezed Siobhan's chest.

'They told me I was having extra physiotherapy before I came out, but it seemed so little. They walked me up and down the corridor a few times, just to see if I could use the crutches, and told me I would do. Apparently, I have good upper body strength for my age, according to them.'

It was Siobhan's chance to query her mum's age, to ask if she was really as old as she claimed, but her mouth dried up at the thought of challenging her. No matter how gently put, it had to come over as a criticism, as doubt to her mum's integrity. If she put the question out there, she would be calling her mum a liar.

Siobhan let it pass.

Now wasn't the time, when her mum was at her weakest.

Weariness lay heavy in the other woman's expression and Siobhan really wanted to keep the peace. Until her mum was feeling stronger. Then she'd find some way of broaching the subject. If she ever did. She glanced at the closed laptop. She might not have to.

She forced a small laugh. 'It's all that lifting bales of straw and horse bedding, Mum. You've got muscles like iron.'

Grace chuckled. Her good character restored, even if her strength wasn't. 'I think that's why they chucked me out so quickly.'

Siobhan stopped herself from remarking that most people would have been sent home a couple of days earlier, and it was probably in deference to her cancer diagnosis that they'd kept her longer.

Worry had snappishness lying just below the surface, but she crushed it while she ate, trying instead to listen to music filtering through the radio until Jeremy Vine started talking and she snapped it off quickly, knowing she couldn't cope with anyone else's drama today.

Halfway through the soup, her mum placed her spoon in the bowl and leaned back in her chair, her head wobbling slightly from side to side as though it was too heavy for her neck. 'I think I've had enough for now.'

Apprehension snatched at her and Siobhan leapt up, glancing at the sandwich her mum had barely touched. Hit by a wave of guilt that she'd been so wrapped up in her own concerns, she'd not noticed her mum floundering. 'No worries, Mum. Let's get you upstairs and into bed. I think we may have pushed you too hard.'

'I'm a bit cold.' Her mum shivered, her teeth chattering.

'That's probably the anaesthetic still in your system.'

Grace made a humming sound of agreement in the back of her

throat and closed her eyes for a moment, trying to draw strength, Siobhan assumed.

Her mum despised showing weakness.

Siobhan helped the older woman to her feet, giving her a gentle hug for a long moment, as much for her benefit as her mum's, and then kept a hand on her arm as she walked her to the bottom of the stairs, finding it awkward to avoid the crutches.

Her mum abandoned one crutch and used the stair rail and the other crutch to help her ascend the stairs, a pained grunt coming with each step she took.

Siobhan held on to the abandoned crutch until they reached the landing, her hand on the small of her mum's back for support and comfort.

'Mum, are you okay?'

Siobhan was greeted with another grunt as she shifted, positioning herself behind her mum to steady her with firm hands on her waist.

By the time they reached the bed, her mum was exhausted. She dropped her sticks and lowered herself with caution onto the bed, letting out a low groan. A thin sheen of sweat glistened across her forehead.

Fear ran through Siobhan at how fast frailty had hit.

She eased her mum's clothes off and pulled a soft nightshirt over her head, tugging it into place with tender care and then manoeuvred her back onto soft pillows.

As she pulled the covers up, she noted her mum was having what looked like small seizures. Her teeth were clenched, her eyes screwed shut and she was shuddering in small convulsions.

'Mum?'

She smoothed a hand over the cool, clammy skin of her mum's arm. 'Mum, are you okay?'

She considered calling the hospital, but what would they say? That she should have administered the medication almost an hour before?

Siobhan sprinted downstairs, hearing the ping of her laptop.

She spared it a cursory glance and grabbed the prescription painkillers from the paper bag the hospital had sent her home with and with shaking fingers filled a glass of water.

Out of breath by the time she flew up the stairs again, Siobhan was panting hard as she reached her mum.

'Mum? Here, take these.' She eased the tablets in between the woman's tightened lips, despite her mum's protestations about not wanting to take co-codamol, and lifted her head as she brought the glass to her mouth, letting her take sips of it until she was sure the tablets had been swallowed.

She placed the half-full glass on the bedside table and touched her mum's face with light strokes until the shudders calmed and the woman's muscles seemed to ease.

Grace's breathing slowed, and her jaw relaxed.

* * *

Siobhan glanced at the time. She'd been sitting on her mum's bed for almost an hour.

Her shoulders creaked in protest as she stood, her left foot throbbed, pins and needles stabbing through the numbness from sitting on it for so long. Her own soup would be cold, and the sandwiches probably stale, but her stomach gave a low growl of protest.

She groaned as she took her first step away. Stumbled.

'Who's that?'

She froze at her mum's voice, at once both familiar and strange. The harsh grate of it had Siobhan spinning on her heel to check, almost expecting her mum to be sitting up, her head doing a 360-degree rotation.

Not quite that, but her mum's eyes were filled with desperate horror. Her hand rested on her chest, the back of it bruised black and blue with yellow tinges where a cannula had been inserted right up until the moment she was discharged from the hospital.

Siobhan took a step toward her, and her mum's hand shot out in a stop motion.

'Don't come near me. Don't touch me. I'm not your wife.'

Fear sliced through Siobhan's heart, tearing away at the delicate filigree that kept it together. 'Oh my God.' The words whispered from her lips. What had gone on in her mum's life that Siobhan had no knowledge of?

Terrified that her mum would fall out of bed in her desperate attempt to keep Siobhan at bay, she didn't know whether to charge forward and stop her, or retreat.

'It's okay, it's only me. Mum, it's just me. Don't worry, you're safe. I'm here.' She lowered herself to her knees by the bedside so she appeared less intimidating, hoping the threat would seem less physical as she crawled closer.

She calmed her voice. 'It's only me,' she crooned.

Her mum's glazed eyes stared back at her, empty and far away. 'Leonora... Leonora, you need to get away.' Her voice faded to a whisper. 'Take the baby. Escape before it's too late.'

Her hand dropped onto the soft white bedclothes. Fingers loose. Palm up.

Boneless, Siobhan sank onto her heels, her chest aching, heart-beat thrumming in her ears.

'Dear God.' She covered her mouth with her hands as she breathed through her nose to get the hysteria under control. This wasn't some kind of post-operative delirium. Nothing she could call the hospital about.

Her mum might be reacting badly to the anaesthetic and medication, causing confusion and incoherence, but Siobhan refused to believe this was purely fantastical. A psychotic episode.

Something about the way her mum spoke had Siobhan believing a past she had no knowledge of, but was evidently central to, was fast catching up with them both. Spinning out of control.

23

THIRTY-ONE YEARS EARLIER – 1993 – GRACE

'Leave. Right now. You don't have to go back. You don't have to tolerate that kind of physical abuse, or bullshit.'

James's eyes flare with fury, especially when I show him the purple-bruised imprint of Justin's fingers on my pale upper arm.

'He's never done anything like this before.' But he has been sarcastic, and often puts me down in small, subtle ways. Like when I'm on the phone to someone important, he wiggles his fingers in a 'gimme' attitude and then says afterwards, 'Sometimes it's the monkey, not the organ grinder they want to speak to.'

With. I want to correct. You don't speak 'to' someone, you speak 'with'. It's a two-way conversation, unless you're speaking at someone, which is what Justin sometimes does to me.

James's face tightens. 'They do it once, they do it again, Grace.'

I sink to my knees next to him and then shuffle onto my bottom. It's not an easy manoeuvre in a pencil skirt and heels. He budges over to make enough room for me on what looks like a worn-out bedding set. It looks clean, though, so he probably picked it up at the local charity shop.

'He apologised afterwards.' If you could call it an apology. It was delivered fast and gruff from under lowered eyebrows, his expression surly as though he blamed me for his loss of temper.

I dip my hand into the plastic carrier bag full of goodies and hand James a sandwich, desperately trying to hide the shake in my fingers.

'They all do,' he grumbles, accepting the food from me and unwrapping it.

I want to ask if he's okay because it looks like he may have been on a bender. His hands are shaking, too, and he crams the sandwich in his mouth as though he's not eaten for a few days.

I think back to the last time I saw him.

Ten days. Maybe more.

I don't always have time to go looking for him, and he never comes to my place. Not since I moved. I think the idea of him encroaching now that I've moved up in the world, as he sees it, is not something that sits comfortably with him. He would be far more prominent in this new and clean area. People would stare. I don't care, but it's not my sensibilities that are important. I won't upset him.

He draws me back with his quiet voice, filled with conviction. 'I don't trust him. I've never trusted him.'

He's always been a little jealous. Nothing to put my finger on, but he gets a little spiky whenever I mention anything work-related. Or Justin-related, more specifically.

I have the distinct impression he's never liked Justin, even though he's never met him. Perhaps it's the way I have conveyed him. Is that because I've never truly trusted Justin myself? I've projected my image of my boss onto James's mind.

I draw in a breath, almost regretting telling him. But who else am I supposed to confide in? There's no one at work. Although we've a bustling staff, most of whom I'm on nodding terms with, being a personal assistant brings with it a certain distance.

The distance comes from them as well as me. I have no friends because everyone believes my allegiance lies with our mutual boss. It does. No one tells me their secrets. I tell no one else my secrets.

One thing I would never do is gossip either about my employer or their employees. Nor would I tell tales unless my knowledge of someone's misdemeanour is something that would affect the organisation.

On occasion, I must speak to someone, and that person is James, who I trust implicitly, but I feel a little spiky myself today. Defensive. Not so much of Justin, but of my dogged persistence in believing this is still the job for me.

'It's not easy, you know. Giving up my whole livelihood and just walking away.'

My gaze darts to his as soon as the words leave my lips. I slap a hand over my mouth as though I can take those hurtful words back. 'Oh, James, I'm sorry, I never meant...'

I would do anything to take it back. James did just that. He walked away from his past life and look where he is now. What a bitch I am to have pointed that out to him. He had no choice in the matter.

He puffs out a laugh, although I notice he raises his hand to his neck, where the scar tissue pulls the skin taut. 'Don't worry yourself, Grace. Mine was a whole different scenario. I never made the choice to get blown up. That was taken well out of my hands.'

I take a can of Coke out of my bag and hand it to him. He accepts it without a word. My stomach is roiling with nerves. I have never asked him about his background, never wanted to open up that wound. But with those few thoughtless words, I have ripped the scar off and left it gaping wide open and bloodied.

'What happened?' My voice is soft, reticent. I'm ready to back off and pretend I never asked if he shows the slightest insult.

He does not.

He pulls the tab back on the can, making it pop and fizz. Instead of drinking, he simply holds it in his hands for a long while. His knees are pulled up to his chest with his bare forearms resting lightly on them, his head lowered, his eyes studying the can of Coke. He pings the ring pull several times as though he's deep in thought, or maybe contemplating some wisdom.

I start to wonder if he heard me.

If he did, is he just ignoring me? Hoping I won't pursue the matter.

I don't move. If I had, I believe I would never have heard his story.

With a sigh, he tilts his head back and rests it against the wall he's propped up against.

The stubble on his face rasps as he rubs a hand over it.

'Did you know you can join the army when you're sixteen?' He rolls his head, looking into my eyes with his blue ones, brighter because of the redness tainting the whites. 'There was a gang of us. Seven. We all applied when we were fifteen and a half. I think that's the age, if I remember rightly.'

'Still babies,' I whisper, horrified that children are allowed to join the army at that age.

He snorts.

'Boys. Not yet men. I don't think I was even shaving at that time.' He takes a sip of his Coke and shakes his head. 'It shouldn't be allowed. Not that young. It's instinct for youths to be aggressive, to want to run and fight, especially in the name of country and freedom. A banner to wave over the heads of feisty little fuckers who want to get drunk and beat the shit out of each other. Then the army harnesses that aggression and points it in the direction of most use.' He lets out a derisive laugh. 'By our sixteenth birthdays, we were dressed in uniform, proud as punch. Champing at the bit to get stuck in.'

He takes another long pull on his Coke and then puts it on the ground by his side, dropping his hands down so they hang loose between his knees.

'What a balls-up.' He shoots me a sideways glance, shaking his head. 'Nobody even speaks about Aden. It was a brief flirtation with war, but never amounted to much, so no one remembers it. We had basic training in Detmold, Germany. We had the time of our lives there, thinking it was all a game. Running around, learning to duck and dive. We thought it was all a great laugh being Jack the Lad. Until we were shipped out to do our job of protecting Queen and Country.

'All seven of us. Benny, the eldest, was drafted into the army medical corps, disappeared off and we never saw him again. He might be alive.' James gives a disinterested shrug, looking off into the distance. I don't like to interrupt him, so I just listen. 'We never heard a single thing from him. He was simply MIA, missing in action,' he says, in case I don't understand the meaning of the acronym. But I do.

'The remaining six of us were selected for the 45 Commando Squadron. We were supposed to be the elite, but I think they kept us together because we'd trained all that time together. Training! Christ, it doesn't prepare you for real war.' He raises his hand and swipes fingers through his hair. 'We were so flaming proud.' I know he swears, but I rarely hear it from him – he keeps it a mild blaspheme in front of me and I'm quite impressed he's managed to do so now. 'Strutting like peacocks.' He stops for a minute, puffing out a long breath. 'Peacocks,' he repeats, sadness tinging that word. 'The objective was Bakri Ridge, eight miles east of the Dhala Road at Thumier. We had a convoy of over one hundred and fifty vehicles, together with amphibian landings. God, we thought we'd been sent to beat back the insurgence, break the enemy.' He closes his eyes for a long moment as he screws them up, the scar tissue around his eye tightens and turns white.

'We were the ones who were beaten. Savaged.' In an automatic move, he raises his hand to his scarred neck and cradles it as I wonder how far that scarring goes. I've never seen him wear short sleeves, not even on the warmest of days. Even now, he wears long sleeves, turned up. Nothing naked above his elbows. Pale, thin scars streak down the inside of one forearm as though whatever burned him had run out of energy, sending one last lick of flame.

We sit in silence for a long moment before he speaks again, his voice gruff and wistful.

'It was bloody chaos. When they taught us to run, duck, dive, roll in training, it wasn't to the constant accompaniment of being shelled by an army that was better prepared than us for the terrain.'

He puts his hand over his mouth. 'Reg.'

He stops, reaches for his drink and takes a sip as though his throat is dry. 'I grew up with Reg. We were born in the same hospital just two days apart. He was like a brother to me. We did everything together.' He fiddles with the can, staring at it as though it holds history in its distorted reflection. 'Turned out, we'd also been sleeping with the same woman.' He puffs out a light laugh as though he's still incredulous. 'So had Ben. All three of us seeing the same bloody woman, and none of us knew. All three of us in love with her.'

In the silence, I could barely whisper the question, so palpable was his pain. 'How did you find out?'

He sucks air in and shakes his head. 'Because Reg saw her the night before we were shipped to Germany for training. She was pregnant. The stupid fool promised to marry her.'

My heart thuds in my chest as memories of Thomas wrench at me, tearing into me, so I'm left raw and bloodied, sympathy oozing like slow-moving lava.

'When did you realise she was seeing all of you?' I whisper, not sure if I can bear the answer.

'Not until we were on the ship on our way to Aden. He'd managed to buy a ring in Germany.'

He makes a move, a light touch to his chest, and I know with certainty that the ring is there, against his heart. Because he always wears a shirt with the collar done up, I've never seen a chain, but I know.

He glances sideways at me and his eyes glisten in the soft, fading light.

'What happened?'

'He'd asked Ben and me to look after her. You know, if anything happened to him. Make sure the baby was well cared for. That's when we realised. When he told us her name. Ben wasn't too bothered. He'd have moved on, and he knew for certain that he wasn't the father in any case.' James glances sideways at me, as though he was embarrassed to impart the information, even though it was relevant to his story. 'We all knew he'd had mumps when he was fourteen. He wasn't able to father a child.'

Maybe James's discomfort is for my situation. For the fact that I cannot have children. Whatever the case, I see a burnished red flush his cheeks.

It hurts each time I think about it. So, I make sure I don't think about it. It's becoming more difficult, though, with having a constant reminder of Leonora's advancing pregnancy. All the tests I've been party to, arranged. I'd been dragged into their issues and only now the toll is beginning to tell.

In the dark recesses of my heart, I'm desperate for a child. Somehow, I think James knows. If he does, then he is the only one. I keep it well enough disguised.

James blinks and I realise I am simply staring at him. Hypnotised by my own internal monologue.

I blink back at him. Wait.

He continues as though he was waiting for me to come back to him. Giving me a moment for my own thoughts, and I appreciate that, even though we don't acknowledge it. This is his story, not mine.

'Reg and I had a major bust-up. We had to be torn apart by Ben and a couple of the other lads. By the time they did, we both had bloodied lips and black eyes. We'd fought like maniacs. All over a woman.' He snorted. 'Not even a woman. Just a girl. Like we were just lads. Turned out, she was still only fifteen, just a couple of weeks off her sixteenth birthday, but all the same, what we did amounted to a crime, no matter how—' he pauses '—enthusiastic she was. We could have all been sent to prison if we'd been found out.'

I smile at that thought. A wry smile, not really humour. If he'd been imprisoned, it would have saved James going to Aden, would have meant he didn't suffer from shell shock, or PTSD as we now call it, if only fate had dealt him a different hand.

If only it had dealt me a different hand, I wouldn't have fallen for a married man who'd give me gonorrhoea, an ectopic pregnancy and infertility.

Bitterness briefly swells inside me.

Fate is a bitch.

I rail against her with every move forward I make, every success, promotion and pay rise I get. But she's the winner. In the end, it's her who decides what becomes of us.

What became of James.

For some reason, I hold back on making judgement on that young girl. Not yet. Not until I know the whole truth.

'Did he return from the war?' I had to know. I felt I already did. A strange lurking suspicion that this story would not end well.

James shook his head. 'The Radfan rebels pushed back, day

after day. They knew their terrain. We were supposed to do a helicopter assault, but there was such a shortage of helicopters, the idea was abandoned.' He squeezes his eyes closed and shakes his head. 'Bloody army. Bloody government. We were so ill-prepared. We were stuck on the side of a hill, blazing sun during the day, and enough to freeze the brass balls—' James stopped himself as though he remembered who he was talking to. 'There was a barrage of artillery fire, mortar, snipers. If you put your head above the parapet, it would be shot off. Two of my pals went that way. Duncan and Trent.' He blows out a breath as though it's been lodged in his chest for a while. 'We were cut off for a while, and the insurgents kept coming. Thirteen days on the trot and there were barely any of us holding position when backup arrived and we pushed and pushed back.'

Confused, I wait for him to continue.

'It sounds like it was a success.'

'It was. For the British army. We held position, despite the constant bombardment. The lads and I were told to fall back in the eery silence of the aftermath. Ben went first, followed by Reg, then me.'

I reach out to touch his arm. It seems to jolt him back.

'One of our sergeants lay wounded on the field and all three of us went to his assistance. I dug in the first-aid bag I'd managed to grab and found morphia. I handed it to Reg as he knew how to administer it.'

James closes his eyes as the memory sweeps him along. Too caught up in his own thoughts to even be aware of me.

'The first missile struck Ben full in the chest, literally throwing his entire body high in the air in an explosion of blood and guts with nothing left of him. Reg and I were sprayed, splattered with bits of him.'

James drops his head, so his chin rests on his chest. 'I grabbed

Reg's hand, tried to pull him down, away from the wounded sergeant when the second missile exploded alongside him.' James put his hands over his ears to block out the sound raging inside his mind. He's shaking now, as though the scene is playing through his head, vivid and real, and I understand for the first time what demons come to haunt him. 'I hear the screams. My best friend.'

Tears prick the back of my eyes, and I touch my neck, to indicate his, my voice hoarse with distress. 'Is that how this happened?'

He raises his hand and cups the side of his face, then runs it down his neck and all the way down his arm.

'I never even felt it. My uniform was on fire, and I never knew. The bomb blast ripped away my skin, but I was numb. It was like we were in a bubble of white noise, no one else but us.'

He turns his head and tears stream down a tortured face. 'I hear his voice every time there is silence. I can't bear to be alone in a room. When I close my eyes...' He gulps down the tears.

He drops his hands from his face and makes a circle of claws with them. 'My name was the one on his lips as he screamed his final words while I held his hand in mine.'

James's hand slackens into a gentle cup. 'I was still holding his hand... but it was no longer connected to his body.'

I close my eyes and squeeze them tight as I try to stanch the flow down cheeks already wet with tears. My stomach rebels at the image ingrained on the back of my eyelids and I open them wide, unable to bear it. A sob catches in my throat. 'Oh, James.'

'I still feel the warmth of his hand in mine, every single day.' His voice thickens with emotion. 'Still hear his last words as he pushed the morphine into the sergeant, crouching over him to protect him. He stared at me as he depressed that syringe and said, *James, keep the pact.*'

I pull in a breath and swipe at my wet cheeks. 'He still wanted you to look after his girlfriend? The one you fought over?' I'm shocked at how far love can carry a person. I've never experienced a feeling that intense for anyone. I thought I had for Thomas, but his infidelity had snatched away any love I felt for him and left me cold. Heartless. Only I'm not heartless because James's pain is tearing me apart, and I would do anything to stop it.

James turns tortured eyes to mine and gives one slow nod, his hand going once again to his chest. Before I can say anything, he dips the tip of his fingers inside his shirt and yanks on a thin linked chain, dragging a plain gold band out of his neckline.

'It wasn't so much the girlfriend, as the baby we agreed to look out for, whichever one of us lived through that nightmare. We knew we wouldn't all make it. I think somehow by this time we knew there was no redemption for her.'

'What happened to the other one? The seventh boy who went to war?'

James gives a crooked grin and a quick shrug. 'He got out alive. Undamaged in many ways. He's still in the army. On a posting to Germany at the moment.' He pauses, his eyes meeting mine as his lips twitch into a wry smile. 'A good friend of mine. He's a document specialist.'

It occurs to me to question this line further but James unfastens the chain and the ring drops to join the wet streak of tears on the palm of his hand.

'You never gave it to her,' I whisper, somehow knowing there is more to this story than I could possibly guess.

He shakes his head. 'No. When I got out of hospital, months later, she took one look at me and ran a mile. Told me to take a hike.' He barks out a derisive laugh. 'She couldn't get away fast enough.'

'What about the baby?'

He slants me a look. 'She was holding her in her arms when she opened the door and told me where to go. I never even got a chance to offer her the ring before she slammed the door in my face. Apparently, she already knew about Reg. His mother had let her know. Quite frankly, she couldn't give a shit, pardon my French. Except when Reg's mum showed her the Victoria Cross he'd been posthumously awarded. Apparently, she almost snatched her hand off in her eagerness to get it.' He smiles. It's sad and wistful. 'Reg's mum was no pushover, God rest her soul. She snatched the medal back and kept it herself. Said the girl didn't deserve it.'

'Didn't she want her to keep it, for the child's sake?'

He snorts this time. 'No chance. She'd have sold it. She was already shacked up with another man. With another couple dangling on the line. She's never done without a man. Always has the next one in her sights.'

'Poor child.'

He reaches for my hand and turns it palm up in his free one. His warmth seeps through to my cold veins.

'She seems to have done quite well for herself.'

My voice is slightly unsteady.

'She sounds just like my mum.'

He tips the ring into my palm and curls his fingers around my hand, closing it into a fist, the ring clutched safe inside the layers of both.

'Not *like* your mum. She *is* your mum,' he murmurs with finality.

And at last, I understand.

24

PRESENT DAY – TUESDAY, 9 JULY 2024, 12.30 A.M. – SIOBHAN

In the silence, Siobhan raised the lid on her laptop and then opened first the email relating to her mum's DNA.

She stared at the screen. Her gaze cruised over the information. It meant nothing.

Or did it? She narrowed her eyes against the glare.

It was all very pretty. Coloured boxes flagging up relationship possibilities and centimorgans between each connection, or generation.

She expanded the chart on the screen. What the hell was a centimorgan?

Siobhan rapidly typed the question into Google.

A unit to measure genetic links. Hmm. Interesting.

Her mum had no link with any children according to this.

Siobhan didn't let the slide of apprehension take hold. Looking at the way the DNA website worked, it didn't mean she didn't have children, it meant that none had registered with the site at this point. Except her. Perhaps her information hadn't updated. Once it did, would that link show?

She studied the information. The instructions. She scrolled

further and there did appear to be considerable connections to relatives on her mum's side. Not that distant either. That wasn't what interested her currently, although a small flicker of curiosity lit in her stomach.

All her life, Siobhan thought there was just the two of them. And yet here they were. Connections indicating relations. Or, at least, on her mum's side.

She knew she should go to bed. The day had stretched out while she divided her time between running up and down stairs, making tea, coffee and meals and administering drugs, all in addition to feeding the animals and bedding them down for the night.

Her mum would need her in the morning to help her get up, showered and dressed, but Siobhan couldn't take her eyes from the information she'd downloaded. Frustration nagged at Siobhan as she opened her own information. The spit dried in her mouth as her gaze raced from one table to the next, her heart racing.

With a low groan, she lowered her head onto her hands, curled her fingers into her hair and tugged at it.

'No. No. It can't be true.' Because however well she thought she'd prepared herself for this over the past forty-eight hours, the shock rocked her to her core.

She raised her head and checked again.

The screen on the laptop glowed with bright ferocity without the kitchen lights on.

She swallowed.

Her mum's words had been true.

Without a doubt, she was not her mother's daughter.

Side by side, she'd loaded her own details next to her mum's on her laptop.

There was absolutely no connection, no overlap of centimorgans, or so few that they may have a distant great-great-great-grandparent, although even that was doubtful.

She flopped back in her chair, the screen wavering in front of her as her eyes filled with tears.

How did she not know that she was adopted?

Why had her mum never told her?

She scrambled in her pocket for a screwed-up tissue with no knowledge or care for how long it had been there.

If what her mum had said in her delirium the first time in hospital had been correct, then what about today? What if her mum had a dark secret?

Siobhan dabbed at her eyes, then blew her nose before automatically reaching down to scratch the top of Beau's head as he wandered through the still-open back door to lean against her leg.

Siobhan turned to look through the door, a sudden shiver raising goosebumps over her flesh.

She came to her feet and made her way over, Beau at her heels as usual.

She stared out into the dark night, narrowing her eyes to scan the length of the garden, and strained to listen for sound, to watch for movement. Normally, she would step outside and stare up at the night sky, appreciating layer upon layer of stars unhindered by light pollution where they lived.

Tonight, she closed the door and locked everything out there. Her world was strange enough without the dark intruding.

Siobhan sat back down, looked at the screens. Nothing. There was no connection.

She read the instructions from the DNA company again, just in case she'd got it wrong, she was looking at it from the wrong angle, then peered at the screen again.

There was no connection between herself and her mum, but there were relatives on both sides. She looked at the matrix which explained the connection between each relationship and ran her fingernail across the screen on her laptop, knowing she shouldn't but unable to stop herself. According to this, the closest relationship registered on *her* side was an aunt.

There was no mother, no father listed.

It didn't mean she didn't have them, merely that they hadn't subscribed to DNA testing.

An aunt was listed, but there was no contact information.

There was for a cousin. She had a first cousin according to the centimorgans on the chart.

This was crazy.

She had a cousin. And the cousin had provided contact details.

Siobhan looked at the time. It was 1 a.m., and she really needed to get off to bed. Her body was about ready to drop, but her mind still raced.

Before she had time to think, Siobhan's fingers raced across her keyboard, rushing out a quick message. She read it through...

> Hello, I hope you don't mind me contacting you, but I've recently discovered that I am adopted, and I have no idea who my real parents are or the reasons behind my adoption. I've recently taken a DNA test and the whole process is quite a mystery to me. I notice from the information that you appear to be a first cousin of mine which I assume from the chart is on my birth mother's side of the family. I'd really like to research into this further if you are willing to help. Thank you so much for any assistance you can lend. I look forward to hearing from you. Kind regards, Siobhan.

Siobhan stared at the message. Read every single word to make sure there were no mistakes. 'Recently discovered', that was the understatement of the year.

She tapped the fingers of one hand against her lips as she transferred her attention to her mum's DNA profile.

Once more her fingers made a mad dash.

This was crazy. From the look of it, her mum had either half-siblings or first cousins on both her mother's and father's side. According to the information supplied, with the number of centimorgans each of them had, they could be either, as there was an overlap. Six on her mother's, three on her father's. Only one on the father's side had contact details, but three on the mother's side.

Not giving herself time to think, Siobhan bolted off another message.

> Hello, I hope you don't mind me contacting you, but I've recently discovered that despite believing I had no living relatives, it appears that I do. I have recently taken a DNA test and the whole process is quite a mystery to me. I have given permission for my adoptive daughter to contact you on my behalf. I notice from the information that you appear to be either a first cousin, or a half-sibling, neither of which I was aware of. I was also under the impression that my dad was no longer alive. I'd really like to research into this further if you are willing to help. Thank you so much for any assistance you can lend. I look forward to hearing from you. Kind regards, Siobhan, pp Grace.

Siobhan copied and pasted the message and also addressed it to her mum's maternal side of the family, making a slight adjustment so it fit.

She had no idea what possible reason her mum could have for cutting herself off from her own parents, so she would take it easy on her approach. Test the waters, so to speak.

She hesitated, unable to actually hit the send button.

Was this disloyal to her mum? A woman she adored and who adored her. The only person she had ever known as her mother.

Was it fair of her to rock the boat?

Surely there had to be a genuine reason for her mum not to want her to know she was adopted?

Siobhan pressed her lips together.

Unless she wasn't adopted.

Unless her mum had lied to her all her life and there was something more sinister. Something her mum definitely didn't want exposed. In which case, did she deserve Siobhan's loyalty?

Had she taken Siobhan? Bought her?

In all the papers she'd looked through of her mum's, there was no evidence of an adoption. Nothing.

A snake of suspicion curled in her stomach. What if her mum had somehow bought her on the black market? It wasn't unheard of, especially when her mum was younger. Or perhaps an underage child got pregnant, and her mum came to her aid. She'd rather think of that scenario, than any other.

She drew in a breath as a thought occurred.

Photographs of her were kept in an old-fashioned album, not on a database, or a hard drive like they did these days. She didn't need to search for them. She pretty much knew where they were kept.

Before she pressed send, she drew her chair back and came to her feet in one smooth movement, lifting the chair so it didn't scrape on the floor tiles and wake Beau, or her mum.

Perhaps she needed a moment longer. Time to consider what she was about to do. The consequences that would follow. Would this ruin everything she had ever known? Destroy her world?

It was like the time Christopher Hardiman had lobbed a stink bomb at the Year Six teacher in the classroom one hot summer afternoon when they were still at junior school, only ten or possibly eleven years old. He'd thought it a laugh. A naughty schoolboy prank.

The stench had been so overwhelming Kathy Stark had thrown up instantly, causing another three of the girls to do the same.

A thick yellow fog had encompassed them, stinging their eyes, and closing their throats. Instead of evacuating as he should have done, the incandescent teacher had walked out, fury etched in every muscle in his face. He'd stood on the outside of the door holding the handle so none of the children could escape. He'd watched as Christopher peed his pants, and allowed children to choke and cry and collapse on the floor while he stared, dispassionate, through the window in the door, his eyes burning with hate as the entire class became hysterical.

Of course, he'd been dismissed for doing so, banned from teaching for life, but that didn't lessen the trauma for those children locked in a stench-filled room, with eyes stinging and hysteria spreading. If it had not been for the next-door teacher coming to investigate what all the screaming was about, Siobhan had no idea how long they would have been locked in there. How far that teacher would have gone to punish them.

That one thoughtless prank carried out by a young boy with more enthusiasm and mischievous glee than sense had set off a long sequence of events that would affect every single person in that room for the rest of their lives.

Less affected than most, it had still left Siobhan with a dislike of enclosed spaces. Not exactly claustrophobia, but she avoided lifts, taking the stairs wherever possible, knowing her heart would begin to race the moment those doors closed on her.

Now, Siobhan had to consider whether it was worth lobbing that stink bomb into a roomful of relatives. Before she pressed the send button, she needed to consider the consequences.

She opened the double doors in the sideboard and drew everything out, so it scattered across the floor in front of her.

With care, she picked up her baby album. This would give her all the information she needed. She could remember seeing it in the past, long ago when she was a child. She'd looked through it. Truth was, she had never paid that much attention. What child does look at their own baby album? It was normally mums showing it to boyfriends or future in-laws, neither of which Siobhan had. She dated regularly via a dating app, but really, she still hadn't met the man of her dreams. Most princes turned out to be frogs in disguise.

She'd not given up hope, but she wouldn't settle. Not for the sake of having a man in her life. Not just any man. Not every woman needed someone. Her mum hadn't. She couldn't remember her seeing anyone when Siobhan was younger. There had been a couple of men along the way that she'd dated, but no one she remembered her mum having anything more than a mild affection for.

She thought she was genetically predisposed with the same personality.

It appeared she wasn't.

Not genetically, in any case.

Kelvin had been nice. Too nice. A pushover. Someone Siobhan had initially thought would make a good husband and father. In the end, he'd have made neither. His distinct lack of interest in anything had almost bored her to death. The first flush of romance had brought dinners out, flowers, weekends away. That lasted all of six months before he was sitting in her mum's living room, feet on the coffee table watching football and eating whatever her mum provided, his midriff becoming wider by the week.

Siobhan had begun to wonder which of them he preferred, which was when she came to the conclusion that he didn't want a girlfriend, or wife. It was all too much effort. What he wanted was another mother.

Three months it had been since she last saw him and there was no sadness, no regret. She didn't miss him in the least. It was a relief. She enjoyed her freedom.

She'd seen a couple of men recently and there was one she quite liked chatting to from one of the dating apps. Greg, he was called, but he lived in Devon, and it all seemed such an effort to arrange a meet-up. There was the dilemma of deciding whether to stay in a hotel overnight. He'd offered for her to stay at his place. But what if they took an instant dislike to each other?

In any case, everything had to go on hold for now. Until she sorted out her mum, and her life.

She flipped open the album her mum had kept. Kelvin wouldn't be seeing it.

Oddly, the first page had virtually nothing written. Most of the information was left blank.

Siobhan frowned. Was that usual, for a young first-time mum to go to the effort of buying a baby album, but to not complete it?

It had her full name. Siobhan Sarah Martin. Her date of birth. Her birth weight. Even the length of her, which came as a surprise, as she never had any recollection of babies having their length measured in hospital. Not that the fact was relevant.

What it didn't have was her progress. Gaps where her weight and height should be. Small details that now she looked closer were missing where you would expect them to be.

She flicked over the first page to look at her baby photographs.

There wasn't one of her straight after her birth, nothing to show she was in hospital. Admittedly, social media hadn't taken the leap into photo frenzy at the time Siobhan was born – indeed, there was no social media – but looking at these, the first photo of her was in a cot. At home. She had a full head of hair and looked fairly well-developed. Round-faced, rosy-cheeked. At the very least, she would have expected one photograph of her mum holding her in a hospital bed.

She realised hospital had never been mentioned.

Siobhan closed the sideboard door and leaned back against the piece of furniture, raising her knees to bring the page closer to her face.

'How strange.'

She flipped through the pages of the first two years of her life.

There was nothing abnormal. Not if you ignored the first few weeks of her life.

She stared at the first photo again.

So, when did the adoption take place? There was no evidence of it. Unless her mum never intended for her to ever find out. Evidently, she didn't.

Why?

Her mum didn't strike her as backward thinking. If anything, she was a progressive woman. She had her finger on the pulse, normally, when she'd not been flattened by cancer and a broken hip. Even now she was starting to show shades of her former self.

Not used to signs of weakness from her mum, Siobhan was aware the woman had a core of steel.

Siobhan chuckled with dark humour. Well, she had a hip of steel now.

Which was what Siobhan would have if she didn't get up off the floor.

She closed the book and rolled over onto her knees so she could open the cupboard and slip everything back inside.

Upright, she walked stiff and flat-footed to the door, turning to check the place before she switched off the lights, and wended her way through to the kitchen to do the same thing there. She reached out a hand to close the laptop and paused.

'Sorry, Mum, but I have to know.'

With a decisive tap of her finger, she sent the messages winging their way to their intended recipients.

Heat rushed through her as her stomach clenched with anxiety. She'd done it, now. There was no turning back.

She closed the lid, turned out the remaining lights and made her way upstairs to check on her mum before she went to sleep. Tomorrow she would gather the courage to speak with her mum about her adoption.

For tonight, she would content herself with the fact that she'd set plans in motion.

Or had she just lobbed that stink bomb into the room?

25

THIRTY-ONE YEARS EARLIER – 1993 – GRACE

On occasion, I know James is right. More often than not, in fact. There are moments when I am astounded that such an intelligent, insightful person can be reduced to nothing by a twist of fate.

I check my hair and make-up in the ladies' room before I leave work. I'll pop into Sainsbury's on my way home and buy a microwave dinner. I can't be bothered with cooking tonight, but I'm beyond hungry. I skipped lunch. Not intentionally. I've not stopped all day. Organising a charitable event on this scale is nothing to be sneezed at. To be truthful, I can do this kind of thing with my eyes closed, it's the others who cause issues.

The caterer whose premises have just been flooded and will no longer be able to accommodate us.

The star guest who put the event in the wrong month of their diary and is subsequently double-booked as they'd also not informed their agent that it was their best friend's wedding.

The boss who is currently uncontactable to run anything by.

I lean in close to the mirror. Large almond-shaped eyes stare back at me with irises such a dark blue they could almost be violet. Thick, sooty lashes emphasise the depth of my eyes. James's eyes.

How had I never spotted that?

It all makes sense now. It certainly did once he showed me a photograph of Reg and I realise there is nothing about him even vaguely resembling me. No wonder James knew the moment he spotted me. Our eyes are the same, so too is the hair colouring. Reg had a thick mop of black hair and eyes as dark as nutmeg. James had known. Now I do.

The whole reason he'd kept an eye on me. Possibly the reason he'd never entirely gone off the cliff edge. Maybe I'm the reason he pulls back. So he can look after me.

Like he's trying to look after me now, knowing how uncomfortable I am at work.

In the silence of the immense Hall, I totter back to my desk on new heels which may be a little high, but God, do I love them.

I'm late as usual, and my stomach gives another grumble, hinting that I should hurry. I'm pretty sure I'm the last one here again, even though I've made a concerted effort not to be. I don't think Justin needs that much dedication any more and I've pulled back on the number of hours I put in. When I checked my contract, it is only forty hours a week. I put in closer to sixty and don't get paid overtime unless it's for a specific official engagement. Working over my lunch break, arriving early and staying late don't count. I have never claimed it and have never been expected to do so.

Perhaps I need to reassess, maybe pack up my bags and leave. There's a strange atmosphere here of late and I can't quite place what caused it, other than Justin's insistence to his two closest allies that Leonora is a raving lunatic.

Tensions obviously ran high while Leonora and James were trying to conceive, but I would have thought as her pregnancy is now well-advanced that they'd both have relaxed somewhat and be enjoying the journey.

It seems my opinion is wrong.

Justin is... tetchy.

He's never been that way with me in the past, but ever since the day he grabbed my arm, he's been quite standoffish. As though it was me who had over-stepped the mark. Admittedly, he's never discussed the fact that I stood my ground against him, again, and maybe that is a major factor. Perhaps I undermined his masculinity. Just as Leonora may have been perceived to have done.

We've chipped away at that fragile ego of his, each of us in our own way. Not deliberately, but the fissure has widened. Where once he was all-powerful, he's now diminished.

Gordon also has something odd going on. He's not around as much as normal, but when he is, his dark eyes search mine, looking for goodness only knows what. There's a question in his gaze, but I swear I don't know the answer.

He's never intimidated me. Not since that first day when I soon realised it was more of a lark to him to have me tearing around to the other side of the Hall. I think my driving abilities impressed him. Gained some kind of respect. I have, also, always had a quiet respect for him in return. I hold him in high esteem, because he is clever, and he is hugely loyal to Justin. An attribute I find very noble, because Justin is not an easy man to deal with all the time. Oh, Justin has charm aplenty. At events I organise, making sure everything runs not just smoothly, but with precise precision, I slip through the crowds unnoticed. A ghost. A light touch to Gordon's arm, a dip of my head. We understand each other. Read each other.

I'm not reading him now.

Something inside of him has closed off. Changed forever, I feel. Not just with me, but this is the other thing, I think his relationship with Justin has changed too. Skewed. Ever since that day when he stepped in claustrophobically close. Although he never touched me, never threatened me, I felt the menace, whether it was meant for me, or Justin, I don't know. Something between the three of us has broken.

Am I the catalyst? Or is it Leonora?

I scoop up my handbag and loop it over my shoulder. I'll lock up behind me, because from the glance I make out to the empty car park, everyone else has already left and neither Justin nor Gordon will be back for a few days. Perhaps I should start leaving early on a Friday, too.

Ironically, the phone from the domestic quarters peals and I pick it up, hoping to hell it's not Leonora calling to ask me to do one last thing before I leave. She rarely asks me to do things for her, but once in a while when Justin is away, she checks his itinerary with me. 'Hello, Grace speaking.'

'Grace.' The voice is short and breathless. 'I need Justin. Get me Justin right now.'

I half shake my head and stop, realising she can't see me, but there's something in her breathy voice that worries me. 'Justin's not here, Leonora.' I hesitate to say anything further because surely she knows that her husband is currently climbing Mount Everest.

I don't really understand their relationship, but in all fairness, Justin has always been at her beck and call until recently. Whenever she has called him in the past, he has gone running.

In truth, I'm not sure having your living quarters combined with work is healthy, Justin is too accessible to his wife, and she definitely has become more demanding of late, even though I deny there is anything mentally wrong with her. I assume with such an enormous Hall, it was more practical and keeps the costs down. Not that Justin gives any indication that costs do need to be kept down.

Not coming from an affluent background, I am constantly stunned at the casual dismissal of his own wealth. Never will I ever put myself in the position of being without again. I watch every penny I spend, save half of what I earn every month and although my work clothes are stylish, elegant and sophisticated, I buy them in the sale. Classic lines that cannot be faulted. After all, I am a personal assistant. My six suits are black, navy, and varying shades of grey.

As a small rebellion, I wear bright silk camisoles with matching shoes. I do love my matching shoes and handbags. It's an indulgence, but one which I temper by, again, purchasing them in the sales. One pair a month.

At no point do I ever take anything for granted.

Unlike Justin and Leonora. She certainly has no qualms about spending his money.

Theirs is a throwaway world. Leonora's outfits are handmade by her exclusive seamstress. Impeccable designs, exquisite materials, styled to perfection. Worn only once. As far as I can tell. Not that I often see Leonora at social gatherings, but I have spoken with the seamstress when she arrives, seen swatches of material, appreciated the swish of a beautiful ballgown as Leonora has floated out on Justin's arm into their chauffeur-driven Rolls-Royce.

How the other half live.

With a casual disdain that only people with dynastic wealth can display.

I'm pulled back to the here and now by Leonora's breathy response.

'Grace, I need him.'

'I'm very sorry, Leonora...' I rarely use her name, but I feel the desperation in her voice. Could Justin be right, has all this hormone treatment leading up to her pregnancy affected her mind?

Not since the day he grabbed my arm has he made further comment about his wife in front of me, but the tension has been there, any time she calls him. I've heard the desperate rise of her voice on the other end of the line, if not the actual words, seen the stiffening of his body.

'Justin is away. He won't be back until...' I glance at the diary, flick through until I find his return flight details. 'Tuesday evening.'

'Tuesday? Tuesday?' The shrill panic in her voice has me sitting upright. I wonder if any of the domestic staff can help her, but they are mainly maids. 'It's fucking Friday, Grace, where the fuck has he gone?'

Has she forgotten?

Justin did indicate how forgetful and strange she had become.

'He's...' I have to tell her. 'He's climbing Mount Everest.' I keep my voice as pacifying as possible, but I can hear the fast-breathing break on a long, high-pitched moan. 'Is there anything I can do for you, Leonora?'

Anyone I can get, because quite honestly, I don't know enough about this woman, my employer's wife. Really, there should be no need to know more than she likes her outfits handmade, she adores champagne truffles from Fortnum and Mason and her favourite flowers are Gloriosa, which according to Justin her wedding bouquet was made from. Another fact I know is that wedding bouquet is kept in a dedicated freezer located next to the vast wine cellars. Her favourite wine is Chateau Landon 1964 Medoc. I know this, not because I am a wine connoisseur, but purely because I had to replenish the stocks in the wine cellar last year and it is not the easiest bottle to get hold of. Nor the cheapest, although according to Justin nor is it the most expensive and as Leonora is not a prolific drinker, the dozen bottles I acquired should last a considerable amount of time, especially as right now she has given up drinking altogether.

Leonora's breath is now gusting down the phone and my muscles tighten. There's something very wrong here, not just Leonora demanding Justin's attention, but she's panting.

'Leonora, are you okay?'

Her guttural groan has me sinking into my chair, elbows on the desk.

This isn't normal anxiety. She doesn't just want Justin, she *needs* him.

'No,' she whispers down the phone. 'The baby.'

The baby? Hairs raise on the back of my neck.

I look again at my diary. This baby isn't due for another six weeks, which was the whole reason Justin had made his last-minute trip, knowing he would be tied to home life once the baby came.

'Are you in labour?'

'I think so.'

'Are you sure?'

The pull of my own womb brings back dark memories I would much rather forget. A shiver runs up my spine.

'Yesss...' I almost hear the grinding of her teeth.

'It's too early,' I say down the phone, regretting it immediately.

Now Leonora starts a keening sob and I come to my feet, reaching for the keys for the domestic quarters. 'I'll call an ambulance, Leonora, then I'll be right with you.'

'Nooo, don't leave me, it's coming. The baby's coming. I need you now, Grace. Now!'

I'm on my feet and running for the stairs.

I should have accepted Justin's offer to buy me a mobile phone, but quite honestly, I don't want to be on call twenty-four hours a day. He gets enough of my time. I may be well-paid, but I work damned hard for my money and put in the hours. At least twelve a day. Every weekday. I have weekends off, but that would all stop if I was accessible then too.

Breathless by the time I reach the locked door at the bottom of the stairs, I plunge the big, fat brass key into the lock and twist.

The door bursts open and I scramble through, leaving it wide. I kick my heels off and sprint up the stairs and along the corridor, the long silk woven hall runner smooth and cool under my feet.

I assume she's in her bedroom, a place I have never visited and, to be honest, really don't want to. This is not my domain. I assume the day staff have left by now and Leonora is alone. Since Mrs Blackwood retired, no one stays overnight. I have no choice. She needs me.

I yell out her name and it echoes along the silent hallways 'Leonora? Where are you?'

'Here. I'm in here.'

Further along the hall in bare feet, I skid to a halt, almost rucking up the silk runner under my feet. I spin and fling the partially open door wide.

A long, expansive living room with floor-to-ceiling windows stretches the whole length which, despite daylight still looming, doesn't overcome the darkness cast by low oak beams and mahogany panelling, chocolate leather sofas and wing-back chairs.

I scan the room, somehow expecting Leonora to be on one of the sofas, one elegant leg crossed over another and a cup of tea in her hand, with no sign of being in labour, but she's nowhere to be seen.

'Leonora,' I screech, high and uncouth, but I don't think the situation calls for diplomacy.

'Here.' That one word is quiet and filled with agonised pain.

I hustle through an open connecting door into another long room, the eighteen-place mahogany dining table pitifully set for two at the far end.

I skid to a halt, my heart ricocheting around in my chest. Flames lick up my face as I try to catch my breath, darting my gaze around the room until I spot her. One fluffy-slippered foot pokes from behind the far end of the table.

'Leonora. I'm here.' I want my voice to be filled with calm reassurance, but it's breathless and unsure.

'Fucking Christ! At last! What took you so fucking long?'

I'm not sure I've ever heard so much as a profanity slip from Leonora's elegant lips, but I'm sure the circumstances fit the need. As I reach her, I fall to my knees and crawl up alongside her body, which is currently curled into the foetal position. I drop down onto my elbows, so my head is level with hers, and reach out for her.

Is she in labour? Is she losing the baby?

I quickly assess her. Sweat beads over her brow and upper lip and she's a peculiar colour. All blotchy red and almost yellow in patches. This beautiful woman certainly knows how to ugly cry. It strikes me as odd how her face has transformed, as though the muscles are contracting along with her womb. Her nose has flattened out and the brackets either side have cut into deep creases. Her eyes are squeezed tight shut with wrinkles flaring out across her temples. There's a blue vein in between her creased brows that seems to be pulsing.

Like a bucket of cold water being flung at me, I am suddenly and completely doused in control.

It's just the two of us, and there is no way I can move her.

There is an icy determination that settles over me as I run my gaze over the whole scenario. Emotions a moment ago raging are parked. Compartmentalised. Just like I do with work matters. This is my calling, right here, right now. This woman, Leonora, needs me like no one else has ever needed me. Not even James.

I stroke her shoulder and shake loose any wobble in my voice. I am strong. I can handle this. I know what she is going through because I have been through it too. Although I pray the end result is not the same for her as it was for me. She needs a firm, calm hand. Just like those midwives. She doesn't need a swift slap on the thigh and an old surgeon telling her she's a no-good slut.

I push aside thoughts of my own disastrous experience and squeeze Leonora's shoulder to get her attention. I look into her face.

My voice is steady. Even. 'I need to call an ambulance.'

She reaches out, long bony fingers grasping mine until I feel my bones grinding together, her nails dig in hard to pierce my flesh and I join her as she lets out her next howl.

I may be calm, but I can't shake off that kind of pain. I'm not bloody superwoman.

'Don't you fucking leave me,' she growls into my face.

'No. It's okay. I won't. But—' I prise her fingers from around my hand '—I need my hand.'

I pop my head up and scan the room for a telephone. A bloody telephone. Where the hell is it?

'Where's the telephone?'

'Forget the fucking phone.'

'Leonora, we are going to need help.' I speak to her reasonably, firmly. 'Where is the phone you just called me on?'

She waves vaguely in the direction of a long, narrow chiffonier, the clawed brass feet visible from where she lies.

I push up from the floor and sprint to the landline. She'd dropped the receiver, so I put my finger on the plunger and depress it several times. I dial 999 and wait.

'Emergencies. Which service do you require?'

'Ambulance, please.'

There is static for a moment and then a clear, composed voice answers.

'Ambulance service.'

'I need an ambulance. My...' Who the hell do I say? What is she to me? 'My employer's wife has gone into labour. It's too early, she's not due for another six weeks. She's too far along for me to move. I think her contractions are coming right on top of each other.' I reel off the address so fast that the woman on the other end of the phone has to ask for it again.

Leonora's screech reaches ear-splitting decibels.

'Can we enter the premises easily?'

How do I describe that it's an enormous Hall? That there are two ways in and that there's not a single person here, apart from Leonora and me. No one to show them how to locate us. That if they arrive at the rear of the building, they can't access the private quarters. What a mess.

'I...'

I blow out a breath. 'The front door. Come to the front door and I'll let them in.'

I'll have to take the chance when they arrive and tear down the stairs. Once I let them in, I can hand over responsibility.

'Hurry. Please hurry.'

'Stay on the line and I can talk you through...'

'I can't. She needs me.' And she does, I think to myself. This beautiful, elegant woman needs me.

I hang up and scramble back onto the floor beside Leonora.

'It's coming,' Leonora growls through gritted teeth.

'Don't, don't...' *push,* I'm about to say, but it's too late, I can feel from the bunching of her muscles that she is pushing. She's curled on her side, and I realise she still has her underwear on.

I reach down and, without preamble, I rip her knickers and tights from her body, taking those fluffy pink slippers with them.

Should she be on her back?

I don't really have any idea, but Leonora seems to have made herself as comfortable as possible.

Her body relaxes and I know it's only temporary, so I leap to my feet, running for the living room where I saw cushions on those hard, informal leather settees, and a huge, multi-coloured crocheted shawl. I snatch them up and charge back to Leonora's side, spreading the shawl on the floor behind her curled-up frame, and dump three cushions on it, which was all I could carry.

If I can just make her comfortable until the ambulance arrives, then at least that would be something.

'Leonora, shuffle over, let me make you comfortable.'

I give her shoulder a gentle push. Obligingly, she rolls over onto her back and I wedge a cushion beneath her head. She is panting softly, and if I didn't know better, I would say she had fallen asleep. Perhaps she has reached the end of her strength.

A quiver of anxiety shudders through me and I knock it back, heartlessly. This is not about me, about my feelings. This is about Leonora and her baby.

I pray the ambulance arrives soon. When I hear the sirens, I'll rush down and open the front door. In the meantime, I stroke sweat-drenched hair from Leonora's forehead. 'You're doing really well, Leonora.'

The air in the dining room has stilled and sweat has started to pool in the small of my back. I'm not doing any of the work, but I feel a strange bond between us.

I strip off my suit jacket and lay it on the carpet next to us.

Just as I turn, Leonora's face contorts again, concentration written over every part of her features. Her neck is pulled taut, lines of muscle standing rigid over her collarbones, and this time she pushes.

I mean, she *really* pushes. Her whole body is consumed by that deep, visceral desire to expel this baby from her body.

A low guttural groan strains from her throat and her knees flop open.

The breath catches in my chest.

In my relative innocence, I have never seen another woman. Certainly not this view.

I am stunned. Every ounce of me concentrates on the importance of my task. There is no one else here, no one to help.

The baby's head is crowning. I'm sure that's what they call it.

I can see it, smooth and covered in some sort of thick yellowish gunk, and bloody streaks.

Instinctively, I grab my suit jacket, turning it so the lining is uppermost, and I slip it under Leonora's backside as she digs her heels into the carpet and bears down.

'Good girl. Everything is fine. Baby is on its way,' I croon to the woman, not knowing if she can hear me, or even if she cares. 'Push.' I feel sure that's what I should say. 'Push, Leonora.' I don't know what instinct makes me place my hand on Leonora's stomach, but as I touch her skin, her whole body writhes underneath and I feel the baby move.

The baby's head literally makes a soft popping noise as it clears Leonora's body, followed by a wet slithering as the body follows, sliding out in a mass of blood and mucus. I have no time to mourn the death of my jacket before my heart swells with something akin to euphoria as I wrap the baby with fast, efficient movements in my jacket, so the first smell it has is of me, rather than its mother.

I swoop the baby up, but it's still connected by the umbilical cord to Leonora.

This is not something I have any experience with, but I reach over and place the baby on Leonora's stomach, my jacket covering it to keep them both warm.

Leonora sobs and I allow myself a brief minute to crawl up beside her, touching my forehead to hers. We look into each other's eyes and her smile is wide and sloppy, reflecting my own amazed delight.

'Congratulations, Mummy. You have a beautiful baby.'

I know the baby should be small, but to my mind it looked perfectly formed.

'What is it?'

I chuckle as Leonora pulls the quiet infant further up her body as far as the cord will allow, so she cradles it skin to skin and we both touch the top of its head. Together our fingers stroke the tiny skull. A strong bond forms between the three of us I know will never be broken. Blood does not have to be shared for you to be family. This is what it is like to be needed.

'To be honest, I have no idea. I was too concerned about keeping it warm.'

The distant peal of sirens sound and I move to sit up. Leonora reaches out to grasp my hand, her face instantly transformed back to her original beauty. Although weariness hovers over it, there is a pride, a maternal delight, the beauty of a butterfly emerging from a chrysalis. It harbours deep inside me too, as though I am the one who has given birth.

'Thank you, Grace. I will never forget this. Never.'

I smile and give her hand a gentle squeeze back. 'Nor me. I've never witnessed anything so magnificent in all my life. It was an honour to be here.'

The smile slides across her face. I release her hand and touch the baby one more time before I get to my feet and discreetly tug her dress down to cover her. She starts to shiver, and I wonder if I have done everything right as I pull the edges of the crocheted blanket up on either side of her.

'Will you be okay for a moment while I let the ambulance crew in?'

She nods, both hands now on the gently snuffling baby, like a kitten or a puppy, I suspect looking for its first meal.

My breasts tingle as I turn to walk away, a strange pull that is reflected in my womb.

As though I am the one who has just given birth.

As though I am that perfect baby's mother.

26

PRESENT DAY – TUESDAY, 9 JULY 2024, 10.55 A.M. – SIOBHAN

Siobhan listened for movement upstairs from her mum. All was quiet in the late morning sunshine.

Beau had ambled his way upstairs after his earlier walk that morning and was sprawled faithfully at the side of her mum's bed. Luckily, he'd never been one for getting on beds and was content just to be near his mum.

Although officially her mum's dog, Beau loved them both equally and in his desperate attempt to please, he wasn't quite sure what to do with himself while they were split over two floors of the house.

It made Siobhan realise how much she and her mum did together. How close they were. Had always been. Their relationship was tight. Tight as a ship's defences.

Yet now there was a breach in those defences.

A distrust. Certainly, on her side. Her mum had no idea of the leak Siobhan had discovered, the slow drip, drip, drip as the ship took on water, although she had a sneaking suspicion there was distrust from her mum too.

She placed the coffee she'd just made on the kitchen table and pulled up a chair, Opening the laptop, she powered it up, sadness almost overwhelming her. Had she frayed the gossamer thread of their relationship by pursuing this?

Siobhan leaned back in her chair. It was too late. She'd made a move she couldn't retract.

Heart fluttering wildly in the base of her throat, Siobhan clicked on the message that had just arrived, and held her breath.

Hey, there.

I'm sorry it's taken me a while to come back to you, but quite honestly your message came completely out of the blue and has left me reeling. I've contacted my mum, Louisa, who was almost hysterical with disbelief. She didn't want me to go on this DNA site as she feels that we as a family are very close and have no secrets. Apparently, we do.

I knew my mother had a sister who died under tragic circumstances not long after giving birth, but it was before I was born, and I never knew the full story which is a very painful one. After a very long conversation, Mum has told me all she knows and we are truly concerned that something vile and inexplicable has taken place. Mum never believed her sister capable of harming her newborn baby, but the British police were satisfied that she had murdered her. My mum has stood by that belief and is distraught to learn that she may have been correct. If you are indeed my cousin, then a crime beyond our comprehension has taken place and it is urgent that we meet as soon as possible.

We live in Australia, but I am currently in the UK tying up some family business. I will free myself up if you agree to meet with me. We will, of course, require further confirmation of your identification. When we meet, you will understand why.

In anticipation,

Megan Saville

Heat raced up her neck as Siobhan realised she'd been holding her breath the entire time she'd read the message. The sound of her own heart pulsed in her ears.

'Oh my God, Mum. What happened? What did you do?'

She leapt from her chair, almost toppling it over before she grabbed it just in time.

She covered her mouth with both hands. 'Oh my God, oh my God.' Her voice came through muffled as she tried not to make a noise.

What the hell had she done? Never mind her mum.

She'd opened the floodgates and now she didn't know how to shut them. Was she supposed to tell her mum now?

Siobhan stood at the open back door dragging in desperate breaths and watched as chickens roamed the garden. She rubbed her hand across her chest where her heart sent out sharp spikes of pain. Was she having a heart attack, or was it simply stress?

What was she supposed to do?

She could barely form a thought in her mind. It was all too overwhelming.

A muffled bump came from upstairs as one of the cats, she assumed, jumped from a surface to the floor.

Siobhan glanced behind her before she stepped outside, slipping on ankle wellies she kept by the back door specifically for mucking-out purposes and excursions into the chicken compound to collect eggs.

Never mind the eggs, she thought, as she snatched up a large white bowl. She needed to collect her thoughts.

Terror chased confusion into a black well of numbness.

She let herself into the compound, unsurprised to find the big black Labrador magically by her side. A ghost. A shadow. Perhaps it was him she'd heard bumping around upstairs, the wag of his tail thudding against a door or a cupboard.

She let him through with her so he could sniff around and pee up the two trees in the compound, always a good deterrent for rats, which were attracted by the scents of food, no matter how many precautions were taken.

Opening up the back of the henhouse, Siobhan leaned in and scooped seventeen eggs, all different colours, out of the fresh straw she'd put in the day before.

She closed the gate behind her and Beau, and then stood for a long time in the garden, her face raised to the sun, her mind shut down for a few precious moments to protect her sanity.

When she moved again, her mind was made up.

She wouldn't tell her mum. What good would that do when she had no idea what information this woman, this Megan Saville, was about to impart to her?

But what if she'd just got her mum into deep trouble? Had her mum committed some kind of crime? What if she'd done something illegal, or God forbid, heinous? Shots of panic hit her like small electric shocks.

The foundation of all she knew rocked. If she wasn't her mum's biological daughter and these people, these strangers, accused Grace of something unthinkable, where did that leave them?

To her knowledge, Siobhan's mum had never told her a lie. Her mum abhorred liars. And yet, if this was true, then surely Siobhan's whole life was a web of lies. One that was in the process of being torn apart because of her. Because of her insistence that she wanted to know the truth. And that truth was about to get her mum into deep trouble.

She paused at the back door, Beau trotting ahead of her as she drew in a deep breath.

No. She wasn't going to tell her mum. It would be better if she made arrangements, met up with Megan Saville and checked the circumstances first before involving her mum.

After all, there had to be a good reason she was with her mum. Didn't there? Her mum would never have done anything bad. She loved her mum with all her heart and soul and if she needed to defend her, she would, but she'd caused this. She'd thrown that stink bomb. It was her problem to sort out without involving her mum. Not yet, in any case.

Siobhan dragged her feet out of her ankle wellies and stepped inside the house, slipping her feet into a pair of slippers. No matter what the weather, the tiles inside were always cool.

She placed the bowl of eggs beside the kettle on the kitchen counter. She'd sort them out later, box them up and take them outside to the 'dishonesty box' where the eggs would more often than not disappear without any trace of remuneration being left.

Her chest squeezed hard as she reached the kitchen table, woke her laptop by tapping the mouse with shaking fingers when a sound at the door caught her attention. A soft grunt.

She whipped her head up, her heart banging into her ribcage.

'Mum!'

She slammed the lid of her laptop down, fear overtaking guilt as she raced around the side of the table to where her mum wilted against the doorframe into the hallway.

'Mum, what are you doing down here?'

Frantic, she wrapped her arm around her mum's waist and took some of her weight, while her mum got her walking sticks under her properly.

'I called. I thought you'd gone out.' The woman's voice held a weakness Siobhan wasn't used to. It sent a tremor of terror through her. This strong, vital woman. Her mother had never needed her help before and now she was leaning on her as if Siobhan was her saviour.

Siobhan supported her mum as they made their way to the kitchen table, her heart trembling when she thought of the damage that could have occurred. 'Oh, Mum, I would never leave you alone without letting you know. I only went to collect the eggs.'

'Oh.' Her mum quivered, sweat soaking through the soft cotton of her nightdress.

'Come and sit down.'

Siobhan lowered her mum into a chair and let her lean against the table. Role reversal had come fast and furious. Something that had hit like a punch to the gut. She wasn't sure she was ready to deal with it yet but had no choice in the matter.

Despite the fact neither of them was reserved about nudity between them, she felt a shift of discomfort witnessing her mum in just a pale-yellow nightdress and slippers. It revealed a frailty Siobhan still hadn't adjusted to.

Normally her mum was up and dressed, having walked the dog and tended to the smallholding before Siobhan had even stepped foot out of bed to get ready for work. It was her mum who had strong black coffee ready when Siobhan came downstairs. Her mum who had a packed lunch prepared for her, and fresh fruit peeled and sliced in a bowl with Greek yoghurt and local honey set out on the table.

Her mum who adored her. There wasn't a day of Siobhan's life that she could remember her being anything other than the perfect mum. There was no doubt in her mind that she was adored. Not spoilt, never that.

Siobhan wasn't prepared for this. This was not on their 'to-do' list. It hadn't even been on their horizon.

Despite the heat, her mum shivered. Siobhan opened a cupboard and took out one of the throws they sometimes flung over their knees in the winter when the temperature in the old cottage dipped and draughts sneaked through, to curl around their ankles and creep up their legs.

She smoothed it over her mum's shoulders and gave her a gentle hug. 'Do you think we should get you back upstairs?'

'No. I'm supposed to get moving.'

'I'm not sure they meant you were supposed to free-wheel downstairs on your own.' She tapped her mum's shoulders lightly and then moved away before the tears that threatened could take hold. 'I'll make you a cup of tea, then we'll see how you feel.'

'I'll be fine, Siobhan. Stop fussing, love. I'm not as fragile as you seem to think. And I'd rather have coffee, if you don't mind.'

Siobhan filled the kettle with cold water and glanced at the woman as she dabbed the corner of the throw over a forehead that was pale and clammy. 'Nor are you as robust as you believe.'

Her mum leaned back in the chair and stared, glassy-eyed, up at Siobhan. 'I'll get there. Don't you worry about me.'

'Of course I worry about you. It was horrible, Mum, seeing you fall like that. Getting the news about you having bone cancer.'

'It's not bone cancer, it was a tumour, that's all.'

She knew her mum wasn't ignorant, and if they were to move forward with her care, she had to acknowledge she had cancer.

'It's cancer, Mum.'

'They cut it out. It's gone.'

'They've not confirmed if they're going to give you chemo or radiotherapy yet, so don't set yourself up...'

'For another fall?' Her mum gave a lopsided grin. 'I'm pretty much prepared for all that's coming my way.' With a derisive smile, she nodded down at her legs. 'One step at a time, hey?'

The kettle clicked off and Siobhan turned to pour water into the cafetière she'd tipped freshly ground coffee into, taking two mugs down from a shelf while she gave the coffee a moment to brew.

She turned around and leaned against the kitchen counter as she watched her mum's face closely for any sign of discomfort. Not a physical discomfort, but a tell. Something to show Siobhan if her mum was being honest with her.

'The doctor did tell me that you were generally very fit, which we would expect, because you are, but he also said you had the kidneys of a much younger woman.' She waited a beat. 'Funny, that. He seemed to think you were younger than the date of birth I gave them.'

Her mum shrugged and reached for the mug of coffee Siobhan placed in front of her, no flicker of guilt on her face. Nothing.

Either Siobhan was wrong, or her mum was the greatest liar of all time.

27

THIRTY-ONE YEARS EARLIER – 1993 – GRACE

Something has changed. The dynamics have altered between the four of us. Justin, Leonora, Gordon and myself. A shift of sand under our feet. Each of us has changed with the birth of this baby, this precious bundle.

Justin has become even more surly than before. I barely see Gordon and I wonder if that is due to his boss's bad humour. Their issues don't bother me.

I feel inexplicably protective towards Leonora.

I cradle the baby now, my heart melting as I study the perfect rosebud lips, making that sweet suckling motion babies do, rooting for a feed and turning its head towards my breast.

Her head.

Her perfect, smooth, round head covered in soft downy hair, which the midwife has told us will undoubtedly rub off on the pillow, leaving fine hairs which will probably make us believe a cat has sneaked into her cot.

Not that Justin would have a cat in the house. Or any pet, for that matter. Justin is not an animal person. Not unless he's hunting them on the plains of Africa. It's not an aspect of his personality that I like, but it is not my business. I am his employee, not his conscience, despite filling that role on many occasions.

What I am, now, is important to Leonora. Over that one dramatic event, we have bonded, the three of us, Leonora, the baby and me. There's something special being part of a baby's birth and we silently acknowledge this.

'I think she needs feeding.'

I hand her back to her mum and watch while Leonora holds her close, letting the baby latch on to her exposed breast.

'I thought I would call her Grace Crystal Savannah Schneider. What do you think?'

My heart can barely stand the joy and a burst of heat floods my face as I blush madly. 'Oh my God, Leonora, I can't believe you'd want to name your baby after me.' I cover my mouth with my hand for a moment to control my excitement; after all, I don't wish to disturb baby Grace.

'What's this?'

We both turn as Justin appears in the open doorway, and there's a certain lack of anything akin to the desperate love I feel for this baby. On the contrary, he shows no interest in her whatsoever. There's a certain aloofness ever since he returned from his trip.

He'd not hurried back but taken his time and it was a full four days before Gordon and he arrived home, his excuse being he was halfway down the mountain when he eventually received notification. By which time, Leonora and I had spent time getting to know one another. At her request, I had moved into one of their six guest bedrooms, so she had company at night. Only until Justin arrived home. So she wasn't lonely.

I think the death of her mother and father two years previously, in a car accident in the South of France, prompted her desperate wish for a baby before it was too late. Before her time ran out.

Perhaps that was the reason she'd been so frantic, so impassioned. All that desperation seems to have lifted now.

During the peaceful moments of bathing the baby, feeding her, changing her, Leonora tells me so much about herself. I have very little to tell. What a plain, boring life I have led so far. All my ambition and determination to succeed and yet I am the one with nothing. An empty life full of empty ambitions that mean nothing to anyone.

Leonora doesn't seem to notice. Her life is consumed with her newborn daughter, and she is happy to include me.

Leonora has a younger sister, Louisa, who emigrated to Australia seven years ago because of her work as a marine biologist, and although they are in constant contact, according to Leonora, it's not quite the same as having someone with you to help out.

Her sister had scheduled to come in another six weeks and stay for a month which was when they believed the baby was due. This baby, to my mind, is not premature. Because of her work commitments, Leonora's sister can't shift that timeline. In the meantime, as Leonora says, she has me.

She appreciates me. She constantly reminds me that I saved the life of both her and her baby, and I am flattered. Whilst that may sound a little melodramatic, perhaps it's true. Perhaps if I had locked up and gone home, no one would have discovered Leonora and called an ambulance in time. Because by the time they arrived, she had gone into shock. Apparently, this is nothing unusual when a baby comes so quickly.

I shudder as that's something I cannot bear to think about. That gorgeous baby perishing through a slight twist of fate. No, I push aside that thought and choose instead to think about the positive outcome.

During the day, I continue to work for Justin. After hours, I sneak upstairs for a cuddle and chat with my two favourite girls.

Strange how never before have I formed a bond in any way remotely like this one.

Don't get me wrong, I love James, but our roles are different. We have looked after each other, supported each other through bad times. Seen the worst of each other. Our connection is strong, and I do love him, but we are independent people. We live our own lives, with our paths crossing regularly, but we don't live for each other.

This is different. Having done what I did, I have a fierce desire to protect and nurture. Not just the baby, but Leonora too. Something connected between us that day and I have become her ally.

Before Justin returned, I would cook the two of us a hearty meal. I've never really been a brilliant cook, but it's surprising what you can achieve if you're trying to impress someone. And I do like to impress Leonora. There are such easy recipes to follow, and Leonora sent one of the house staff out to do the shopping each morning with a list full of items I supplied her with.

All that changed once Justin arrived home and I moved back into my lonely house again.

I feel a little awkward as Justin leans against the doorjamb, arms crossed over his broad chest, awaiting an answer.

Leonora raises her chin, and I realise there's a certain defiance to the angle of it.

'I was just telling Grace that we're going to name the baby after her.'

Surprise springs into his eyes as they dart towards me and then back to his wife.

I don't think I've ever seen him speechless, but there it is. Right in front of me.

Oh, no. This is awkward.

She hasn't discussed this with him. It's evident from his expression.

I blink, wishing I was anywhere but here. This is not my business. I don't want to be here between my employer and my new best friend. There is no escape for me, though, as Justin blocks the open doorway.

I squirm inside.

Justin bows his head. 'As you wish.' With a leisurely push away from the door, he saunters away. The muffled sound of his footsteps on the thick hall carpet receding.

I turn to stare at Leonora and her face is fixed. The baby is making soft, contented noises as she gets her fill of milk, her little body relaxing until her rosebud mouth pops open, milk gently oozing from the corner of her lips and she rolls slightly in Leonora's arms, contentment written all over her features.

I wait, but evidently, Leonora isn't going to broach the subject.

I have to.

'Leonora, this is awkward.'

'What is?' She raises her head, feigning innocence.

I'm not going to let it pass, though. Leonora and I have been very honest with each other. As far as I am aware. I wave my hand in the general direction of Justin's departing back. 'Did you even discuss the baby's name with him?'

'I did.' Her mouth quirks in a sour smile as she tugs her clothes back into place. 'He wanted me to name her after his long-departed mother. Ethel.' She blinks. 'I am not calling my daughter Ethel.'

I don't quite know how to respond. I try for diplomacy. 'It's a little old-fashioned.'

She snorts.

'I come from a family of aristocrats, Grace. We are not going to use the name Ethel in our title.'

I'm not quite sure what she means by title.

'But you must have had this discussion, about using my name, surely?'

Leonora shrugs and shuffles the baby in her arms so she can

hand her over to me, knowing I'll take the greatest of pleasure having a cuddle while I burp her. I fling a terry towelling square over my shoulder so I can do it without getting milk all over my suit jacket.

'We did have this discussion,' Leonora replies. 'I suggested we call her after you, seeing as you saved our precious lives. Justin didn't answer, so I took it as a "yes".'

I close my eyes. The scent of baby Grace fills my senses with talcum powder and rose petals.

'He seldom answers me these days, so I do my own thing.'

And here, I also need to be clear and honest with her, because the uncomfortable feeling that I could lose my job over my friendship is starting to grow. And I can't afford to lose this job. Nor do I want to lose my friendship.

I am so torn.

'You know, Justin is my boss.'

I have to make this very clear to Leonora.

There is a line we are crossing here, due to the circumstances, but it is a line I have never before crossed. I have never become involved with any of my employers' personal lives on this level. Oh, I've been the woman responsible for sending flowers to my bosses' wives, in the pretence it was my boss sending them. I've been invited to the occasional party. But I have never formed a relationship to this degree before now and the lines have become blurred.

'I feel really awkward, and I have to be careful, I really can't afford to lose this job.' And I really can't. I am paid a very healthy salary and there aren't many positions around that could match this one. I know I have a considerable amount stashed away for a rainy day; after all, when you've lived through the storm, you never forget to prepare for the next one. I don't want to weather another storm. It may not be my ideal job, but I am good at what I do, and I ooze confidence with it. I do love it. At least, I did, right up until

Justin grabbed me that day. I still haven't managed to forget that, but I can put it to one side most of the time. It was not just the grab, but that momentary slip of control showed me Justin. The real man behind that mask.

Leonora shuffles herself into a comfortable position before she pushes up from where she was propped up in bed. She's recovered really well, but I still notice the wince that passes over her face from time to time when she makes a sudden move.

As she stands up, I pass baby Grace over to her, glancing at the bedside clock. It's time for me to go home. My stomach gives a low grumble, and I start moving towards the door.

'You know, if you ever want to jump ship and come and work for me, I'd be very happy to have you as my personal assistant.'

At first, I think she's joking. Then I cast her a second glance.

'I don't think that would go down well with Justin.'

She pulls a face. 'You do know it's not Justin who holds the purse strings.' She tilts her head to one side, her gaze delving into mine. 'Besides, he may not be around for very much longer…'

Startled, my mouth drops open, and I stare at her before glancing at the doorway to make sure he doesn't suddenly come through and demand to know what we're talking about again.

I lower my voice, a conspiratorial whisper. 'Really? Why would you say that?'

She lays Grace down in her Moses basket and pulls a thin white cover with yellow trim up around the baby, who makes sweet squeaking noises and has my heart rolling over in my chest once more.

When Leonora turns to look at me, her face is set.

'I know it's unfair of me to burden you with my marital problems, especially as you do officially work for my husband, but Justin hasn't been the same since I fell pregnant.' She falls silent for a moment as though contemplating whether or not to continue.

Her eyes fill with tears and her feet shuffle as she walks to the window. She sinks into an over-stuffed tartan wing-back chair that makes her tall, slender body look slight and frail.

She dabs at her eyes with the tips of her fingers.

My throat tightens in response, and I feel a lump forming, ready to choke me.

'We had such a difficult time conceiving.' Her voice is thick.

I walk over and sit on the end of her bed facing her. I know she's given birth ten days earlier, but she does look beyond tired. Shattered may actually be the right terminology. Not merely exhausted but broken.

There's a ghost shadowing her gaze as it meets mine.

'The worst of it has always been his inability to conceive, rather than mine. Stupidly, though, they put me through the most horrendous tests before we discovered the issue wasn't with me but with Justin.' She squeezes her eyes closed. 'You wouldn't believe how angry he was. Furious. I tried to console him, but he became really withdrawn. I don't know whether you noticed it in his work life, but he's been spending more time away from home than here.'

She took in a long, shaky breath and glanced over at the Moses basket.

'He seemed to believe once he'd "donated" his sperm that he was no longer needed. We tried and tried with ICI, but nothing seemed to happen.' She swallowed, her teary eyes meeting mine. 'The last time, he said would be the final time. That it was humiliating for him to do what was required.' She snorted. 'It's nothing in comparison to what I had to go through before they even tested him. He was convinced there was no problem with his sperm.'

I fidget because the subject matter is uncomfortable. This is my boss we are discussing and really, it's too much information. I hope she doesn't go into any really intimate detail, because quite honestly, I don't think I'm up to that.

Maybe she senses this because she falls quiet. When she speaks again, it's barely a whisper. 'It changed us.'

Her sadness washes over me in waves. I know she could be suffering from baby blues, but this isn't so much about that. This is about her relationship with Justin.

'It changed both of us. His ego has been damaged. Battered.' Her lip curls with distaste. 'Funny how he was quite comfortable believing that the fault lay with me, but the moment we discovered it was his sperm with no fight, it was like a light flicked out. Now, I'm not sure we can carry on the way we have been.' She shakes her head, her lips pressing together to stop the tears from turning into a full cry. Her pain fills the room. 'I don't know if our marriage will survive this.'

I lean in closer to her, rest my elbows on my knees. 'I'm so sorry.'

I'm not apologising and I'm not entirely sure what I'm sorry for. The whole situation, I suppose. It's sad. When I first came to work for Justin, I truly believed he was besotted with his new wife. Everything he'd done, arranged, organised had been with her at the forefront of his mind. This is a tragedy of epic proportions if they can't get over it.

'I'm sure you can work things out.' I think of my own mother. A horrible creature with not a care for me. Leonora is different, but I do wish she could keep their lovely family together, for the sake of the baby. Coming from a one-parent family, I am almost desperate that this one doesn't split up.

'Perhaps you should go to marriage counselling.'

She lets out a delicate snort as she wafts one hand in the air.

'Justin would never agree to that. Since the day I told him I was pregnant, we've not slept together.'

'That's surely not insurmountable,' I say, and I'm not sure how I could possibly give marital advice, having never even been in a stable relationship for more than five minutes, but I continue to try. After all, I've read *Cosmopolitan*, and that's an eye-opener.

'Surely you can repair things, once you're feeling better, recovered, you can perhaps work on your relationship, see if you still feel how you used to about each other.'

'That's the problem, Justin no longer feels the same about me. I think I pushed him too far and he's fallen out of love with me.' Eyes damp with tears meet mine. 'He also knows that I love our baby far more than I love him.'

My brow twitches into a frown. 'That's surely a different kind of love.'

She scrubs the back of her hand across her nose and sniffs. 'Grace.' She drops her hand back down onto her knee and meets my gaze. 'The problem is, I did something really bad.' Her face flushes at the remembered guilt.

What could she possibly have done that was so bad?

She cups her face in her hands and shakes it slowly, a soft groan coming from her.

'I'm sure it can be put right, whatever it is.'

Devastation glints through eyes that peer at me from between her long, slender fingers.

'I don't think it can. This is beyond my control.'

28

PRESENT DAY – TUESDAY, 9 JULY 2024, 5.10 P.M. – SIOBHAN

Siobhan scanned the email again.

When she sent her messages off, she'd never thought any further than getting a reply, a connection, and now she had, she wasn't absolutely sure what to do about it.

This woman, not much younger than herself, wanted to meet her. Almost demanded to meet her. Siobhan wasn't sure she cared to hear what Megan had to say. Scared to be told of something her mum had done. Her mum, who she was devoted to. Who she had just betrayed.

Megan claimed to currently be in London on family business, but her latest message declared she was happy to travel in order to meet with Siobhan. After all, distance to her, she claimed, meant very little. She lived in Australia where it was pretty much taken for granted that travel was a major part of their lives.

Fingers on the laptop keyboard, Siobhan listened for movement from above.

Her mum had gone upstairs to rest a while. Stairs that she'd proved remarkably adept at negotiating, even according to the physiotherapist who had called around that afternoon. No more home visits after today. Her mum was considered a special case initially, but since she'd shown how fit and capable she was, she'd been left to her own devices. All further check-ups would be carried out at the hospital.

Despite this, her mum had been left exhausted and wrung out from the visit and the exercises she'd been asked to demonstrate.

Pride rippled through Siobhan at the thought of her mum's progress. The inner strength that had carried her that far, and her physical fitness. Her mum's physique came from hauling bales of straw and hay, mucking out, lifting and carrying feed, digging the vegetable plot and walking the dog up more than just hills. She'd always loved trekking through the quiet of the challenging Welsh countryside, a backpack on with a full picnic inside. Prior to her hip breaking, Siobhan had considered her mum a veritable workhorse. A woman whose strength had always filled her with such pride.

Siobhan hesitated, her fingers hovering while she considered how traitorous she was being by even considering meeting up with this young woman who was her first cousin. It wasn't like she'd committed to it. She still had the choice to pull out, to back off. She'd not given her address or any real personal information to Megan Saville. Just an email address.

Her heart quaked. Could she be tracked down by an email address? Was it better to meet Megan, or simply disappear back into the ether where no questions could be asked or answered?

There was a window of opportunity still open to stop this. She could if she wanted to. She simply didn't want to, though. The balance tipped in favour of her finding out the truth about what had really happened.

Emotions see-sawing, Siobhan typed her reply, dovetailing the meeting with her mum's appointment at the hospital which she'd been told not to hang around for. With her consultant review, together with a physio appointment, her mum considered it a waste of Siobhan's time.

'You'll be hanging around for hours. I'm perfectly capable of going to the doctors on my own, Siobhan. Don't fuss. I'm not an old woman yet.'

She certainly wasn't. In fact, very possibly she was considerably younger than she claimed.

Siobhan typed the message to Megan Saville and hit send before she could change her mind.

At the exact same time, another message came through with a soft 'ting'.

Thrown at the speed of the response, it took Siobhan a moment to process the fact that the incoming email wasn't from Megan, her Australian cousin, but someone else entirely.

This one was the one she'd sent on behalf of her mum.

> Hello. I am Linda Marie Francesca Kerr and I believe your mum is my half-sister. Our father's name is James Mabbott. He is aware that I have sent off my DNA but wishes to be kept out of it. He says that he has all the connections he needs. He is a very private man with a past he rarely speaks of. All I know from my mother is that it was traumatic. My father was born 27 September 1947.

'Oh my God!' Siobhan clapped her hand over her mouth, eyes wide as she stared at the text. 'That's not possible.'

That would make James Mabbott ten when her mother was conceived. With the best will in the world, that was impossible.

She squinted at the screen and read the message again. Letting out a sigh, she rested her forehead on her hand. Eyes closed, her mind raced before she raised her head and looked again.

It was possible.

Her mum absolutely did lie about her age. This was confirmation. James Mabbott would have been sixteen, not ten, when her mum was conceived if she believed the more ragged birth certificate.

Siobhan raised her head and skimmed her gaze over it once more. Sixteen. Barely a child himself. But possible.

She leaned forward and read on.

> All my family know about your mum is that when he left to join the army, her mother Maureen was somewhat younger than him and pregnant with you. We only know this because we managed to track down certain details of her through friends of friends. I don't know if you have managed to have any contact with Maureen, but I do know she went on to have a further seven children.

Siobhan rocked back in her chair, eyes wide.

'Eight children altogether! Blimey. Who does that?' Siobhan continued reading.

> When we contacted Maureen, she refused to talk except to say she wanted nothing to do with any of it and that the past could remain in the past.

Siobhan chewed her lower lip as she regretted that bloody stink bomb she'd lobbed into the room and the consequences which were about to consume all of them. Including her mum, if she chose to tell her.

Not that she had to. She wasn't obliged to involve her mum in any way.

Except... she was pretending to act on Grace's behalf and with her permission and the subterfuge gnawed at her conscience.

How was she supposed to follow this line of enquiry?

Siobhan brought up her mum's DNA details and stared at them for a long time. She ran her finger over the screen, where the long list of first cousins, as she believed, were. But they weren't first cousins. She double-checked with the chart the DNA company had provided. There was a crossover in centimorgans between first cousins and half-siblings. Which meant they could be either.

These weren't her mum's cousins, but her half-siblings. Seven of them.

Siobhan picked up her cup of tea and took a sip.

Was her mum even aware? What had been so bad that she had been obliged to change her date of birth? Did she run away from home? If so, why?

A million questions chased through Siobhan's mind. The truth could only be told, though, by the people who were there.

And James Mabbott was there. Even if 'Maureen' refused to talk. He'd also said he wanted nothing to do with it, but... could he be persuaded? The only other person who knew the truth was her mum.

Siobhan returned to the message and read on.

> I am married with three children. I have an older brother, Simon James Mabbott and a younger sister Catherine Swanwich who is married with two children of her own.
>
> It would be such a delight to meet up with you to try and piece together this fractured history we share. I'm aware it may be intimidating for us all to meet together, but if you let me know where you live, I'd be thrilled for just the two of us to meet initially.

Siobhan lowered the laptop lid and sat for a long moment until Beau nudged a cold, wet nose under her elbow to remind her it was his dinner time.

She glanced at the wall clock. It was also time to make dinner for her mum and her too.

She scooped kibble into Beau's dish, opened a can of sardines in oil and mashed them in. His once-a-week treat that kept his joints supple and his black fur shiny and soft.

Her mind not quite on the job, she placed the bowl on his mat in front of him without getting him to sit and stay patiently for one moment. As he leapt on it and started wolfing it down, she wandered to the sink and stared out of the window over the parched ground of their land.

The moral dilemma she had was not so much finding out *her* heritage. She had every right to know, even if she should possibly discuss it with her mum beforehand. If she did, though, she might hurt her unnecessarily. Despite the dishonesty, she truly believed the past actions her mum had taken would have been in Siobhan's best interest.

She loved her mum. Circumstances couldn't change that fact.

Her mum, whether blood-related or not, adored her like she was her own child. There was never any doubt of that. Theirs was a relationship with a foundation of love and mutual respect.

At least it had been until Siobhan had found the lies, discovered the hidden fissure in their lives and poked her fingernail into it until it widened.

She needed to know where she came from. At the other end of the scale, Siobhan had no right to dig into her mum's ancestry. Did she? Now she knew they were biologically unconnected, that part of her mum's life had nothing to do with her.

Or did it?

Closing her eyes, she breathed out a long, slow breath.

Surely she had a right to know. Wasn't she also embroiled in this web of deceit her mum had woven?

29

THIRTY-ONE YEARS EARLIER – 1993 – GRACE

I slip off my heels and bolt on silent feet up the rear stairs of the Hall into the private accommodation, tucking the key that Leonora gave me back into my pocket. Heat is rising in my face as annoyance with myself for leaving a highly confidential file upstairs when Leonora had called me up earlier gets the better of me. Hugging it to my chest as I left the locked file room, I'd had no time to return it and would never normally leave that kind of information lying around even for the shortest of times.

Concerned that Leonora was upset, I took it with me to save time, knowing it was safe when I placed it next to me on the coffee table in the lounge.

Leonora had been tearful and upset that Justin had thrown a strop that afternoon and had left in a fury.

'I refused to allow him any further money from my funds. He seems to be spending it like water. I think he's gone off the rails, Grace.'

The words echo in my mind now. He'd gone. Without telling me. Which means he no longer trusts me, either.

When I left Leonora, I completely forgot the file. So unprofessional of me, and an ideal excuse for Justin to discipline me, or worse, dismiss me. It's not so much the dismissal I hate the idea of, but if I do decide to slide over the fence to work for Leonora, I'd rather it was on good terms and my reputation was still intact.

The one rule that's so fixed in my mind is to always make sure files are locked away in secure cabinets. Information in some of these fundraising files is highly confidential. Names of people who may not wish to be known, donating vast sums of money, and in my cynicism, I believe, often purely for the tax break rather than the charity itself.

Silence greets me as I sneak back through the long corridor I'd been along earlier that afternoon, not wanting anyone to hear me, to question why I'm up there. I don't want to disturb Leonora and the baby, and I don't want to have to explain my error. I don't make mistakes normally and I'm completely aware that Justin is watching me closer than normal, as if every move I make somehow attracts his disapproval.

I know he's not happy about the baby being named after me, but that's not my fault, not my issue, and secretly I am rather thrilled that Leonora overruled him on the matter. I'm not entirely sure she isn't going to ask me to be godmother too, as she has hinted, asking what religion I am. I know she will ask her sister when she arrives to visit, so I am fully prepared to be required to make arrangements for a christening.

There's been no mention of it from Justin yet, though, so I hope they're not going to leave it until the last minute, leaving me to scrabble around trying to put it all into place. I think I'll start enquiring tomorrow, put the feelers out. Just as long as they don't insist on having somewhere like a minster or cathedral, which are going to be difficult to book.

My heart is saddened for Leonora's distress. I'm torn between my loyalty to and deep affection for Leonora, and my dedication to my job and my boss. If truth be told, Justin has become even more thoughtless since the birth of his baby. Snippety. Bitter. A bit of an arse, I think.

Leonora isn't just suffering from postpartum depression as he insists, quite vocally, I might add, but there's a sad desperation about her. The crumbling of a marriage she'd once cherished, the thought that it was all her fault, somehow, for wanting a baby so desperately.

I pause halfway along the long twists and turns of the hallway and listen. I hear nothing, no gentle music, no cooing of the baby, no sweet murmurings from Leonora.

My mind races as I wonder how tenuous my position has become when evidently Justin has arranged for someone else to sort out his travel arrangements. My hands tremble, not because I'm sneaking through the domestic quarters, but at the conflict of interests that is tearing me apart.

I know I'm good at my job. I know how much Justin has valued me in the past. That value seems to have deteriorated along with his relationship with his wife and now I'm standing alone in their home, feeling like some kind of thief.

I know I should have phoned ahead, let Leonora know I was coming up, but I didn't want to wake the baby who has been fractious because of the atmosphere between her parents.

I relax a little. If she is snoozing, then hopefully Leonora can also catch up on sleep. Hopefully, the soft dark bruising under her eyes caused by exhaustion will dissipate, although I fear it will take far more than sleep to dispel the sadness lurking in those deep, beautiful eyes of hers.

I won't disturb them. They don't even need to know of my visit. I'll just collect the file and be gone in a flash.

I hesitate as I pass the closed door of the nursery, pausing as I consider taking just one little peek at the sleeping infant.

With a slow turn of the antique brass knob, I give the door a gentle push.

The light in there is dim with heavy brocade curtains covering huge Georgian sash windows. At the top of the window where the curtains are not fully closed, leaving a narrow vee, dust motes dance like fairies in the shaft of light, bringing a gentle smile to my lips so I forget for a moment why I am there.

I tiptoe across and spend precious moments peering into the cot at that exquisite, sweet infant, her cherubic face serene, her skin milky white with the soft purpled eyelids of a baby who is in a deep, deep sleep.

My heart squeezes, sorrow at my own lost opportunity flooding through my senses to bring tears to my eyes. Since I lost my baby all those years ago, I have never looked back, never mourned the inability to have children. Until recently. Until I've spent time with Leonora when she was pregnant, until I helped birth this serene, incredible being. Until I heard the cry of a newborn infant and my soul wept.

These are the moments, when that desperate pain rushes in unexpectedly, that I know without a doubt that I want a baby. That I would do almost anything to have one of my own.

But that ship has passed and I'm unable to get pregnant. I am, in the old-fashioned sense, barren and I know that, feel the barrenness with every fibre of my being.

I cover my mouth with a hand to stem the sob that wells in my throat. Tears drip onto the back of my hand and I know I should turn and walk away, but I can't. This baby, this wondrous being, has melted my heart and I will never be the same.

Tempted to touch her, I wipe the tears from my hand on my skirt and reach over the cot. I stroke the back of a gentle finger across the cool, downy skin of her cheek and can't help the smile that stretches over my face, drying my tears and lifting my mood.

Precious little bundle that she is. Much as I desperately want to give her a cuddle, I simply stare at her, not wanting to disturb her, or her mum.

A muffled sound in the bathroom beyond has me jerking my head up and I hold my breath, knowing that this will not look good should Leonora come through and find me here looming over the cot at her precious baby. No matter how well we get along, I don't have permission to be here.

Terrified I may be discovered, I tiptoe to the door which leads to the Jack and Jill bathroom beyond, shared by both the nursery and the master bedroom on the other side.

Filled with indecision and the sense of deep foreboding, guilt races through me, as I know I'm in the wrong. I raise my hand to knock, feeling it best now to reveal my presence, hoping Leonora understands when I explain what brought me back upstairs.

I stop myself mid-movement. Leonora may not appreciate me coming through from her baby's bedroom into her private bathroom in which she may be indisposed. I hesitate a moment longer, chewing at my thumbnail. It's best if I go back into the hallway and just bypass the bedrooms and bathroom and continue on until I reach the lounge where I left that damned file.

A further sound makes me hold my breath and wait, sure the noise I heard could not possibly be Leonora.

A whispered curse followed by a short bark of a cough that didn't sound female.

Oh, hell. I straighten up and frown. A little quiver of fear dapples my skin with goosebumps.

What am I doing?

I'm intruding on their privacy where I shouldn't and there's no easy way out.

That definitely sounded like a male voice to me. One I'm not sure I recognise.

Who would be in Leonora's bathroom, other than Justin?

But Justin has gone.

I press my lips together to stifle any noise in case the person on the other side of the door can hear me breathing as I could hear their sounds.

I realise too late that Justin must have returned home and perhaps Leonora and my boss are taking advantage of the fact that baby Grace is asleep, and they are having make-up sex. They would be mortified to know I'm here. I certainly don't want to be here.

Terrified of being discovered in such an embarrassing situation, I glance towards the door I have left open onto the landing. It casts an elongated beacon to spotlight me where I stand, and I realise if someone comes through from the bathroom they will see me immediately and if I make straight for the door, I will be highlighted. Feeling stupid and juvenile, I sneak to the floor-to-ceiling curtains and slip behind them.

I am mortified. There is no way I want to get caught in this position. My cheeks are burning at the thought.

I was sure Justin had gone. In fact, I know he had. I saw him speed off as I walked past the enormous windows dominating the entrance hall earlier today on my way to the file room. Just before Leonora had called in tears. He'd slipped into one of his three Ferraris and revved the engine until the gravel spat out as the car kicked up and almost sonic boomed down the drive when he sped off.

I am positive it was him in the driver's seat. Although I can't recall seeing Gordon.

I was sure he'd not returned. When I went to my car, just before I realised the mistake I'd made and rushed back, there were no other cars in the car park indicating all the staff had gone home. This irks slightly because once again I've worked well over my hours and have to lock up the whole business side of the Hall.

Justin's car had been parked next to mine. He has his own little sign, as does Gordon, so nobody else parks in their spaces right outside the door to the Hall.

I can't peer out onto the car park from here to check, as I'm on the wrong side of the building.

When did he come back? How could he possibly return without my knowledge?

With the curtain wrapped around me, I hold still, turning my head to hear better.

The gentle slosh of lapping water indicates that whoever is in the bathroom has got into the bath. With a sigh of relief, I push the curtain away from me, briefly glance at the baby to check she's still asleep and dart on swift feet to the door leading back out onto the landing, knowing I'm unlikely now to get caught.

I hesitate on the other side, the brightness blinding me as I blink away the shadows behind my eyes.

If Justin is in the bath, then I have time to sprint along the hall to the lounge, grab the file and dash back out before I'm seen.

Thankful that I kicked off my shoes in order not to wake the baby, I hurtle along to the end of the hallway, keeping my heels high like a pre-shaped Barbie foot, so they don't thud.

I fly into the lounge, snatch up the file from exactly where I left it on the coffee table, turn and race back along the hallway like the hounds of hell are on my heels. Which, to be honest, I feel they must be. My chest is heaving, and I slow, then pause before I reach the door to the master bedroom, trying not to wheeze as I catch my breath.

I need to glide past it, a silent spectre that no one will see.

The door is ajar, and I can't help noticing the dark shadow beyond. I hold breath that now burns in my chest and squint into the darkness. I can't help the small gasp that escapes as instinct fills me with the desire to run. To flee. From what, I can't quite put my finger on, but the fear is visceral.

There's another sound from the bathroom, a slosh of water, a quiet grunt.

Something is not right. My chest is so tight I think it might burst.

I place one hand on my breastbone and feel the violent hammer of my heart through my palm.

I hesitate, undecided. I should move on. It's none of my business. I know it's not, but I can't help this feeling of anxiety. A concern that all is not right in the world.

Decision made, I'm going to leave. I allow my head to overrule instinct, and tiptoe past the master bedroom, past the bathroom and towards the nursery again.

Here, I stop, unable to pass without checking that baby Grace is fine as a soft whine comes from her room and my heart hitches, telling me she needs to stay quiet. She doesn't want to disturb whatever this strange thing is that is going on.

Am I safe? Is she?

I hug the file tight to my chest, creep into the dark room, waiting for my eyes to adjust before peeping into the cot and slipping the small dummy into the baby's mouth.

There. That's it. The sum total of what I need to do here before I get out. Now.

As I turn to go, something stops me. I move closer to the bathroom door and that unease that has stayed with me blooms into conviction that something is definitely amiss.

I know I shouldn't be nosy.

I swallow and pray no one catches me and thinks I'm a voyeur.

God, that would be the most humiliating situation, if I get caught spying on them having sex.

But I don't think sex is the issue here. There is something else. Something sinister. I can smell it as I breathe in. A taint on the air.

Heavy footsteps clunk through one of the rooms, possibly the master bedroom, and again a swish of water. A thud. Why would anyone be wearing shoes if they had just got out of the bath, or were about to get in? Were they kicking them off?

Nothing about this makes sense.

I draw in a breath and then reach out one hand to gently ease the door open enough for me to see inside the room.

My heart simply stops.

30

THIRTY-ONE YEARS EARLIER – 1993 – GRACE

Leonora is stretched out in the bath, her long golden hair fans out around her, the darkened ends float on the water to cover her breasts.

Only the arm flopping outward is any clue to the fact the woman is stone-cold dead. That and blooms of blood-like petals opening to welcome the rain swirling in the water as each drip falls in slow rhythmic throbs, taking with it Leonora's life force.

Horror grips my throat as I stare in disbelief at the scene before me.

A short-bladed sharp knife lies abandoned by the side of the bathtub as though Leonora dropped it from weak fingers after using it on the wrist of the opposite arm, the deep scarlet gouge runs inside her arm, wrist to elbow.

My knees weaken and queasiness squeezes my stomach until I flop against the door jamb, unable to walk further into the room.

There is no doubt, from the amount of blood and the depth of the injury, she is dead. Her face is ruddy like the last of the blood made a rush for the most important part of her, eyes glassy and wide.

I cover my mouth with one hand.

'Leonora! Oh my God.' I breathe the words, desperate pity filling me that this beautiful woman, this beloved new friend of mine should take her life in this way.

I know I should ring someone. Police, ambulance, but I can't move.

If only I'd come in the first time I heard movement. Would I have been able to save her? Would I have been in time?

Devastation weakens me further. The file slips from my numb fingers and falls with a muffled thud on the bathroom floor, leaves of paper scatter across the black tiles and flutter over the blood-stained white bathroom mat. Crimson polka dots soak through the pages.

'Who's there?'

My head rears back and I draw in a shocked gasp at the deep, guttural tones from the room beyond.

I snatch in a breath, terror paralysing my throat, but thankfully not my legs.

At the thud of fast footsteps heading through the neighbouring room in my direction, I spin around. I race back through the nursery knowing I have left that file sprawled across the floor, evidence of my presence there, because with sudden insight I know Leonora has not taken her life, but someone has taken it from her.

Christ alive.

What am I supposed to do?

My head spins as I take in the nursery, the sleeping baby, the situation.

Leonora has not killed herself. She would never leave this beautiful soul alone willingly. But that person beyond in the other room has murdered her.

And this baby has no one but me to save her, because if that individual, that interloper, so ruthlessly killed her mother, what is to stop them from murdering her?

Without thought for my own safety, I snatch the baby up and hug her tight to my chest, her head in the crook of my neck.

She makes a startled noise, a squeak, and then, recognising my scent, settles immediately.

Still with Grace in a deep sleep, I charge out of the room. Leaving the door wide, I belt along the hallway, down the stairs, almost missing my step as my bare feet slip on the stair carpet, skidding from under me. I jerk upright and my back spasms.

I reach the door at the bottom of the stairwell, fling it open, exposing the wide expanse of open hallway of the business quarters, and pause.

Something makes me stop. A sound. A breath.

Holding Grace close, I do a slow turn on my bare heel.

I glance up at the dark shadow that has paused at the top of the stairs. At the face of the man pursuing me. The manic light in the eyes that bore into mine, willing me not to make another move.

The blood in my veins turns to ice.

I slam the door shut, fumbling one-handed for the key in my pocket as my pursuer hurtles down the stairs to the sound of thunder.

My fingers tremble as I ram the key in the lock and turn it, leaving it in so that the person beyond that door cannot immediately get out. The door handle rattles, followed by a loud thump akin to a rhino ramming into a tree.

I back away, horror gripping me.

I glance down at the heels I'd left at the doorway, knowing that at this moment, they would be more of a hindrance if I put them on. I snatch up the handbag I'd left beside them and fling it over the opposite shoulder to the one I cradle the baby against. I sprint with every ounce of energy in my body towards the front door.

This, I don't bother to lock but slam it open wide and fly out. I charge towards my car, horror chasing me down.

I don't have a baby seat in my car and all I can do is snatch up the coat I keep on my backseat for emergencies, and cushion baby Grace in it, lying her down on the front seat. I stretch the seatbelt over her and use my handbag on the outer edge to anchor her into place.

She lets out a mewling whimper, but I can't do anything about that now. I need to go.

My hands are shaking so hard, I can barely buckle my own belt up.

Grace's whimper turns to a moan.

Panic slices through as I rattle my key into the ignition and fire up the car, conscious I have a baby in a very precarious situation. Instead of flooring the accelerator, I trundle off at a steady speed, knowing there is no car behind me. No car in the car park.

I ponder whether there's a car parked at the opposite side of the Hall or in the barn with the other collectable cars. Was that a deliberate move to disguise the fact that there was someone still in the building? In the private quarters.

At this point, I don't care. My only concern is to get out of here.

I power my vehicle down the long, narrow driveway without looking back, terrified of what I might see if I do glance in my rearview mirror. Will I see those demonic eyes again boring into mine? Accusation and fury combining in a melting pot of evil.

I will not look. Not until I reach the main carriageway and then I will allow myself a quick glance, but for now, the most important thing for me to do is escape.

31

PRESENT DAY – WEDNESDAY, 17 JULY 2024, 11.35 A.M. – SIOBHAN

Tall, slender and elegant, the woman who walked into the coffee shop they'd agreed to meet in was immediately familiar.

Just two years younger than Siobhan, according to the messages they'd continued to exchange over the past few days while her cousin finalised travel and hotel arrangements.

The shape of her nose, the tone of her skin. All recognisable from when Siobhan looked in the mirror.

Siobhan came to her feet, noting that Megan's face reflected the same surprise as they met eye to eye, almost exactly the same height.

'Oh my God. If there was any doubt that we were related before this, it's totally dispelled.' Megan grinned, her lips forming the same smile, a look of wonder crossing her face.

Stunned into silence, Siobhan held out her hands, palms upwards, and took Megan's into hers. 'I can't believe it. We could be sisters.'

'Or first cousins,' Megan qualified with a puzzled smile, sinking into a chair without releasing Siobhan's hands.

For several moments, they did nothing but stare at each other, the small table between them. Megan shook her head as though trying to release herself from a spell. 'Mum said it wasn't possible, but here you are.' Her soft Australian accent swam across the words. 'She said not to trust anything, because you could be trying to wheedle your way into our family.'

Siobhan let out a soft huff at the insult, let go of the other woman's fingers and leaned back in her chair. The sound of hundreds of bees buzzed in her head.

'Sorry, that kind of came out wrong.' The other woman sent her a regretful smile. 'We never knew you existed until a few days ago.'

'Same here.' Siobhan paused.

'Go ahead. You tell your story first. Then I'll tell ours and we'll see where the lines got crossed in our history.'

Siobhan nodded. It was the only way. 'Shall we order a drink first?' Siobhan felt she needed a distraction while she gathered herself.

'Absolutely. What would you like? I'll get it.' Megan sprang to her feet, supple and agile.

'I'll have a frappé, please.'

Megan let out a hoot. 'It's tea for me, every time. Mum's a tea snob. It's just not the same in Oz. I have to take her the proper stuff back, so I have a spare suitcase to fill before I return.'

As she turned her back and walked to the counter in the small café to place their order, Siobhan stared out of the window at the bright sunshine that never seemed to dim at the moment. Air shimmered above the heat of the pavements, distorting everything a little like the wobble in her brain that could barely cope with the whole prospect of this woman being here. A relation she had no knowledge of.

The only reason she'd chosen to sit inside was because the place had the cooling breeze of air conditioning, and she couldn't be more grateful at this minute as heat licked through her veins.

Megan returned, placing the frappé in front of Siobhan and taking her seat once more opposite her, the cup of tea rattling in its saucer as she put it down. A small sign that she was also full of nerves. This couldn't be easy for her either, but at least she had her mum to confide in.

They sat for a moment in silence. Siobhan took a sip of her ice-cold frappé and Megan stared at the bubbles that circled on the surface of the tea she'd stirred.

Siobhan took in a long breath and started.

'My mum recently had an accident. She broke her hip...' Siobhan didn't see the point of going into all the details, she wanted to stick to the more relevant line of her story. At the sympathetic frown on the other woman's face, she continued.

'When she was just out of recovery, something she said made me doubt I was her daughter.'

Megan leaned closer. 'Do you mean you didn't know?'

Siobhan shook her head and she felt tears prick at the back of her eyes. 'I never had a clue. Not until last week.'

Megan reached out to place a cool hand on top of Siobhan's hot, clammy one and made her want to cry even more.

She swallowed back the tears and acknowledged that the stress of the last couple of weeks was probably getting the better of her.

She turned her hand over and held the other woman's. There was a strong pull towards liking this woman already, an instinct telling her she belonged. Yet she was still cautious in what she revealed.

'Because Mum threw this spanner into the works, I felt I needed to prove to myself that she was my biological mother.'

'Instead, you proved the opposite.'

They unlinked hands, both of them reaching for their drinks at the same time, and Siobhan nodded her agreement. 'Yes. My mum has an entirely different family tree than I do. There is no crossover, nothing seems to intertwine.'

Megan sipped at her tea, her eyes narrowed in contemplation. 'Strewth, that puts you in a pickle. Have you confronted her?'

Confrontation wouldn't be the approach Siobhan would use, although there had to come a time when she sat her mum down to have a heart-to-heart. 'No. I don't think the timing is appropriate. She's recovering from the hip operation.' Least said...

'But you will?'

Siobhan pressed her lips tight. *No*, she wanted to say. 'I adore my mum, whether I'm adopted or not.'

'Well.' Megan placed her cup back on her saucer and leaned back, looping her arm over the back of the wooden chair in an overly casual manner that had Siobhan stiffening. 'I can tell you straight, you are not adopted. Well, in any case, certainly not via a legal route.'

Air compressed in her lungs and Siobhan looked towards the door and then back at Megan. She raised her shoulders in a deep shrug. 'Then I have no idea how my mum ended up with me.' She could not believe her mum would ever do anything illegal. Her mum was the perfect upright citizen.

Megan leaned down and picked up the handbag she'd placed on the floor at her feet and delved inside. She took out a sheet of white A4 paper, folded in two, and laid it flat on the table between them. She placed her bag back on the floor.

'Let me tell you Mum's story. Then, I'll show you this.' She tapped her finger on the paper.

'My mum emigrated to Australia back in the 1980s with Dad. She's a marine biologist and he was a merchant banker, now retired.' She rested both hands on the sheet of paper and linked her fingers. 'Her sister... my aunt... your biological mum, also married, but she chose to stay here on the family estate.'

'Family estate?'

Megan flicked her well-manicured fingers. 'That's not currently relevant.'

Like her, Siobhan had the impression Megan was being frugal with the truth, as though she too had things to hide.

Megan continued. 'As I said, your mum married too, and for several years tried unsuccessfully to fall pregnant. The last time my mum saw her, she had embarked on some kind of IVF treatment. Mum said Aunt Leonora was desperate.'

'Leonora.'

Megan gave a nod, by now already wrapped up in the story and didn't notice Siobhan's jerk of recognition. The name her mum had said in her delirium.

'She came to visit Mum in Oz while her husband, Justin, did some kind of trek out there. He was always one for the outdoor life. It was a short stay and by all accounts an unhappy one. Your mum was intent on having a baby, come hell or high water.' She shook her head. 'And that also included risking her marriage. Your dad wasn't happy. She put them under a lot of pressure. In the end, just as the steam almost blew, she was suddenly pregnant. Mum says Leonora was wild with joy.'

Siobhan rested her elbow on the table and cupped her chin in her hand. 'So, what could possibly go so wrong?'

'Postnatal depression.'

'What?' Siobhan jerked upright again hand against her chest, her memory flickering to the message Megan had originally sent, stating that Leonora had died under tragic circumstances. 'Post-natal depression? Did she harm the baby, or herself? Did they take the baby... me, away from Leonora?' She knew there had to be a logical explanation as to why her mum had ended up with her, something above board, but this didn't make sense. She'd had a father, an aunt, even though she was no longer living in the UK.

'No. They didn't need to. Until now, we've always thought she did something bad to you. To the baby my mum knew as Grace.'

Siobhan gasped as her own mum's name came out of this stranger's mouth. This was crazy.

Megan continued, so wrapped up in the story she was relating that she didn't seem to notice Siobhan's reaction. 'The police thought she must have accidentally killed you, dumped you. There was never any trace of you. The police set up a search. You disappeared into thin air.' She clicked her fingers. 'Gone. You and your snuggle blanket. That was it.'

Siobhan covered her mouth with her hand. 'Oh God. What happened to Leonora, my real mum? I thought you said she died.'

Megan's smooth brow wrinkled. 'No. Sorry, Siobhan. I maybe didn't make this clear. Your mum committed suicide.'

32

THIRTY-ONE YEARS EARLIER – 1993 – GRACE

I'm absolutely terrified. Bricking it, as the boys on the construction site used to say. There are stronger descriptions, but I think this one is appropriate, all things considered.

I don't know why I responded the way I did. Why I snatched up that little baby and ran with her, not willing to leave her there. But every instinct in my body told me to do it, to run. To run and not look back. But I did look back. And when my gaze locked with his, I knew I had done the right thing.

Baby Grace snuffles and shifts about on her makeshift car seat.

Relieved that the motion of the car seems to have settled her, I keep driving, because if I stop, I don't know what I'll do, I'll fall apart, and I can't afford to fall apart right now.

What I need is to be able to think straight.

What I need is an ally.

I need to find James, but he's not been around so much lately and he's not as easy to find since he managed to get enrolled on that ex-servicemen's rehabilitation course. He'd disappeared for twelve weeks and when he'd returned, he was a different man again from the one I have always known.

No longer does he sleep on the streets, but he has a house-share with other discharged servicemen. He has support. A network he can depend on, even when he falls off the wagon, which we know will continue unless, or until, his demons are vanquished.

I'm not sure they can be any worse than my demons at this precise moment. James is in peril of drinking himself to death. I'm in peril of being murdered.

I need him now, and I can only pray that he's not fallen off the wagon, because he did warn me when he does, he's back into rehab. That's the way it works.

As panic grabs my throat, I pull onto the drive in front of my house.

I bolt out of the car, ignoring the quiet whimper that starts up from Grace. She's going to have to wait because I am on a mission.

Locking the car with Grace inside, I tear through my small house, slinging essentials, clothes, shoes, both my birth certificates and passport, my building society book with all my savings, and my bank book where my latest salary has just been paid in.

I glance at my watch and already three minutes have gone past. Time is flying and I have none of it to waste. I know with absolute conviction that I haven't been followed here and I'm positive I never updated my personnel file at work with my latest address when I moved to this house just a couple of years ago. So, hopefully, they won't be able to track me down immediately.

A panicked snort of laughter slips from me as the thought occurs that it's probably a disciplinary offence, not keeping home addresses updated.

I stand for a moment, my breathing heavy in the quiet air of my home. A home I cherish but will never return to.

Right now, I haven't a moment to dwell on that, but I know the time will come when regret will hit me hard. I have worked my arse off to achieve the position in life I've come to. I have dragged myself from the gutter with nobody's help but James's.

And yet here I am.

Fate can be a bitch.

With one last look, I turn and race out of the house. Locking it behind me, I bolt the short distance down the tarmacked driveway, heat singeing the soles of my bare feet and I leap inside my car.

Baby Grace is grizzling now, and I have nothing. Nothing. What am I supposed to do?

With no time to think, I throw my car into reverse.

It's nearly seven o'clock on a Friday night. There are very few shops that are open at this time. I'm pretty sure Carrefour will be, though, they've extended their hours and I think you can shop until nine on a Friday.

I head towards the hypermarket, parking my car as close to the entrance as possible.

I lean across and scoop a pair of flat brogues that I wear for driving instead of my stiletto heels out of the passenger footwell and slip them on my feet, feeling the burn of my skin against them.

I lift the baby out of the car. My hands shake. My stomach is so queasy and I daren't close my eyes for longer than a blink for fear of that image of Leonora flashing up. Gossamer hair floating on scarlet liquid.

I shut that thought, that memory down.

Swallowing hard, I hope like hell no one recognises me. I haven't worked here for years, but some of the women are there for the long run. If Brenda Batshit sees me, it will be all over that I've had a baby. Everyone will know. And once that type of information seeps out, lines of communication will widen until I'm found out.

I think I'm going to throw up if anybody speaks to me. If anybody looks any closer than below the surface, I will crumble into a pile of dust.

With gentle care, I lay Grace in the baby seat of a trolley and march with purpose through the store. It's relatively quiet at this time of night. Most shoppers have already gone home. I smell the scent of the ready-roasted rotisserie chickens and my stomach gurgles. I'm not sure if it's hunger or simply the drop in adrenaline that tells me I haven't eaten since lunchtime and that was only a small salad.

I can't believe I even want to think of food, but I do. My body tells me I'm in dire need of energy because I have spent all of it.

I scoop one of the sealed bags with a whole hot chicken up and place it in the front section of the trolley. I follow it with a bag of roasted potatoes that have been reduced for the end of the evening and have lost their heat slightly. I don't care. I am actually working on automatic, in survival mode. I throw in a bag of ready-washed salad, a bottle of orange juice and then head straight for the baby aisle.

With barely a glance, I snatch up essentials. I can't deny that I have looked before. When I lost my own baby. When there was that thought that I could never, ever have one again. I scoured the aisles back then, reaching to touch items I would never buy for a baby I would never have.

Leonora had said, just this morning, that her health visitor had been so pleased with Grace's increase in weight as normally they drop a little in the first few days, especially breastfed babies. The drop had been a little scary, but after another couple of weeks, it had bounced back. Grace was flourishing and at nine pounds and two ounces she was doing exceedingly well. Not exactly the premature baby they thought Leonora had given birth to. Nothing about Grace appeared prem.

I look for the appropriate size of clothes and shove four double packs of baby grows in my trolley, followed by two pretty frocks with matching knickers, a leggings and little blouse set and two bonnets. She may need the bonnets to cover her hair.

There's a little padded jacket, but it's really too warm for that right now, and what if she has a growth spurt and it doesn't fit her?

Essentials. That's what I need. That's all I need. Time enough for luxuries another day. Right now, I have to get what I need, get out of here.

Don't get distracted. Don't slow down. Move on.

I look at the trolley with items piled high and still I know there's more. It's not as though I have anything that I can make do with.

There is no pleasure in this shop, I am an automaton. Just doing what has to be done.

Relief beats a trapped wing against my chest as I spot a baby car seat all boxed up and ready to go. I place it in the trolley and as Grace lets out a high-pitched squeal, I snap up a pack of dummies.

Ripping them open, I push one into her mouth and pray that it will keep her quiet just for a little while longer, until I can reach a place of safety where I can make up milk for her. I'm pretty sure I should have sterilised it first, but what germs would it have on it straight from the factory into a shrink-wrapped package?

God only knows how it will affect her without her mum's milk but how am I to do anything else? It's not as though I could feed her myself. But the baby milk formula I dump in should be adequate. I quickly scan the label and it's definitely age-appropriate. I pick up a box with baby bottles and steam steriliser. I place that in my trolley too, taking a moment to give Grace's kicking legs a soft, reassuring rub while I assess my prospective purchases.

The trolley is fit to burst. I can barely balance anything more on top of what I already have.

It's not as though I'm short of money. I've got plenty in my bank, even more in my building society. I need to buy things and I need them now. Because I may have to go into hiding if I am reported for snatching this beautiful, precious baby who I have to protect with the whole of me.

I don't have a list, just thoughts of items babies may need rolling through my head in a frantic loop, pushing past the panic, throwing any thoughts that would stop me in my tracks to one side while I study everything in front of me in this vast aisle of products. I'm sure I don't need everything, but is that everything I need?

I turn the trolley and head towards the checkouts, my head spinning with too many thoughts.

Changing my mind, I turn again and round the corner of the next aisle. I lob in a toothbrush, toothpaste, a flannel, more flannels in case I need them for changing Grace and then I suddenly remember I have to get nappies.

Where the hell were they? Surely they would be in the baby aisle?

I charge back up the baby aisle, then down the one next to it and with a cursory glance at the sizes, I hook bags of nappies over the back of the trolley.

I can barely fit any more in this trolley, but I manage to balance a changing mat across the top and then head towards the checkouts.

The young, uniformed policewoman who steps out in front of me gives us a surprised smile as I almost mow her down.

My heart explodes in my chest as blood drains from my head into my feet.

She's holding a packet of sandwiches and a bag of crisps, and she raises it to indicate my fully laden trolley in comparison and gives me a wide grin.

'My goodness, you've got a lot there.'

My smile by contrast is tremulous. Terrified. I can feel my lips trembling, ready to spill the whole story out to her, if only she asks.

It would only take the question and I will blurt out a confession. But she's already looking at the baby as she leans down.

'Oh, she's so cute.'

'Yes,' I manage to stammer.

'You're going to have your hands full with her.' She laughs.

I force a laugh back. 'Yes, I'm sure.' I try to make my tense face relax. 'She's already tripped me up. She's six weeks early. You know, I was rather—' I indicate the trolley '—unprepared, to say the least.' I hope the soft warble I hear in my own voice isn't as obvious to the policewoman.

The police officer's eyes widen with surprise and maybe I've said too much because we're now engaged in a full conversation, rather than just drifting past a stranger in the supermarket. My own stupid fault, but I'm soon to learn that babies do that, attract attention and often unwanted advice. Especially beautiful babies like Grace.

The police officer looks at Grace and then back at me, taking in my suit, which even if I say so myself somehow still looks impeccable, crisp, despite the sweat that must have soaked into the lining, from the outside of the jacket it probably looks fresh. After all, that's why you pay extra for these things. My fuchsia camisole peeps from the V-neckline of my jacket and even my flat shoes don't look ridiculous, although it's not a personal choice I would make for business.

'You do look incredible for someone who has just given birth. I looked ravaged after I had my son.' Her forehead wrinkles as she peers closer. 'Although you're very pale. Are you okay?'

The irony of it is that I'd just applied a slick of lipstick as I was about to leave for the day, so I may well look okay, but for the fine layer of sweat she may mistake for a 'dewy' look.

'I'm fine. I'm fine.' I indicate Grace with a flick of my fingers and dig myself in deeper. 'Her daddy left me, though. Just before I gave birth. So, it's all on me.' I give a careless shrug. The lies rolling off my tongue so easily, just like the lies I've told in the past about my age, about my date of birth, about my experience at being a PA. Funny how it all comes back. Yet here I am, the person who cannot bear a liar.

The policewoman gives a sympathetic murmur and looks skyward briefly and I almost hear her thinking 'men', then she reaches over and touches Grace's head.

'I'm so sorry,' she says, placing her free hand on the one I have resting on the trolley, and my eyes start tearing up, not because of the situation she thinks I'm in but because of the sympathy that oozes from this woman, making me want to put my head on her shoulder and whisper the heinous truth of the matter.

Instead, I shake my head. 'Thank you.' I assume she thinks my tears are for my husband leaving me. It occurs to me that all these lies I am piling up could easily come back to bite me in the arse when Leonora's death and missing baby are reported to the police. I will hardly be able to plead innocence, or ignorance.

My tongue thickens in my mouth, and I can barely speak as the next thought tumbles on top of that first one. What if I am accused of murdering Leonora in order to take their precious baby? A baby I have made no bones about thinking the world of. A baby I would die for. But would I kill for her? I'm sure that would be the question.

My face burns and I can feel two spots on my cheeks that must be florid.

'I'd better get a move on. I need to get home.' I stammer the words out.

The policewoman opens her mouth to reply and I think she may be about to say something that will surely bring me to my knees. I am teetering on the brink of a full confession here.

'Thank you,' I mumble as a tear rolls down my cheek.

I turn and briskly walk away.

I pay for the goods, not even blinking when the cashier tells me how much they're going to cost. I hand over my card and she processes the payment.

'Can I have cashback, please?'

'Cashback?' She raises an eyebrow, judgement in the twist of her lips as I pile the last of my purchases into the trolley. Perhaps she doesn't believe I should have a baby out this late at night, but it's not like I have a choice in the matter.

'We can only give fifty pounds, you know.' The way she looks at me makes me think I can't afford all of this, but I paid for it with a cash card. I've never had a credit card. Never had a loan, except my mortgage. I don't like to be beholden to anyone.

'Fifty pounds will be fine,' I reply and tuck it into my purse when she hands it over, dipping my head so I don't need to have eye contact with the woman. Why couldn't everyone be as sympathetic and kind as the police officer? This woman hasn't even glanced at Grace. For which I should be eternally grateful, but instead a little anger stirs in me at her obvious disenchantment at the whole world.

My hands shake so much that I can barely unbox the baby seat, when I get back to my car, never mind anchor it in the passenger seat. Why do they make these bloody things so complicated? The strap only just reaches across, so I have to ram the buckle hard to get it to click in place. Still the seat wobbles a little, but I don't have any more time to waste.

I consider leaving the empty car seat box in the car park, and then re-think it. That would be a red flag to anyone when Grace is reported missing. And I am convinced she will be once the police are informed of Leonora's murder.

I lift the baby up, cooing to her all the time, even though my insides are shaking apart. I'm not sure I can hold it together much longer. That whole compartmentalising is all very well until the sides of the compartments bow and collapse inwards to let the tide rush in.

After sorting out the harness, I clip it closed across her little stomach and put the last of the items in the boot of my car.

Just as I'm about to climb into the driver's seat, the police officer emerges from the hypermarket. She glances over and I hope to God she doesn't realise I never had a car seat before I bought this one.

I pray she'd not taken that much notice, but she's a police officer and she hesitates.

My heart stops. Why hadn't she already gone? I've been ages unpacking my trolley.

'Shit!' I murmur to myself, my hand gripping the open door.

She's got a lollipop shoved in the side of her mouth and she carries a full carrier bag of shopping, which surprises me as I assumed she'd grabbed a sandwich and had left before me.

We stare at each other over the roof of my car. She tilts her head, her brow furrowing and she raises her hand to remove the lollipop from her mouth as though she's about to ask me a question. Like '*How the hell did you get here with your baby and no car seat? You know that's not only illegal but downright irresponsible.*'

The sharp *Neenah! Neenah!* of a police car siren has me almost jumping out of my skin. My neck cracks as I jerk my head around to see a panda car speeding towards us from the bottom of the car park, blue lights flashing, and I'm not sure my heart will hold out.

Adrenaline crashes into my shoes and I sag against the burning metal of the car.

They've caught me.

33

THIRTY-ONE YEARS EARLIER – 1993 – GRACE

The WPC raises her hand and points a finger at me. She waggles it from side to side, like I'm a naughty schoolgirl, a slight frown of disapproval on her face, and I'm pretty sure she knows I'd not used a car seat on my way here.

Then, she turns and leaps into the approaching police car as it barely stops before racing off. The sirens blare, the lights blaze and the vehicle tears away in the opposite direction, speeding out of the virtually deserted car park and I am left alone.

I'm not sure I can cope any longer.

I think my heart might give out.

I wilt into the driver's seat, strap myself in, all the time puffing out my cheeks, trying not to hyperventilate. There's no oxygen in my lungs and I'm lightheaded. I don't know how my luck held, but there was obviously an emergency for the police to attend, otherwise I might be in handcuffs by now. If she'd had time, even if she'd not arrested me for that misdemeanour, she'd have given me the biggest bollocking of my life. At which point I would have collapsed at her feet and begged for mercy, for forgiveness. Not for lack of a baby seat, but for kidnapping Grace. Because when it boils down to it, isn't that exactly what I've done?

I put the car into gear and I'm just about to drive off when I notice the auto bank machines in the wall. Somewhere in the recess of my mind, my inner voice whispers that I could do with as much cash as I can get my hands on. Just in case.

I wonder how much money the auto bank will allow me to withdraw. I glance at the baby, her eyes are on mine. Sweet, trusting.

I switch the engine off and leap out of the car, locking it with my key before charging to the auto bank. I fumble as I punch in my PIN number too quick and have to try it twice more before I get it right. The third try is the last one before it will whip away my bank card and I'll be without money or a card. I slow myself down, press each key with firm determination and the small screen lights up to celebrate my success.

My fingers tremble as I request three hundred pounds and let out a whimper as it rejects that. The limit is two hundred pounds daily through the auto bank. A sign flashes up which would have been more helpful had it informed me prior to attempting to take more than the limit.

I grind my teeth and plumb in the two-hundred-pound limit. The machine chugs and grinds as if it's counting each ten-pound note individually and licking its finger in between. Aren't computers supposed to speed things up?

At last, it spits the notes out and I rip them from the metallic teeth, not bothering to check if it's all there. If the machine is defective, I hardly have time to put in a written complaint.

From the wad of notes, I'm reasonably sure it's correct and I cram it into my handbag and race back to the car.

Grace has fallen asleep, and I can only assume that she had not long been fed before her mother was murdered, which is why she appears so content, although the baby has been mild-mannered from the very first moment she made her dramatic explosion onto the scene.

I drive through the enormous, almost empty car park and tears roll down my cheeks. I scrub them away with the back of one hand while my fingers grip the steering wheel with the other.

This has gone too far.

I'm not sure I can do this.

I follow the one-way system which takes me out past the brick and glass monstrosity that is the police station, built only ten years previously and already looking outdated, and consider if it would be better if I go in and report it to the police. If I tell them all I know, will they believe me?

This time, I swipe the back of my hand across my runny nose and let out a few desperate sobs as the car sails past the building and I instinctively continue straight over at the roundabout, barely recognising the landscape of where my first job was on the M54.

I reach to turn on the radio low to disguise the quiet sobs that escape me, so they don't disturb Grace.

I don't really know where I'm going, but it seems there's a sixth sense turning me in the right direction.

I need help.

I head along the dual track of the Queensway, taking the slip road off heading towards Randlay, one of the original estates built in the new town of Telford already suffering because of the poor design and fabric of the community. The last place I'd seen James, knowing that if he's there it could be a double-edged sword because that could be an indication that he's had another lapse. The narrow alleyways and dark corners a haven for drunks and drug addicts.

For this reason, I almost wish he's not there, yet the moment I see him my heart leaps with hope.

James is not huddled under a blanket in the corner, but he is bending over someone who is, handing them a packet of sandwiches and what looks like a hot drink.

The relief is indescribable. Desperate to grab his attention, I jerk the steering wheel and the car almost mounts the pavement behind him.

My breath is hitching and as he turns towards me, his gaze delving into my soul, the weakness I have been staving off hits me and tears course down my cheeks. Floods of them, not just leaking, which they've done since I left the supermarket, but a downpour, a deluge.

I want to put my head on my steering wheel and wail until there is no more weeping left to do, but I have a job. And just as any other job in my life, I need to get it done, to compartmentalise.

The question is, do I have the strength to do it?

James rounds the bonnet of my car and jerks open the driver's door.

His eyes are quick to assess the situation, but he doesn't know the details.

'James,' I gasp, barely able to speak past the sobs. 'I need help.' I dart my gaze around at the interest I'm attracting and the panic tightens my throat. 'I need to get out of here.'

Without judgement, he jerks his head. 'Out.'

The word is quiet, but indisputably a command which I don't hesitate to obey. He is a man of few words. This is what I need. Direction. Assistance.

He slides into the driver's seat, and I climb into the back of the car.

'Good Christ.' His voice is pure gravel. 'What in hell's name is going on?'

'I can't! Not yet, James. Give me a moment.'

I can see baby Grace better now, her sweet contentment as she rhythmically sucks on her dummy, stops, then sucks again.

My heart steadies as James drives with casual confidence, rounding several bends in the road before he pulls onto the motorway without saying another word. We know each other well enough to realise when we need space.

The drama that unfolded before me needs no exaggeration, and I impart it to him, step by miserable step. He asks no questions, just listens until I finish. Exhausted, spent.

I know the wheels of his mind are turning, desperate to find a solution, and can only be thankful as mine seems to have collapsed. A black hole swallowing up the universe.

We are silent. My exhausted body has turned weak. I have no more tears to cry. I close my eyes, and when I wake, I realise James has been driving for a couple of hours before he pulls over into the car park of a Little Chef motel. I've never stayed in one. I've only ever stayed in five-star hotels for work purposes. The place looks eerily quiet. Then again, it would be at this time of night, and I wonder if they will even let us have a room.

James gets out of the car and when he returns, he has keys in his hands. By the look of it, we have separate rooms.

My heart skitters as I think of being alone with this tiny baby.

It's not like I haven't changed her nappy. But I've never been alone with her, never taken full responsibility for such a small being. Certainly, I haven't fed her and from the way she's smacking her lips and turning her head blindly from side to side, evidently looking for a breast, she's quite desperate for a feed.

I have no idea how to feed a baby, or how often. I've had no contact with anybody else's babies but Leonora's, and Grace has always been breastfed. She's a mere few weeks old.

Panic is spiking through me.

James opens my door as I remain motionless. I turn my face to him. I am dry-eyed now, but fear is banging down the door of my sanity.

'What have I done?' I speak the words that have been whispering through my mind from the moment I took Grace.

If I expected sympathy from James, I was wrong. His eyes are stony, his mouth set.

'You've witnessed the murder of a close friend, and possibly saved the life of that little baby.' He inclines his head to the passenger seat, where Grace is now thrashing her legs and making snorting, whimpering noises.

He moves his hand to direct me. 'Now you need to get out of this car and go and feed her before she starts crying and possibly attracts attention.'

He dangles one key in front of me and I automatically take it.

I can barely lift one foot in front of the other and he must see that as he circles the car and lifts Grace, baby seat and all, out of the passenger side.

Wordless, he waits as I swipe up my holdall and as many shopping bags as I can carry. I stumble to the room, slide the key in the lock and James bumps the door open with his hip.

With barely a murmur, he places the baby seat with Grace inside on the floor. There is nowhere else to put her. There's no cot in the room and the chair would be too small, the bed too soft and possibly too high should the baby seat not be stable.

I give him a weary, thankful smile and he hums in the back of his throat as though contemplating something before he slips out.

Barely a heartbeat later, a light tap sounds on an internal door and I realise he has managed to get connecting rooms. He smiles as I open my side of the door and he holds it wide, indicating to me a small, neat travel cot in the corner of his room.

'I asked for a cot. Thought it was in your room.'

He picks up my bags and transfers them to the room he came through and as I bend to take Grace from the car seat, he fills the small kettle and switches it on and then wordlessly starts to open the box containing all the feeding bottles and steriliser.

The man works with quick efficiency, as though he's done it before as I jiggle Grace in my arms and hope that the soft sobs she's emitting don't morph into hysterical cries.

I nod at him. 'You look like you have experience with that.'

He flushes as he shakes the bottle and drops a tear of milk onto the inside of his wrist, presumably to test the temperature.

'I do. I used to do it for you, when your mum couldn't cope.' His eyes harden. 'Or when she wasn't available.'

I take the bottle from him and lower myself onto the small bucket chair and with James's help manoeuvre the baby into position. He grabs a pillow from the bed and pushes it under the elbow I have braced under Grace to make me more comfortable.

As Grace starts to suckle, a little cautiously at first, feeling the difference I assume between a real nipple and a rubber one, her hunger gets the better of her and she sucks with voracious intent. My body wilts and some of the tension of the day drains to leave me exhausted and yet somehow comforted.

I am not alone.

James has always been with me. He always will be. And despite the fact that I have never given him the title, he is my dad.

34

PRESENT DAY – WEDNESDAY, 17 JULY 2024, 1.05 P.M. – SIOBHAN

Siobhan's lips were numb. She could barely move them as she stared at the woman opposite.

'Is this for real?'

Megan reached across the small table and touched the back of her hand. 'I'm so sorry. I didn't mean to shock you. I thought somehow you would already know something of the truth before we met. That you had researched the case.'

'I know nothing.' She swallowed. 'I wasn't even aware there was a "case".'

The woman's eyes filled with tears. 'I'm so sorry,' she repeated.

Siobhan hauled in a shaky breath, not knowing whether to stand and run from the café. She wasn't sure she could continue the conversation as fire rushed into her cheeks. On the other hand, she couldn't guarantee her legs would hold her up.

She shook her head. 'It can't be true. It's impossible. My mum has a beautiful, kind heart. I can't imagine she would have anything to do with something so... grotesque.'

Megan tapped her fingers on the folded sheets of paper she'd placed on the table between them. 'Mum messaged these over last night and I printed them off.' She picked up the papers and unfolded them.

She placed them on the table in front of Siobhan.

'Your birth mother was Lady Leonora Constance Schneider. You may have heard of her.'

Siobhan shook her head, too deep in shock to do much else. She'd never heard of the woman. Why would she? She drew the papers towards her.

The first page was a photograph of a young, beautiful, vital woman. Laughing into the camera with a view of a mountain behind her.

'This.' Megan tapped the picture. 'This was Leonora. The woman you claim to be your mother.'

Siobhan opened her mouth to protest. She didn't 'claim' to be Leonora's daughter. The DNA site claimed it for her. Perhaps they were wrong.

She closed her mouth without saying another word as she stared at the woman whose face was so like hers. If she squinted her eyes, it could be her. The way Leonora stood. Her deportment.

She tuned back into Megan's voice.

'She married Justin Schneider, the father of her baby, and this was taken on their honeymoon.'

Siobhan reached for her frappé and reconsidered, pushing it away from her. She wasn't sure she could stomach it.

'What happened to Justin?'

There was a slight flicker, something Siobhan couldn't quite identify in Megan's eyes. Was it distaste?

'He's still alive. Still living in the Hall where Leonora's body was found in the bath.'

Siobhan's eyes widened.

This might be her story, but she'd never lived it. It was like hearing about someone else.

'According to him, he's never forgiven himself for your mother's death.'

'According to him...?'

Megan gave a slight shrug. 'Mum knew there was some kind of friction going on. She was due to visit a couple of weeks later. Instead of coming to see her niece christened and become a godmother, she came for her sister's funeral.'

Siobhan drew back, placing her hand on her chest. 'That's horrendous.'

'Yes.'

'But she thinks he had something to do with Leonora's death?'

'Well, she thinks he didn't take good enough care to ensure she didn't take her own life. Obviously, there was a thorough police investigation. He didn't kill her or anything dramatic like that. He had a watertight alibi for the night. Came back and found her on the Sunday morning after he'd gone on a trip shooting deer in Scotland.' She wrinkled her mouth in revulsion, and then her face cleared. 'I'm sorry, this is your dad we're talking about. I shouldn't try to influence your opinion one way or the other. He was traumatised, no doubt. Never married again...'

Siobhan sensed an underlying... 'But...?'

Megan crooked her head to one side. 'It wouldn't be in his best interest to marry. He can have as many mistresses as he wants, but the trust set up by my grandparents—' she dipped her head towards Siobhan '—our grandparents, is such that should Uncle Justin ever remarry, or, under the terms, live with someone, he loses Crest Park, Leonora's family estate.' She shuffled the papers and brought another one to the top. She tapped on the picture of an immense Georgian-style mansion.

'Whoa!' Siobhan gripped the table with both hands as she stared at the incredible building with manicured gardens to the side and a large fountain in the middle of a circular driveway. Blood pumped a heavy thud, thud, thud through her head. 'You wouldn't want to lose that,' she whispered faintly.

She raised her gaze and caught the slight narrowing of the other woman's eyes and couldn't stop herself from letting out a small wince.

'Oh. I see.' The laugh that came out was tinged with bitterness.

Megan's own smile reflected the emotion. She picked up her tea and took a delicate sip. 'You see our dilemma? You've come out of nowhere.'

Siobhan almost heard the accusation. No one from nowhere.

'Call me cynical, but what is it you do for a living?'

Megan's smile widened. 'I'm a solicitor. I deal predominantly in dynastic wealth.'

'Inheritance?'

Megan gave a delicate snort. 'Of sorts. But for the exceptionally wealthy. Landowners, et cetera. Trusts, mainly.'

'And my biological father isn't included in the trust.'

Megan nodded. 'He is. He is entitled to live in the Hall until his death. He gets no allowance, though, and according to the trust he must maintain the upkeep of that Hall.' She gave a sharp smile. 'It means he has to continue working, just like he did before he met Leonora.'

'Hmm. Complicated.'

'Which... and I beg your pardon for this... is why my mum wanted me to meet you.'

'Scope me out. See if I'm trying to nab the dynastic wealth from under your noses?'

'Ha!' Megan leaned back, looping one arm over the back of her chair. 'You'd have to have big balls to try.' She tipped her head back and laughed. 'It's not unknown for people to turn up out of the blue and claim to be the long-lost Queen of Sheba to grab their share of the inheritance. It's my job to find out if the Queen of Sheba is genuine.' Megan straightened with a suddenness that took Siobhan by surprise as she un-looped her arm and smacked one hand on the table, making her cup rattle in its saucer and attracting the attention of the surrounding patrons. 'But I can tell already that unless you are an award-winning actress, you're as staggered as we are by this turn of events.'

Siobhan nodded. 'I have no idea who you or your dynastic family are. I just want to know who I am.'

'So do we.' Megan swept a critical gaze over her. 'You look so much like the photographs of my Aunt Leonora. Obviously, I never knew her. The nose, the mouth. Your eyes are nothing like hers, though. Yours are hazel. She had blue eyes.'

'Blue.' Siobhan absorbed the information for later dissection.

'Uncle Justin has blue eyes, too. So...' Megan raised her hands.

'So...?'

'So. We need to carry out our own DNA test to verify what you're telling us.'

'In case I somehow lied? Fiddled the results?'

'It's been done before.'

Siobhan shrugged and then reached for her own drink at last. She needed to wet a throat that was totally dry. 'I'm happy to take another test.'

'Good.' Megan picked up her own drink. 'We've let Justin know. He's desperate to meet you. Meet your mum. He can't for the life of him think who she might be. Like the rest of us, he's desperate to know what happened that day.'

35

THIRTY-ONE YEARS EARLIER – 1993 – GRACE

Aristocrat Lady Leonora Constance Schneider takes her own life after the disappearance of her baby girl

Police were called to Crest Park, residence of entrepreneur Justin Schneider and wife Lady Leonora, late on Sunday morning. It is reported that Schneider returned with his butler, Gordon Taper, from a short trip away to find his wife dead in the bath at their home having slit her wrists and bled to death.

Lady Leonora was granddaughter to Toby Charles Winnipeg, a Lieutenant Commander in the Royal Navy, and Sienna Maria de Lara of Spanish aristocracy. She is believed to be the goddaughter of British royalty.

Lady Leonora was pronounced dead at the scene.

On further investigation, it was discovered that their newborn baby, Grace Crystal Savannah Schneider, was nowhere to be found.

Sources inside the police station have led us to believe that Lady Leonora may have murdered her baby girl, disposing of the body, and then, filled with remorse, taken her own life.

Justin Schneider declined to comment, although it is believed that Lady Leonora was suffering from severe postnatal depression after giving birth unexpectedly at Crest Park with only a secretary in attendance. Sources revealed that it had been reported on more than one occasion that Lady Leonora had threatened to hurt her baby.

Mr Schneider is believed to have thought his wife had someone in attendance with her, but that she must have dismissed them for the evening.

The search continues for the baby.

James and I stare at each other across the small table in the Little Chef. The full English breakfast loses its appeal and I push it away from me and draw my steaming, weak coffee towards me.

Grace is in her car seat on the booth seat next to me.

I draw in a breath, but it's shaky. 'What do we do now?'

James looks down at the newspaper and I can see he's deep in thought as he scratches stubble on his chin, making it rasp in the quiet of the café.

He leans in closer, so he can whisper. 'We need to move your money.'

'But why? The police aren't looking for me. Has Justin let them believe Leonora killed her own baby?' My breath catches in my throat, and I take a minute. 'Why would he do that?' I close my eyes and picture the quick snatch I caught of a shadowed figure at the top of the stairs glaring down at me. Who had it been? 'If Justin and Gordon have a watertight alibi, who was it?' I am convinced he is behind it, but it seems he has the ear of the police.

I reach out to rest my hand on Grace's stomach, full from the feed I've just given her.

She's such a good baby. I'm pretty sure babies are supposed to sleep lots, but she is particularly well-behaved and considering how stressed I am, it doesn't seem to have affected her temperament.

Maybe it's because I'm not her mum. Perhaps she doesn't pick up on my anxiety. Whatever the reason, I am grateful for her gentle nature. She'd slept through until 3 a.m. and then again, once I'd fed, changed and burped her, until almost 7 a.m.

James looks at her and then back at me. 'The police may not be looking for you, but without a doubt, Justin will be, if, as you believe, it has something to do with him.'

I expect him to berate me, tell me that he warned me before about this man. The boss who grabbed me and bruised my arm. Whose insidious bullying had grown exponentially over the past year. But James doesn't. He's not a 'told you so' kind of person. This may be horrendous, but I guess he's lived through worse.

He puffs out a breath. 'This could go two ways. Justin has either convinced the police that Leonora did something vile to her baby, and then took her own life, in which case he will be looking for you, because you are the only witness.'

'Or?' I question.

'Or—' he taps the paper '—the police have withheld information as they frequently do when trying to track down a suspect who has gone underground, and Justin has convinced them that you have a hand in this. Without knowing what information the police have, you may be in danger either way and we need to get that money moved.'

'Surely he can't track my bank account.'

James blinks. 'Don't be naïve, Grace.'

'He doesn't even know I have a building society account.'

This time, James simply picks up his mug and blows the steam off the top of his tea.

'I think your man has the power of the rich behind him. So, we need a plan.'

'Do you have a bank account?' I ask him. 'Could we put it in there?'

I trust him implicitly.

James shakes his head. 'No. For two reasons.' He holds up one finger. 'One, I don't have a bank account because I don't want to be traced by anyone.' He holds up a second finger. 'Two, do not trust me with your money. If I go on a bender, there's no promise I won't do something stupid with it.'

I gasp at his brutal honesty.

'You've not been on a bender for ages. Months.'

'I'm still an alcoholic, Grace. I will always be. I still fall off the wagon from time to time, and when I do it's bad.'

'I saw you giving food to that chappie in the shop doorway.'

James inclines his head. 'It's getting worse here. There are more people on the streets than ever before. When I'm in a good place myself, I help them. At some point, I might need their help. Right now, I earn a little money doing odd jobs and Crisis has given me a proper job. It's only part-time, but it seems to help me when I help others.'

The pride throbs through his voice.

I stretch a hand across the table to take his in mine.

He smiles and his calmness communicates itself to me through our touch.

He is not frightened. Fear is something he has come face-to-face with and survived.

It's my turn to survive.

I think of the police officer I'd seen in Carrefour, of the lies I willingly told her spilling from my lips with such ease. Of how incriminating those lies could now be. They could even believe I murdered Leonora and kidnapped baby Grace.

I can barely breathe as I stare at James, the horror of the situation pressing down on me.

I could spend the rest of my life in jail. Then what would become of this poor, vulnerable baby?

'If I can't trust the police with this, what do I need to do?'

His expression hardens. 'You need to disappear. Disappear so no one can ever find you.'

36

PRESENT DAY – WEDNESDAY, 17 JULY 2024, 6 P.M. – SIOBHAN

Siobhan couldn't believe how stupid she'd been. How naïve. Why on earth did she give Megan her address? They'd exchanged information and yet in the quiet of contemplation, Siobhan now felt she'd been railroaded.

She wasn't ready to meet her biological father. Not yet.

She needed to breathe. To collect herself. She felt like she'd been run over by a forty-four-tonne truck.

Not least of all, she was concerned about her mum's reaction to the whole crazy scenario.

What would she say?

No matter what the situation, she was her mum. Siobhan had known nothing but this life. Nothing but the unquestionable love her mum had lavished her with.

Panic fluttered through her. It was all going too fast. This life she'd always known had screeched to a halt and now she was presented with a crossroads. There was no going back, but that was her own fault. Maybe she should never have opened that Pandora's box.

Be careful what you wish for.

'What are you thinking about?'

Siobhan jumped so hard that her chair scraped back, screeching on the tiled floor, and Beau leapt up from where he'd been asleep at her feet, his deep bark resonating through the cottage.

'Jesus Christ!' She snatched at the mug she'd almost overturned on her laptop and hot liquid spilt onto the back of her hand. 'Beau, quiet!' Her voice barked out as loud as his.

Unused to Siobhan's sharpness, the dog slinked off to garner their mum's protection. The woman stood in the doorway, a look of confusion on her face as she reached down to pet silken black ears that were flattened to Beau's head.

Guilt stabbed at her. 'Oh, Beau.'

Siobhan dropped to her knees on the floor and called him twice more, her voice soft and yielding before he slunk back to her. She buried her face in his neck and snuggled in, tears threatening to fall.

What had she done?

She wrapped her arms around Beau and gave him a hard squeeze, determined to swipe away the tears before her mum spotted them. 'Sorry, lad.' In typical Labrador fashion, the dog took on an ever more pitiful expression, his liquid brown eyes filled with sadness, and then flopped on the floor in front of her, turning on his back so his belly was exposed. Siobhan spluttered out a desperate laugh as she obliged him by giving him a rub.

Aware of her mum's slow, cautious movements across the room, Siobhan raised her head.

'Sorry, I was deep in thought.'

Her mum smiled, but her gaze searched Siobhan's, full of hidden questions.

She chose to ignore them, and instead came to her feet and pulled out a chair for her mum to sit in as Beau rolled onto his front and watched her with pained suspicion in case she shouted at him again.

'I'll make dinner.'

'That would be nice. Something light. Chicken salad, maybe.'

Siobhan moved to the fridge to take the leftover chicken from the night before out. As she prepared the salad, she glanced at her mum. 'You're looking better.'

Her mum gave a weak smile. 'You're not. I think it's time you got yourself back to work, instead of nursemaiding me.'

Shock at her mum's firm tone made her lay down the knife she was using to slice a cucumber.

'I...'

'I don't think it's doing either of us any good. You need to occupy your mind with other things, not dwell on this situation 24/7.'

'I don't mind.' It wasn't work that occupied her mind, but the sick slide of guilt and betrayal.

'I know you don't, but it's not healthy and it's not fair on you. You need to get out. Not be stuck here with me all the time.'

And there was that guilt again. She had got out while her mum was at her appointments and look how that had turned out. Should she tell her? She picked up the slices of cucumber and divided them between each plate. 'I have been working from home.'

'No. I don't think so. You haven't been able to concentrate fully and you don't need that extra stress, my darling. I want you to return to work tomorrow. For my sake as well. I feel as though you're forever at my beck and call, and quite honestly, Siobhan, I'm not ready for this—' she flicked her hand towards where Siobhan prepared lunch '—role reversal.'

Siobhan almost smiled at the 'role reversal' reference, her mum's mind obviously synced with hers. She wasn't ready to give in to that yet. There was the strong woman Siobhan recognised. She wasn't lost to her, she'd just been hiding.

She was right, too. They both needed a little space. The atmosphere had become claustrophobic. Her mum didn't need to be reminded every minute of the day about her situation. She needed to get as healthy as possible for the upcoming chemotherapy treatment she'd been informed she needed to undergo at her check-up. That didn't mean she wanted to think about it continually and with Siobhan hovering, perhaps it provided a constant reminder.

A cool wave of relief hit her, and she picked up the knife again to chop the chicken into cubes, sneaking a piece to Beau as an apology.

As she rinsed her hands, she nodded. 'Okay. I'll go back to the office tomorrow, probably work a shortened day from there, as long as you promise to call me if you need me.'

'I will.' Her mum bowed her head in satisfaction.

Perhaps she needed to apologise to her mum, too.

She drew in a breath, sprinkled the cubes of chicken on the salad and reached for the packet of Parmesan shavings as she made up her mind.

She'd message back to Megan and ask her to put everything on hold. She wasn't ready to take another DNA test, to make things official or bring everything out in the open. She definitely wasn't ready to meet her biological father.

If her birth mother's death had attracted that much attention, what was the discovery of her long-lost daughter going to do?

Siobhan reached for Beau's kibble and measured it into a bowl, placing it on the floor. As he waited patiently for the word to go, she placed both plates on the table.

'Go on, boy.'

Beau leapt on his food and Siobhan moved to the table, pausing to give her mum a quick squeeze.

'I don't mind looking after you. You've done it for me for long enough.'

Her mum's voice thickened as she returned the hug. 'I appreciate the sentiment, but you know it makes me feel weak and pathetic. I need to get my own confidence back.'

Siobhan's heart squeezed in her chest and hot tears threatened again.

Her mum was the most important thing in her world.

She withdrew and gave a light stroke to the back of her mum's hand. The bruising, now faded to a sickly yellow, had spread and started to dissipate. Her mum smiled back at her, turning her hand so their fingers linked.

A surge of love pushed aside every other emotion. This was her mum.

No one else counted. Just the two of them.

No matter what the past entailed.

37

THIRTY-ONE YEARS EARLIER – 1993 – GRACE

I can't control the tremor in my fingers as I push my building society passbook through the paying-in hatch and the clerk looks at me over the top of her glasses. She reminds me of one of my old schoolteachers. Scary. Like she can see what I'm thinking.

'Don't be intimidated.' James's words echo in my head.

He's outside with the baby. He's just sold my car for cash, and we're about to buy a new one... for cash. Easy.

'I'd like to withdraw my money and close my account, please.'

The clerk pushes her glasses further up her nose. 'May I ask if there is a reason?'

I look down so my rapid blinks can't be seen. 'There is.'

James has coached me on this but I'm sure I can't carry it through. *'Look, we have to wash the cash.'*

'Wash the...?'

'Clean the money. So it's not traceable. You have to do it, Grace. I can't do this bit for you.'

It's all so complicated. I knew this question would come. Building societies do not like you to withdraw your entire savings in one go. It's not good for business. They don't like to upset important clients, and my savings are substantial enough to attract attention.

I look back up at her.

Tell as few lies as you can.

'I've decided to buy a car.'

'A car?' She opens the passbook and peers at the balance. I have saved over the years in excess of eighteen thousand pounds. Her eyebrows almost shoot through her hairline, her eyes are wide when she looks back up at me.

I'm prepared for this. I smile. 'Don't worry, I'm not buying a Porsche. I only want a thousand pounds in cash, the rest I will take as a cheque. A deposit on my new house.' I hand over a slip of paper with the name of the recipient of the cheque, dropping it in the paying-in hatch as I notice my hands shaking so hard I could start an earthquake.

I have to calm down.

We'd expected this. James had researched it. This particular building society will only allow you to withdraw one thousand pounds in cash per day. I can't keep coming back daily to get all my money out.

James knows someone, but they're going to take 10 per cent. It grieves me, but it has to be done. I hand over my cheque and they hand over cash. Then I open a brand-new account in a totally different building society in a totally different part of the country.

I see the disapproval move over her face, but what business is it of hers? It's not like the money belongs to her. It seems to take forever for her to process the money and the cheque as I stand with a fixed smile on my face that feels like it might just crack.

At one point she excuses herself and disappears behind a locked door, her keys jangling at her waist as she goes through.

My mouth dries out. Has she gone to call the manager? Phone the police?

I lick my lips and glance at the exit, trying to decide whether or not to run.

I hear the rattle of keys again and the woman returns. She has a bundle of money in a cotton cash bag which she takes out and slowly, painfully slowly, counts every note out in front of me.

For a moment, I think she's going to count it a second time, but she places it to one side, takes a cheque from the same bag and puts them together. She then opens my account book and slams an ink stamp several times over each of the pages. Flipping them over so that I can never use it again, every bash of the stamp vibrating through the counter to make my nerves jangle and jump.

Red letters state 'ACCOUNT CLOSED' to eliminate any doubt, just in case I try to come back.

She slips the money and cheque inside and pushes the passbook back through the paying-in hatch, all the time mirroring my stiff smile with one of her own.

I turn and the queue behind me is now six deep, with people glaring at me as though the delay is my fault. I look directly at the elderly woman who has edged too close behind me. 'Gosh, wouldn't you think they'd have more staff on at busy times?'

I lift my chin and walk past the queue.

I stride out of the stifling building and drag cool air into my lungs.

James is on the other side of the street, walking towards me. I cross the road and join him, fumbling as I try to push all that money into my handbag. Stuff it inside. I should have done it while I was in the building society, but I just needed to get out. To escape.

I take control of the pram, admiring James's taste. It's navy blue with green piping and it's one of the brand-new easily collapsible ones that have become so fashionable.

A gust of wind gets up and I push my hair back from my face and turn away… and freeze.

Across the road, dressed in a Giorgio Armani suit distinguishable in its elegance from all the dressed-down males in the vicinity, is Gordon.

I bow my head and take long strides, my hands gripping the handle on the pram as I almost break into a run in the opposite direction.

A hand on my shoulder makes me gasp.

'Slow down. Act natural. Don't attract attention.' James's voice is close to my ear, soothing, calm. If anyone knows how to linger in the shadows, it is him.

'It's Gordon,' I hiss, continuing at a fast pace, although I have slowed down marginally.

'I could do with getting a look at him. See what we're up against.'

'I'm not going back. He'll see me. I don't stand a chance of getting away with a pram if he spots me.'

'Keep going. I'll catch up.'

And just like that, James has gone.

38

THIRTY-ONE YEARS EARLIER – 1993 – GRACE

I cradle Siobhan in my arms. That's what I've started to call her. I don't need to call her Grace any more. That's my name and I wouldn't call my baby after me. That's an old-fashioned idea and remarkably confusing.

Besides, I don't want her to be immediately identifiable, do I?

If her name crops up in the newspapers or on the news, I don't want anyone to take a second look.

Despite the fact that the police believe Leonora did something sinister with her, they are still scouring the surrounding area, looking for her little body and appealing for any help for the distraught husband who hasn't been seen since. Through a representative, most likely Gordon, the family have asked for privacy so that they can come to terms with recent events and grieve in peace.

Siobhan is the name I would have chosen for my little girl, given the chance, and it's pretty. It's not a difficult change to make and I think Leonora would approve.

That's something James will get his military friend to do. A new birth certificate.

We've booked into another Little Chef motel, locally, as we

weren't sure how long all the bank matters were going to take. It's a good job we did, really. No one is likely to look for me in a Little Chef.

James only wants me to go out when absolutely necessary in case anyone recognises me, although he may not think so soon. I look very different since he saw me a short while ago.

He's going to be really surprised when he comes back. I'm no longer a dirty blonde, but I've dyed my hair a beautiful, rich chestnut and cut a fringe in. It actually suits me. I'm so used to seeing myself wearing my hair up, pulled back away from my face to expose a narrow forehead. My hair normally has a neat twist in it, to give me the elegant maturity I need for my position. Although I'm mature enough now not to need that neat little trick, it comes from a habit of a lifetime making myself look older.

This colour makes me look younger, wider-eyed, rounder-faced. It seems to warm my skin and I look so much less like my mum, which I was starting to worry about. Although she seemed scrawny and emaciated by my age.

Having said that, I heard she's settled down and got married. Someone mentioned to James she's had twins. Two lots of them. Barmy cow. I hope she treats them better than she treated me.

When James returns from the bank a few hours later, his face is a set mask.

'What happened?' I prop myself up on my elbows on the bed to see him better.

'We need to get you out of here.' His voice brooks no argument.

Fear sends a lightning bolt of adrenaline through my veins, and I jump up from where I'd been resting when he walked in. I need to take every opportunity to rest while Siobhan naps, as although she is good, I'm not used to being woken at intervals during the night. I've never done this before. It doesn't exactly come naturally. Nor was I prepared for it. Although James is in the next room to me, I don't disturb him in the night. It doesn't seem fair.

James halts as soon as I move. His gaze roves over my face and hair and a slight smile curves his lips.

'Clever girl.' He nods with approval. 'We'll stay tonight. Hopefully that will be enough. I'll have all the documents by tomorrow, but we need to get you as far away from here as possible. This is one hell of a powerful guy you're up against.'

'I know. I could have told you that.' I think I did, but I see now that revelation has only just hit him, and hit him hard.

He huffs out a laugh and rubs his chin. 'Perhaps you should have, the first time he grabbed you.'

'The only time...'

'It was a show of power, and that power is far stronger and wider reaching than you could ever imagine. He has people in his pocket all the way to the top.'

A vision of that file, papers scattered over the floor, comes to me. The names on the file are some of the most influential people in the world. And they are his friends.

'You don't just need to lie low, you need to disappear.' He reiterates what he has already told me, but this time the words hold an edge of steel.

My breath stops.

I don't want this. I never asked for this.

And then I look over at that sweet baby in the travel cot. My baby.

My heart stutters.

Did I wish this upon myself?

39

PRESENT DAY – THURSDAY, 18 JULY 2024, 9.35 A.M. – GRACE

Silence shrouds the place since Siobhan left for work earlier this morning. Honestly, she needed to get out of the house for a while and get to the office. I metaphorically pushed her out of the door. I couldn't physically, I have no energy for that.

Much as I adore her, I can feel she's become restless. She's not used to the responsibility of looking after me and I'm not ready to give up my independence yet. I'm not sick. Or at least I hope I'm not. Tests will tell, but in the meantime, the hospital is getting a preventative chemo regime ready for me and I should start at the end of the month, provided all is well with the surgery side of things.

Funny how I've never given thought to my age since I lied when I was too young for that first job. Once I changed it, that remained my age. After all, at what point was I expected to change it back?

Although my memory is fuzzy around the time of my collapse, I know I told the paramedic the wrong age, and Siobhan corrected me. I was in so much pain I couldn't help myself. I know also that I was vile, but my memory of that is thin and I don't really want to think about it too deeply. It's over. Gone.

What I do have to think about is getting a will written. It's never occurred to me to write one before. I've always had an understanding with James that should anything happen to me, he would be responsible for Siobhan. But Siobhan is an adult now, has been for some time, and James has had his own family to care for, also for some time.

James.

It doesn't matter what my age, James still keeps in contact. He may have his own family, but his wife knows about me. I've met her a couple of times and she is incredible. A mental health nurse, she's helped James weather the storms over the years and rarely does he ever have a relapse. Thanks to her. When he does, it's quickly nipped in the bud as she is so perceptive and intuitive, seeing the signs almost before he does. He adores her and I am inordinately happy that he's found the life he deserves. His past will always haunt him, but he has a present now. A future.

I prop myself up on my elbows and let out a hearty groan. God, it hurts. Everything hurts, not just the site of my surgery but my entire body aches in places I didn't know you could ache. Probably through inactivity, which my muscles aren't used to. They've seized up.

But I have to get up, get dressed. The next best thing to a nightdress, at least, is one of the three lovely summer dresses Siobhan bought me on a quick trip into Asda.

A cruel flash of me charging down the aisles of Carrefour fills my mind as memories of those days return to haunt me recently, since my fall. Events I thought were sequestered away in the recesses of my mind, jabbing at me occasionally in weak moments. Memories which bring such pain and regret.

My heart is galloping.

It's been years since I dwelled on those horrific times. Not since we settled here, and Siobhan was old enough for me to no longer worry about the bad people still searching for us. They will have forgotten after all this time. Won't they? After all, for the oddest of reasons I was never implicated in Leonora's death. The police never pursued me for questioning. My face was never in the newspapers, despite my desperate fear that it would be. There would be a reason for that. Because someone knew that I was a witness, and that means they wouldn't want the police talking to me, so they've kept my name out of it.

I try and push the thoughts aside but they circle like hovering vultures, ever there, even if it is in the periphery of my vision.

I swing my legs off the side of the bed and Beau is already there, anxious to please.

'Hello, boy.'

I scrub my fingers over his head and then rub one silky ear in between them while I gather enough strength to make the next move. He lets out his own soft groan, but this is pure pleasure, not pain.

'Are you going to help me up?'

I reach over for my sticks. I have a walker downstairs, but I can't bring that up and down with me each time. I'm quite proud at how adept I am with the crutches. Upper body strength, I'm told. I reach for one of the dresses, one-handed, and flick it over my shoulder to keep my hands free. I make my way to the bathroom where Siobhan placed a small basket of underwear to save me rooting through drawers.

Occupational Health had offered me a commode, but I'd opted instead for one of those raised, padded seats to go on top of the loo. The NHS one was awful, so I paid extra. If I have to sit on one of those for the next few weeks, I want to be comfortable.

I had a shower last night before bed to cool me down so I could sleep easier. It didn't work – Jesus, who thought it would be so painful when bones knitted together and nerves started to jangle –

but at least I had Siobhan waiting in the bedroom, giving me enough privacy and independence, but there all the same.

Now, I soak a flannel and give myself a quick all-over with it, brush my teeth and hair, which sticks up as I'd washed it the previous night and it was still damp when I went to bed. I tug on my underwear and dress.

It's odd, I'm not used to seeing myself in a dress these days. Ever, really. Dresses weren't so much the fashion when I was a PA. More skirt suits. Smart, businesslike. The feminine version of businessmen. An imitation because we were still at the beginning of the journey for equality back then. Funny how these things have moved on so rapidly, and yet the fight for equality still has not been won, which is evident from simple things like the way Siobhan's boss treats her.

I pick up my phone from the bedside table and slip it inside my bra, just until I get downstairs, as the dress I'm wearing has no pockets. I'm puffing now, almost tempted to lie down on my bed, just for a few minutes before I make my way downstairs, but determination overrules good sense.

Beau refuses to leave my side and makes it a little awkward as I leave my sticks propped against the wall, and using both handrails swing my way down the stairs to where my walker is at the bottom. I'm extra cautious, knowing Siobhan will be fuming if I fall down the stairs and break my neck.

'Mum, if you die, I'll kill you,' were her humorous parting words as she left the house this morning, just after reading me the riot act, in which she made it clear I was not to attempt the stairs without a responsible adult in attendance.

'Ha!'

Breathless, I lean on the walker and wobble slightly before gathering myself. A fine sweat has broken out and my hair is sticking to the back of my neck, already. I make it to the kitchen and slide with caution into a dining chair, exhaustion hitting every muscle, turning them to water.

Maybe Siobhan was correct. I should have stayed in bed. But I don't want to be up there all day and I have things to do. Things I don't want Siobhan necessarily knowing about.

Besides, I also fancied a cup of coffee. Siobhan made me a flask of tea and put it with a fresh cup at the side of my bed, and a sandwich for lunchtime in a cool bag with more ice packs than sandwich.

Tea doesn't taste the same out of a flask and I just fancy a coffee.

I don't have the energy to get up just yet, though. I slip the phone from my bra and place it on the table next to me.

I raise my head, watch the bright light from the window swirl in my vision.

'Oh Christ.'

I lay my head on my folded arms on the table and close my eyes against the blackness swarming in.

When I blink my eyes open again, it's almost 11 a.m. I look at my phone and there's a message from Siobhan.

Is everything okay, Mum?

That was almost forty minutes ago. Just as I pick it up to type a reply, it rings. I answer.

'Hello.'

'Mum.' Panic slices through her voice.

'I was just having a snooze.' It's not a lie. I was. I'm just not in bed.

'Oh, did I disturb you?'

'I've just woken.' It's not a lie. 'I'm going to have a drink of coffee.'

'Oh.' There's a pause on the other end of the line. 'I made tea for you, not coffee.'

I realise my mistake and backpedal. 'That'll do nicely. As long as it's hot and wet.'

'I'll come home at lunchtime if you need me.' Worry makes her voice tremble.

I don't want to be a worry. I have been independent my entire life with only James to rely on from time to time.

James.

I look at the kitchen clock just as he rounds the back of the house, walks past the window and in through the kitchen door I'd told Siobhan to leave wide so Beau could wander in and out. After all, we don't get many people around here. It's safe. And if it's not, Beau isn't likely to let anyone pass him.

At that, Beau leaps up and gives one sharp, ear-piercing woof.

I raise one finger to my lips, and taking his cue, James drops to the floor, opening his arms wide for Beau to rush into. Son of James's Labrador bitch, he never forgets his original owner.

'Mum, is everything okay? Why did Beau bark?'

The dog's tail is wagging so hard, I swear he's going to break it. James grins and backs out the door with him and takes him down the garden.

'Oh, I don't know...'

I can't help grinning myself. It's been an absolute age since I saw James. I've never introduced him to Siobhan. At first, it was a matter of security, that no one could link any of us. We may have been more cautious than necessary in the beginning, but you had to be there to know that kind of terror. The fear of having Siobhan taken away from me, of her being in danger.

'He's run downstairs, so it might just be the postman.'

'It's too early for the postman, Mum. Are you sure everything is okay? Shall I come home?'

'No.' The word comes out sharper than I intended, and her swift intake of breath lets me know that my waspishness got the better of me.

I sigh. 'He's just come back up, love. He's fine. I'm fine. You need to concentrate on work for a while. Don't worry about me. If I need you, I'll shout, I promise.' God love her, I don't want to upset her. I know she's stressed enough as it is, there's no need to make it worse. My heart aches with love for her, but I do need this time without her to sort my life out. Mums don't tell their children everything, and that is for their protection, not just ours.

'I've the book you left me on the side, but I think I might subscribe to this Audible lark and have a listen to an audiobook.'

I've never had a TV in the bedroom, and I declined when Siobhan offered to put hers in here. I cannot bear the idea of daytime television, just a load of drivel. Recently, I've found my eyes too heavy to stay open long enough to read, but it would be nice to have company when it's not the real thing.

My gaze drifts to outside again as James throws a ball and Beau races across the lawn, mouth wide in a wild grin, and I half listen as Siobhan says, 'That's a good idea, Mum, I'll help you set it up when I get home.'

'No need, Siobhan, I'll do it this afternoon.' I relent at her silence. 'If I can't manage, you can help when you come home. There's nothing you can do here, you catch up with your work and we'll sort things out later.'

'If you're sure.'

I know she's torn. After all, I was dedicated to my work... right up to the point where it no longer mattered.

'Of course. See you later.'

'I won't be late.'

'Okay. Love you, bye.'

I let out a long sigh as I hit the off button and place the phone on the table in front of me just as James walks back in the house with Beau at his side.

His gaze roves over me, quick and assessing. I don't want him to see my weakness, but I don't seem to be able to straighten my shoulders.

'You look different.'

I shoot him a weak smile. 'You're not used to seeing me in a dress.'

His eyebrows flick up. 'Not recently, in any case.'

'I never did wear dresses. Not unless I was...' I stop, about to take a long walk down memory lane, and I don't want to do that. This whole mess seems to have triggered all those memories. Ones I don't want to haunt me.

Don't get me wrong, they are always there, but normally I can squash them back into their box. Except Leonora. To my dying day, I will always see her in that bathtub with her wrist still lazily pumping out the last vestige of blood.

As if he understands, James turns his back, walks over to the sink, letting me gather myself. 'I'll put the kettle on. What are you drinking?'

'Coffee. Strong. With a shot of whisky...'

His head whips around so fast, I gasp. I put my hand over my mouth at my own stupidity. My insensitivity. 'Oh, James, I'm sorry...' It was a joke, nothing more, but I am mortified at my own tactlessness.

He raises a hand, his eyes a sea of tranquillity. 'No worries, I thought you meant it for a minute. I should know better.' He grabs the kettle, filling it so the white noise covers any silence that might have fallen between us.

When he turns back, he takes a leisurely measure of me again.

I push my hair back from my face. 'I'm fine. I told you on the phone.'

'You should have called me when it happened.'

I want to say, *I wasn't in a fit state*, but that would worry him even more and it suddenly comes home to me that we should have a procedure in place for the future. If something happens to me, he'll be devastated not to be informed. He's always been down as my next of kin on paperwork, but Siobhan naturally has taken that position since she was of age. It would never have occurred to her to check old papers. As far as she is concerned, there are only the two of us.

I nod. 'I've always been rather robust. I didn't expect something like this. I didn't want to worry you. You would have come rushing to the hospital and how would we explain that to Siobhan?'

'We should have told her the truth in the first place.'

'We couldn't. She didn't need that burden.'

'And now?' His mouth tightens. I've told him everything about the tumour and I know he's worried.

I can't face other people's emotions at the moment, my own are already stifling me. On top of that, my worry for Siobhan is foremost in my mind.

'I need to make a will.'

The kettle clicks off and with a nod, James turns to make the coffee. He stirs in sugar and hands me a mug, just the way I've always liked it. Strong, sweet, black.

He settles in the chair opposite me and I think he catches my wince as I shuffle on my own seat.

'Do you need a cushion?'

'We might be better in the lounge. I have a special cushion on the sofa that Occupational Health recommended.'

He comes to his feet again, swipes up both cups, and with a few long strides he disappears, knowing exactly where he's going. After all, he has been here many times over the years.

Before I'm even properly on my feet, he's by my side and he

walks next to me as I do my shuffle, bump, shuffle, bump along the hall into the lounge.

I lower myself gingerly and wonder if I'm expecting too much of myself as my body demands another sleep. I haven't got time to be weak, though. I point at the bottom drawer in the old sideboard.

'Most of my private paperwork is in there, and behind the double doors.'

James gets on his knees and the creak and groan of them has me smiling.

'You're getting old.'

He turns his head, insulted amusement flickering over his face. 'I'm not that much older than you.'

I laugh as he pulls a huge bundle I could have sworn was neater than that out of the cupboard and it drops to the floor.

'I can't remember the last time I sorted through it. Years ago, most likely.' When we first moved here. After all, I've had no need of it for some time.

I didn't want the memories of what I did forever torturing me.

He gathers everything in his arms and dumps it on the sofa next to me.

My fingers instantly touch on the birth certificates, which I'm sure weren't on the top. I hand them to James.

He studies them. 'You know you could revert to your old one.'

I shake my head. 'Not without answering a whole host of questions. Everything is related to my latest birth certificate.' I don't say *forged*. 'My national insurance number, hospital number, everything. It would complicate matters.'

'You're never going to be able to claim your state pension.'

A sob catches in my throat as I consider the possibility of that never happening in any case.

I keep my head down and sift through all the paperwork,

reaching the items at the bottom. I edge out a brown envelope and ease the thick wad of documentation out.

I smile at James. 'Two of the three best things I ever did, thanks to your friend.'

He smiles, remembering thirty years ago when his military contact persuaded me to sell my own house back to myself just as mortgage rates dropped, for a little less than I had paid for it, but just more than my mortgage giving me the laundered money via the equity. A little complicated, but, Boom! An overnight profit, which I then sold the house again for an even larger profit some years later, and purchased two smaller houses in its place, using up all my savings. Instant money laundering as I then rented both houses out and lived off the income while I took my first job as a school dinner lady and bought a third property. It's all clever stuff.

What I came to realise is, a job is a job, no matter what. But some jobs are invisible.

40

PRESENT DAY – THURSDAY, 18 JULY 2024, 4.25 P.M. – GRACE

I'm not sure which one of us is more exhausted – James or myself – but we've managed to root out all the paperwork I need. I even discovered the original personal pension I'd touted around for a number of jobs before I ran. It's been so long I can hardly believe James had managed to get his friend to doctor this paperwork too so my national insurance number tallied.

It couldn't happen these days. Anti-money laundering regulations didn't come fully into force until after Siobhan was born. For good reason. Yet, if they'd existed then, we would probably all be dead.

I have that to be thankful for.

James and I make our way into the kitchen, and I watch while he deftly whips up scrambled eggs on toast. It's difficult to describe the pride I feel watching him. Way back when I was an executive PA and he was homeless, I'd never imagined how far he would come. So far that he's happily married with children and can cook. Even if they are only simple meals.

When we finish, he washes the few dishes and I disappear to the bathroom.

Exhaustion creeps over me and I wonder if I shouldn't go to bed for a while, but I know I may only get this chance to sort through things with another adult. After all, no matter how bright and intelligent Siobhan is, she is my daughter. She will not understand.

I shuffle back to the kitchen table where James has laid out all the relevant documents.

I thought I was organised, but I realise I have let things go in the last few years. I need to remedy that.

Each pile of paperwork has relevance.

James has contacts through the work he does to help out veterans. Not quite the old military-style contacts from years before, but he knows solicitors, reputable financial advisers, and will writers.

'This is for the solicitor.' I push one pile towards James.

'He'll need to see you in person.'

'I know. Once he has it drafted, perhaps he can arrange to come here, but for now, once he has these, he can call me.' I scribble my number on a sticky note and smooth it down on the top sheet of paperwork.

James draws it closer and flicks through. 'Everything should be in order.'

I bob my head. 'I think I can deal with the pension myself. I just have to log in online. I think I did it years ago when it first went computerised, but I need to update all the details. I don't think they even have my current address.'

'Do you want to do that now?'

Again, I give a nod, but I'm weary and I'm not sure how much longer I can do this.

James's eyes narrow. 'I think maybe another time. You've had enough.'

'No, it's fine. I need to take some painkillers. This won't take long, though.'

James gets to his feet again and I feel a pang of worry for him.

'You don't need to run around after me, James, you're not a spring chicken yourself any more.' Although inwardly I do admit he looks remarkably healthy for a man of his age and despite the years of alcohol abuse, he has also been sober for more years now than he was drunk. If I didn't know better, I'd wonder if he'd also had his birth certificate doctored.

'No worries. I just creak a little.' He walks to the sink and fills a glass with water, then reaches over to where I point for my painkillers.

As I swallow them down, I pull the laptop towards me and open the lid.

I know the moment I do, from the background photograph, that I've got the wrong one. Siobhan doesn't always take it to work as she tends to use a desktop with a double screen there in the old-fashioned world of estate agents.

'What's wrong?'

I realise I huffed out a sigh. 'I've got the wrong laptop. This is Siobhan's. Mine is upstairs.'

He makes a move to stand again, and I wave him down. 'No, I'll use this. It's fine.' We aren't precious about using each other's laptops if we have to, although we tend to stick to our own. I wouldn't dream of poking into anything that had nothing to do with me.

'I'm only going to log into the pension portal, change what I can and verify who I am, if I need to. See how much of a pension I have for my old age.'

He lets out a quiet laugh.

I tap in Siobhan's password and the screen opens to a beautifully colourful page of small boxes.

I blink.

'YOU' it states right in the middle of the screen.

'Hmm.'

'You okay?' James frowns and leans closer to me, but from his angle he can't see what I can. I slant the laptop so we can both see the screen.

His frown deepens as he fishes a pair of glasses from where he has them looped over the neckline of his T-shirt and then pushes them up his nose, his gaze fixed on the screen.

He leans back, his gaze bouncing to mine, and then back to the screen, his hand going up to his face. I notice how his fingers have thickened about the knuckles with age and arthritis as he pinches his bottom lip between his thumb and forefinger.

He points at the screen. 'Is this a DNA chart?'

I nod. I've toyed with the idea before but thought it too dangerous. I maybe wanted to find out what had become of my mother. Even though I don't particularly want to see her, I am curious. Funny how time and distance dilute circumstances and increase the desire to make contact with loved ones. I did love her. In a way.

I lean over and minimise that screen.

Another screen is open behind and I gasp. 'Oh God. She did it.'

This isn't just the example screen containing centimorgans for each layer of relationship relevant to 'YOU', this is the actual chart.

Not my chart, but Siobhan's.

Jumbled memories leap out at me. Me thrashing out at the woman in a green paramedic uniform, screaming that I couldn't have children. Was Siobhan with me?

Siobhan holding me close in the hospital while I spat into a tube.

I lean on the table and turn the screen fully to face me, reduce that window and stare at her emails.

James is silent.

My heart is crushed.

Beau comes to his feet and stretches, making a strange squeak as he straightens, his tail, giving a hard thump, thump, thump against the kitchen table.

I read the latest email out loud to James, barely able to breathe so it comes out as a tortured whisper.

Dear Siobhan,

It was an absolute joy to meet you yesterday. I cannot tell you how thrilled my mum is with the news and she's desperate to come over to the UK and meet you. I do understand your reticence at the speed at which this is progressing and can only apologise that I have already passed your address on to Justin. He is desperate to meet you.

I will contact him again and suggest that we give you some space.

Until then, kind regards,

Megan

I swipe at the thin coating of sweat that has formed over my top lip and raise my gaze, letting it connect with James's, transmitting every fear, every regret.

Beau lets out a soft, welcoming woof and races towards the open back door, where Siobhan stands, sunlight streaming in behind her.

A band squeezes my chest, crushing all breath from me.

All these years, all this effort.

My head is moving side to side in denial, and I raise a hand to my mouth.

'Oh, Siobhan. What have you done? You have no idea what danger we are all in.'

41

PRESENT DAY – THURSDAY, 18 JULY 2024, 4.25 P.M. – SIOBHAN

Mum's face is ashen, her lips devoid of all colour. I make to step inside and she points a finger, like the barrel of a gun, straight at me so I freeze. The blood drains from my own face and dizziness washes over me. Beau is fussing, but I'm too busy dividing my attention between my mum and the quiet stranger who sits at the corner of the kitchen table with her, his fingers almost touching the clenched hand she rests beside the laptop.

My laptop.

With all the coloured rectangles blurring across one half of the screen, and an email open on the other half.

'Oh God.'

Dark blue eyes, sharp enough to slice skin, clash with my own gaze, which skitters away, unable to meet the accusation in my mum's eyes.

'What. Have. You. Done. Siobhan?'

She almost rises from her chair, but the man covers her hand with his and with a slight squeeze gains her momentary attention before she turns the laser blues back on me.

Anger stirs in me too.

I turn and look at the man and draw in a gasp, trying not to show the horror I feel at the thick scarring down one side of his face. He shows no response to my reaction. There's a serenity about him as though he's an observer rather than a participant and I wonder what suffering he's endured to remain so calm.

He's not much older than my mum. If I didn't know better, I'd say she'd got herself a boyfriend. But I do know better.

As I meet his eyes, reflective pools of my mum's stare back at me. Deep, dark indigo blue with soot-black lashes, thick and lush. Lashes I'd kill for, but instead have to apply layers of mascara to get mine like that.

Eyes so unlike mine that in that instant I know. I still have to ask.

'Who are you?'

This time, I do step inside, far enough to wilt against the kitchen cabinets.

Without taking my attention from him, I fold my arms over my chest and it reminds me of when I was a teenager and Mum would ask me to explain why I'd not finished my homework on time, and why should she write a letter of apology when it was my misstep, not hers?

He doesn't answer me. Instead, he turns to face my mum. Her misstep, not his.

Mum presses the heel of a hand against her forehead and closes her eyes.

When she opens them again and lowers her hand, I can see she's got that iron control back in place that only ever slips on occasion.

She flicks her hand to the kettle. 'Grab a coffee, come join us.' Her tone is casual, like our whole lives weren't suddenly on the line.

I don't want coffee. I'm too hot and bothered for that. I reach for a glass and run the cold water for a moment before I fill it. When I pull the chair out and sit down, it's opposite the man.

'Are you my uncle?' I direct my question to him, but it's my mum who answers.

'As you probably know, that would be impossible.' She flicks her fingers at the screen in the first acknowledgement of our relationship.

'Do you want to explain? Who is he?' I dip my head towards the man again. One side of his mouth quirks up.

'James is *my* dad,' Mum quietly states.

Stunned, my gaze darts from one to the other. 'Your *dad*? But I thought you didn't know who your dad was.'

'No. I think I told you my *mum* didn't know who my dad was.'

I lift an eyebrow and she shrugs. 'There's a difference.'

'Infinitesimal. I think that's classed as splitting hairs.'

Unperturbed, Mum tosses him a glance. 'I never lied.'

'I think you did. My whole life has been a lie.'

I catch sight of the paperwork on the table that had been hidden by the laptop until I sat down. My birth certificate lies face up on top of the others I'd discovered a few nights before. I wave my hand over them. 'These. These are all lies.'

'Not all of them, and those that are were a necessity.'

I reach over and slide my birth certificate towards me. I tap the print on it. 'But you're not my mum.'

Pain creases her face and I know I've caused hurt. But what damage has she done for this to have occurred? Has she deprived my biological family of me for her own selfish motives?

She shakes her head. 'No. I'm not your biological mother. But for all intents and purposes, I have been a mother to you, your entire life. You're the daughter of my heart. And sometimes blood isn't thicker than water. That's the truth.'

The weight on my chest increases and I almost cry out, remembering Megan's words about my real mum.

'But not the whole truth.'

'No.' A bittersweet smile twists her lips. 'Not the whole truth. I'm not sure you want to know the whole truth, Siobhan.'

I know I'm twisting the knife, but I deserve to know.

'I think I know most of it. I met with Leonora's niece. My cousin. She filled me in about my real mum committing suicide.'

Mum's brow creases in a delicate frown and I know that barb about my real mum has hit home, but my hurt is so deep, I am oblivious. 'She wouldn't know the circumstances. Nobody knows but me.' Her gaze slides across to James, but she doesn't acknowledge whether or not he knows the full tale.

'So, you tell me your side of the story.' I raise one eyebrow at her, my voice filled with disdainful challenge. 'Please, do.'

She pushes damp hair back from her forehead with a shaking hand, and my heart squeezes, knowing it's not just due to the heat. But I am relentless. I am fuming with her, and I want to know the truth.

She takes a sip of coffee, her direct gaze meeting mine. There is no fear there, but a reflected fury of my own anger.

She licks her lips. 'Everything I did was for your own protection, Siobhan. You have no idea. Your mother never committed suicide, she was murdered.'

My mouth drops open and the blood rushes from my head so fast that I sway.

I'm so intent on my mum, I barely notice the darkness that fills the sky to blot out the light coming through the open door.

'What happened?' I force the words from my lips.

'Yes, Grace. Do tell us what happened.'

I whip my head around at the sound of a deep, gravelly voice as Beau launches himself from beneath the table, teeth bared. A feral growl bursts from deep inside his chest as his lips pull back from long, white teeth.

For a moment, I think he might just take a bite out of one of these two interlopers.

A sharp yelp comes from Mum as Beau bumps her leg on his way past.

I leap up, overturning my chair as I fling myself at Beau. Grabbing hold of his collar, the hard vibration of his growl rumbles through his bunched-up muscles and I hold on.

'Wait!' I yell, but I deliberately don't give the command to *leave*. Simply to *wait* while I decide whether the two huge men in the open kitchen door deserve our trust or not.

Beau seems to think not.

42

PRESENT DAY – THURSDAY, 18 JULY 2024, 4.25 P.M. – GRACE

Pain tears through my leg into my hip as Beau smashes past me, catching my knee with his shoulder, ironically in his efforts to protect me from the two tall, dark shadows in the doorway.

It takes a moment for my eyes to adjust. Although my heart leaps with fear, I knew it was my destiny that we would meet again.

Siobhan hangs on to Beau's collar, but he gives one last threatening snarl before he lowers his haunches onto the tiled floor, hackles still stiff with rage. He's not about to let his guard down, not for one minute, and for that I am grateful, because one of these men is dangerous beyond words. The question is, who? Or is it both?

From the corner of my eye, I notice James slip from his chair and move away, into the cooler shadows of the room. I know he's no coward. He's moved to a better vantage point and made himself less vulnerable by standing.

James is not a big man. He's shorter by a head than both of the other two. Justin and Gordon stand at around six foot two and three respectively. What James lacks in stature, though, he makes up for in experience. You don't live through a war and survive life on the streets without being a scrapper. If nothing else, I feel safer with him around. He has always been my protector.

I draw air in through my teeth as my hip throbs. It's only a knock, nothing damaging, I'm sure, but it feels like someone shoved a red-hot poker into the base of my spine and gave it a twirl.

Justin's gaze falls on me and shock eddies in his eyes.

'Justin.' I force a smile. 'It's been a while. What brings you here?'

His attention bounces to Siobhan and then back to me.

Something inside me stirs. He didn't expect to find me here. Did he think Siobhan lived here alone?

'Grace. Good to see you again. You're looking...' He pauses and his lips twist in a sneer I recognise from the days I worked for him, only now realising what a spoilt brat he'd been. '...older,' he finishes.

I sweep a gaze over him. Although his hair is still blond, it's thinned and he wears it swept back, giving him a high forehead and accentuating a nose I'd remembered as short and straight.

He's a little older than me, but it looks as though life has taken its toll on him. I suppose bad things come back to haunt you. Where he was muscular and lean, I wouldn't say he's run to fat exactly, but certainly those muscles have relaxed so he's gone soft in the middle, a slight paunch over expensive trousers that evidently haven't been made to measure recently.

'You're not looking so good yourself.'

There's a slight intake of breath from my daughter and I spare her a quick look. She's shocked that her mother would dream of being so rude. As far as she's concerned, I've always been quiet, polite. A pacifist.

Not precisely a shrinking violet, but a wallflower through necessity of not wanting to attract attention to myself. It may not have come naturally to me, but I've lived the life I dreamed of when I was a little girl. I've had a little girl of my own and cherished her the way I never was cherished.

Justin's eyes dust over Beau and he holds out his hands, palms up, meek and submissive, but I'm not fooled. Nor is my dog, who gives a low growl, forcing Justin to withdraw.

'May we come in?'

I nod. I won't be offering them a drink of any kind. I really don't want them to stay. This is not a scene of my making. I am thunderously annoyed with Siobhan, but that's not their business right now. I will be having words with my daughter alone later. Because whatever the nature of our biological beginnings, this young woman is my daughter.

For now, let's see where this little scenario is going.

I don't offer them a seat either, but Justin pulls out a chair. He's turned a funny colour, a sort of yellowish-grey, and I idly wonder if he's about to have a heart attack when he raises one hand to his chest and gives it a rub.

Concern ripples over Siobhan's features as she straightens up and orders Beau into his bed. He slinks off, but I know he's not about to doze. That dog of mine would put his life on the line for Siobhan or me.

'Are you okay?' Siobhan touches his elbow and I wonder for one mad minute what the hell she is doing. 'You don't look very well.'

He curls his shoulders inwards and presses a hand against his heart.

'Let me get you some water, it might be the heat, combined with the shock.' Siobhan moves over to the sink and, filling a glass, returns, placing it in front of him on the table.

I'm not totally insensitive, but it occurs to me that it may be an act.

I'm surprised Gordon doesn't react. In the past, he would have gone straight to Justin's aid. Now, he hangs back in the doorway. Dark sunglasses hood his eyes, but his head moves as though to look at Beau and I wonder if he's afraid of dogs. He's certainly got a healthy respect for this one.

Siobhan crouches in front of Justin, her hand on his knee. 'Are you okay? Do you need anything?'

I think she might have missed her vocation in life. She should have been a nurse. She's been incredible with me.

Still, her concern for this man is worrying. She's harbouring the illusion that Justin is her long-lost loving father. I know better.

Justin places his hand on her shoulder, and she tilts her head back to look up at him.

'I'm fine.' The thread of a smile stitches his lips. He lets out a soft huff. 'It's come as quite a shock.'

I want to interject, say *I'll bet it has*, but instead I catch James's eye and he gives the slightest shake of his head. He's right, of course. I need to play my cards close to my chest and find out what Justin wants.

My hip aches all the way down the length of my leg and I'm sure if I move it will relieve it, but I'm not ready to let these men see my weakness.

'Justin.'

He turns away from his study of Siobhan with reluctance.

My daughter's anger is palpable, and I can't blame her being annoyed with me. After all, she doesn't know the whole story. She has no idea of the peril she was in back then, and the danger she could be in now.

'I assume you've tracked Siobhan down through the DNA site?'

Justin nods. 'Indirectly, yes. Megan contacted me.'

'Who is Megan?' I've barely had time to process the information that flashed up on screen before James and me. I'm like a fish, floundering on dry land.

Siobhan opens her mouth to reply, but Justin gets there first, the colour rushing back into his cheeks to make him florid, his eyes wild and glassy.

The thought of how convenient it would be if he dropped dead now is overtaken by the amount of questions the police would have.

'If you recall, Leonora...' His voice breaks on her name, and I'm stunned by his acting abilities. Thirty years later and still he seems torn apart by her death. Her murder.

The breath I take in catches in my throat as it all comes rushing back as though it was yesterday. When I blink, I see her, naked in that bath, scarlet plumes feathering out around her.

Acid burns my stomach.

Justin's voice pulls me back. 'Leonora had a sister.'

I nod. 'She lived in Australia.'

Siobhan is watching first Justin and then me intently as she straightens, pulling out a chair between us so she's included in the inner circle.

'She still does. She has a daughter called Megan Saville.'

'Okay.'

'It's my understanding that Siobhan contacted Megan through some DNA tracking site.' His abhorrence of this shows in every stiff muscle in his body.

My gaze slides to Siobhan and guilt creeps over her features as her cheeks pinken.

Pain crushes my chest that she'd not seen fit to tell me, but I still have the urge to give her a good telling-off. I can't help myself. I am her mother and it is instinct for me to admonish her over this.

'Megan and Grace—' he indicates Siobhan '—now calling herself Siobhan,' he corrects, 'met yesterday and Siobhan agreed for Megan to pass on her address to me. This address. I assumed this was Siobhan's house.'

I incline my head. We own it jointly, but that's none of his business.

'I thought you would contact me first, via email.' Siobhan still looks mortified as she glances between us, but her tone holds steady. 'I was going to tell you, Mum, but everything happened so fast, and I didn't expect...' She flicks her fingers in Justin's direction. 'I thought I would have more time.'

Now is not the time to berate her. It's not her fault and certainly she is not the enemy.

'I'd changed my mind,' she stumbles on. 'I wasn't sure I wanted to pursue this.'

Justin's lip curls with distaste. 'Well. To be honest, you appear to have a vague resemblance to my dead wife, but I would want professional DNA verification. I hope you understand, this is not a game we are playing, young lady. To my knowledge, my daughter died when she was four weeks old.'

He turns on me now and a thunderous frown darkens his face. 'This is not a game *we* are playing either. For whatever reason, and I don't care what—' his jaw tightens as he turns his attention back to my daughter '—you have decided you want to claim a fortune. Do not misjudge me. You are playing with fire. There's far more at stake here than you could possibly imagine. A vague resemblance and spit in a pot does not make you the heir apparent of my wife's fortune.'

Vitriol builds in him and his body appears to increase in size as he puffs himself up, confidence returning.

If he genuinely has a dicky heart, I'm afraid it's not going to survive this. Nor am I that bothered if it doesn't. Once again, Justin is showing his true colours. He really is a spoilt brat. I knew it when I first met him.

Back then, money and position meant so much more to me. There's an element of shame that I tolerated him, but that's water under the bridge.

'I don't want to lay claim to anyone's fortune.' Siobhan's voice is quiet, sincere. She probably had no clue when she embarked on this journey what dirt she was going to dig up, what terrible secrets she was about to uncover.

'Good job. Because you're not having it.'

He turns to me. 'I wondered where you skipped off to.'

'I'm surprised you never tried to track me down.' It puzzles me. I thought he'd been pursuing me all these years.

'Why would I?' he sneers. 'You were merely one more in a long line of PAs who bugger off when the job gets too tough.'

I remember my predecessor. He'd never even attempted to ask her why she left.

I want to deny it, but what's the point?

Surprisingly, his words sting. In all, I'd dedicated three years of my life to this man, every hour of every day. I would have dedicated more if circumstances hadn't turned out the way they did. And for what?

To never really be appreciated. To never reach my full potential.

I look at Siobhan.

She means more to me than the world.

There have been moments when I have doubted myself, but watching her now, I know I was not wrong when I took her.

Justin leans forward and the grey pallor hasn't quite dissipated, making me wonder if he does have something wrong with his heart.

'Now, listen carefully, both of you. Grace, I don't know what evil made you contrive to wheedle your way back into my life, but you shot that bolt over thirty years ago when you walked away just when I needed you the most. If you think you can present me with a watered-down version of my wife and expect me to believe she's mine—' he jabs a finger towards Siobhan and I suspect he's just about to lose it if he doesn't lower it as Beau's soft growl vibrates through my chair leg where he's taken up residence next to me '—then you have hard lessons to learn.'

I raise my eyebrows. 'I've had plenty of those in my life.'

'This one could have you going to prison.'

Siobhan gasps and leans back. 'No. She's done nothing wrong.'

He turns on her with a snarl. 'That's where you're wrong. She has.'

'I don't understand,' Siobhan shoots back.

'Let me enlighten you.'

I remember that tone, it was the one he used to put me down in front of the rich and the powerful. Nothing so overt it would be noticeable, but once you recognise it, you hear it every time.

'My wife... note I refrain from calling Leonora your mother at this juncture, as we have absolutely no proof... took her own life. I found her dead in our bath, her wrist slit from here—' he points at the inside of his wrist and draws a line with his finger to his elbow, making the remembered image flash vivid in my mind '—to here.'

He swallows hard and either he's a really great actor, or this memory affects him far more than I gave him credit for.

'By the time I found her, she'd been there almost two days.' His voice breaks and he lowers his head.

The image of Leonora swims in my vision and faintness washes over me at the memory.

Justin pulls himself together, although his eyes are red-rimmed from staving back the tears. 'The police conducted a thorough investigation, concluding that Leonora took her own life. Our daughter was never found and was presumed dead at the hands of my wife.'

Siobhan's jaw tenses, the muscles bunching up inside. 'I'm so sorry,' she mutters through clenched teeth. 'I never meant to cause you distress.'

'Distress?' Justin comes to his feet, and I swiftly lower my hand to Beau's collar. He doesn't like aggressive strangers making quick moves. 'Young lady, you have no concept whatsoever. My wife is dead, has been for over thirty years, and I assume my daughter is too. I have no idea what notion made you think we would ever believe that you're my long-lost daughter. She is dead!'

He is apoplectic and there is nothing I can do but observe. Let him run his course. Because he is right. I could go to prison for what I've done. No matter what my motive. I stole a baby.

Justin takes in a long, controlling breath.

No one moves. We're all observers watching a scene play out on stage.

'Why did you come here?' Siobhan's question is barely more than a whisper, but Justin hears and whips his head around to glare at her.

'To put a stop to this nonsense before you hurt any more people, before the disease you planted spreads. Megan and her mother, Louisa, are distraught. I don't know how you fiddled this DNA crap, but they believe you. They've been offered a carrot with the thin hope that Leonora lives on in you. It is not possible. If you think for one minute that I believe you're my daughter, you're sadly mistaken. The police conducted the most thorough, widespread search. They never found my daughter, but it's not you. You certainly are nothing to do with me.' He streaks a disgusted look from top to bottom of Siobhan and she flinches.

That flinch resonates inside me.

It goes unnoticed by Justin. 'You will tell Megan and Louisa that you were lying, and you will *back off* or I will have the police on to you for fraudulent claims.'

Siobhan gasps, her eyes going wide with horror.

'I assume you thought you were about to inherit a great fortune. Well, you can forget that. You'll not have a bean from this family. You evil, blood-sucking little b—'

'That's quite enough!'

Exhausted I might be, weak and pathetic I am not. Years may have passed, but once again, Justin has underestimated me.

I struggle a little, but I get to my feet. Beau slides up beside me and his tension bonds with mine.

'Get out of my house! I will be the one to call the police if you don't move your arse out of here right now. You were not invited. You are not welcome. *You* are trespassing.' I spell it out very clearly, fury gathering where pity had temporarily resided. Beau trembles with anticipation, but I won't use him as a weapon, purely a threat. I raise one hand and point straight at the door, where Gordon pushes himself upright from where he leaned against the frame as though he has just now taken an interest in our conversation.

'Get. Out!' I growl, between gritted teeth.

A twitch of a smile curves Gordon's face. Is that admiration? I've seen it before when I've stood up to Justin.

I barely acknowledge James, who has stepped forward into the room, quite willing, I suspect, to escort Justin out of there by the seat of his pants, but Justin moves towards the door. He probably thinks he's made his point.

Siobhan's eyes glitter with unshed tears as she stares at me. She can't possibly know the utter havoc she has caused. For more than three decades, James and I have kept this secret. Not for our sakes, but to protect her.

'Out!' I reiterate, my voice cracking with fury on that one word.

Justin brushes past the other man, who steps back into the doorway, like a sentinel.

Gordon removes his sunglasses, dips his head in acknowledgement and then turns to follow Justin out of the garden.

I draw in a soft gasp.

Tension vibrates on silent air as I release Beau's collar and he shoots outside to check our intruders have gone.

I cannot speak as fear takes a hold, almost paralysing me.

After all these years, the final piece of the puzzle slides neatly into place.

43

PRESENT DAY – FRIDAY, 19 JULY 2024, 2.15 A.M. – GRACE

Sleep evades me.

Disturbed by my discovery, I nonetheless run through the conversation again and again in my mind.

For the life of me, I couldn't bring myself to tell Siobhan the whole story when Justin and Gordon left yesterday. I was sapped of all strength and took myself off to bed. I needed sleep to revive me if I am to deal with this.

Siobhan never protested. On the contrary, guilt and concern turned her into a mother hen again and she bustled me off to bed, bringing me a soft, cool flannel to lay across my forehead. She offered painkillers, but James had not long given me some when she'd arrived home so unexpectedly.

James offered to stay, but I told him we would be fine. Nothing was going to happen.

Only now that I've had time to think about it, I'm pretty sure something is going to happen.

It's still such an effort to get out of bed, but I manage, letting out little grunts as I swing my legs over the side and then push up. I hold still, getting my balance before I move off. I am getting better at this. Pain radiates up my leg into my hip, though, where Beau caught me. It's pain that causes the exhaustion, but no amount of exhaustion can persuade my brain to stop whirring.

As I make my way downstairs, I pause to listen.

Silence hangs like a woollen blanket, dark and suffocating.

Normally I love the seclusion of living in the country, the clarity of air, the sweet silence, the peace.

Tonight, though, that silence holds menace, heavy on the air.

I make my way into the kitchen without turning on a light, quiet myself as I don't want to disturb Siobhan. When morning breaks, it will be soon enough for me to explain everything to her. Soon enough for us to make decisions on whether we need to disappear once more.

I reach for the kettle and fill it, glancing as I do at the black shadow asleep on his bed in the corner, so tired I'm not sure he even raises his head. I click the button on the kettle and a soft shushing noise fills the room. I turn my head, scanning the corners for more shadows.

And find one.

'I was beginning to think I would have to come upstairs and find you.' The tone is soft and deceptive.

My hand goes to my chest as I stop breathing, my gaze automatically shooting to where Beau lies, motionless.

The noise I make is halfway between a sob and a wail.

'Oh, don't worry. I wouldn't hurt him. I'd never harm an animal.'

I find my tongue. 'Unlike Justin.' My head spins with the lingering effects of the codeine I'd taken earlier. I'm really not good with drugs. Probably because I've never taken more than an occasional paracetamol.

Gordon moves further into the room, his eyes glittering as moonlight through the window slants across his face to highlight the sharp edges of his features. His bald head glistens with sweat. 'I never did approve of all that hunting Justin used to do.'

'I'm surprised. I thought you used to join him.'

The shadow moves, and I assume Gordon is shrugging. 'No. I don't need to hunt down a defenceless animal to make me feel like a big, strong man.' He bows his head in Beau's direction. 'Typical Labrador. Eat anything. But it's not poison. Your dog's just going to have a really deep sleep for a few hours, maybe wake up with a headache. Time enough for us to sort out this matter without me getting bitten in the arse.'

Much as I want to rush over and check on Beau, this situation is at tipping point. One fast move from me and I might trigger a response I'm not prepared for. Not that I can move swiftly.

I'm not quite sure what is expected of me, but I'm unwilling to sit down, putting myself in an even more vulnerable position as I know I'll struggle to get back up again.

At a soft creak, I glance towards the stairs and hold my breath.

Moonlight spills through a small window Siobhan must have left open, and washes over the stairs to about halfway up, illuminating the shadows.

The bubble and boil of the kettle comes to an abrupt end as the switch flicks off. Perhaps that was all it was.

Nothing. It's nothing.

I turn my attention back to Gordon.

'And what is the situation you wish to sort out?'

'Us.'

I swallow hard but incline my head.

'Would you like a cup of tea?'

A rough snort comes from him. 'This is not a social visit.'

My smile is bitter and cold. 'All the same, I need one.'

I flick the switch on the under-cupboard lighting so I can see what I'm doing. Soft golden light floods the room and I remove the kettle from its base and pour boiling water on top of the teabag Siobhan obviously left in a clean mug the night before. Perhaps she decided she didn't want a cup of tea after all. There was sugar already in, so perhaps she'd been going to bring it up to me.

I leave it to brew and turn back to Gordon.

'You know I took the baby. Why didn't you report it to the police at the time?'

Dark shadows dip into the hollows of his face to emphasise them, giving him a demonic look as he smiles, the creases in his cheeks spreading like the ripple of a pond.

'Because I wasn't there. If I had told them what I saw that night, you running with the baby in your arms, then that would have placed me at the scene.'

I'm puzzled. I tilt my head in enquiry. 'What do you mean?'

'As far as everyone was concerned, I was with Justin. We were each other's alibi.'

Blood starts to drain from my head as the memory rushes in. 'Justin had stormed out, taking you with him.'

'Yes. But I never remained with him.'

'It was you I saw that night.' I gasp, the penny dropping at last. 'Not Justin. I've always thought it was him, but the stairwell was so dark with just a slash of light.' I'd seen a pair of eyes, but in my fear and panic, I had assumed it was Justin. All these years. 'You were supposed to be in Scotland together, on a deer hunt.'

Gordon blows out a breath. 'Only we weren't because Justin was with his whore.'

'Whore?'

'Yes. Prostitute. Woman of the night. However you want to term it. The young woman he paid for sex.'

I raise a hand to my mouth and stop myself from crying out. 'I never knew.'

Gordon shakes his head. 'Of course you didn't, miss goody-two-shoes. He would never have allowed you that much information. You would have gone to Leonora.'

I take one step and open the fridge, pull the milk out, unscrew the cap and pour a good dollop into my tea. When I open the door to place the milk back inside, I see my hands are shaking wildly with fear and pain from standing too long.

'Is that why they argued? Did she find out?' I pick up my tea and take a large mouthful in the hope that it will help. It scalds the inside of my mouth and I swallow quickly. There's a slight taint to it, almost soapiness, and I wonder if the milk is on the turn. I take another sip, and it's hot and sweet and that initial taste seems to have gone. Perhaps there had been washing up liquid residue on the inside of the cup.

'No. At least, I don't think she knew that as well. No, I think what she knew was far worse. Far more condemning.'

A thick roll of nausea churns in my stomach as Gordon quietly pulls out a chair from the kitchen table and slips into it. My heart stutters as light bounces almost blue off the long, thin steel blade he places on the table in front of him. Memories rush in of the one on the flooded bathroom floor and I really don't want to meet the same fate.

I need to keep him talking. Distract him.

Because I know. Have known since this afternoon.

'Justin was right. He's not Siobhan's father, is he?'

I look into Gordon's eyes, the beautiful hazel of Siobhan's. Only, *his* hold a deadly chill.

Only now does it occur to me to ask. 'Did you have an affair with Leonora?'

Gordon shakes his head. 'Far worse.'

'What could be worse?'

He sucks air in through his teeth. 'You honestly don't know? I was never sure if she'd confided in you. That was another reason I never turned the police in your direction. Because it would have come out and then they would have looked at me for her death and the unexplained disappearance of her child. Our child.'

'What would have come out?'

'Everything. Remember how hard Leonora was pushing for a baby? She was relentless.'

'I didn't know her as well back then. I made the arrangements once they decided to get help, but I never had much to do with Leonora until Siobhan was born.'

'You delivered her. No wonder you have a bond.'

'She's my daughter.'

'Not biologically.'

'No.' I narrow my eyes at him. 'Biologically yours, though.'

His smile is sharp and wide. 'You always were too bright for your own good. I knew, the moment I took off my sunglasses today, that I'd made a mistake. I watched the recognition in your eyes.'

'I wasn't mistaken either. I knew you saw it. If you didn't have an affair with Leonora, how did it happen?' But somehow I know. The sick slide of shock has my knees weakening and I lean against the kitchen counter for support. I don't want to sit next to him. I need to be on my feet, although I'm not sure how I'm going to escape. I gulp down another mouthful of tea in the hope that it will revive me sufficiently.

'She was frantic. Justin was right. She was almost insane in her desperation to have a baby.' He shakes his head.

'You did something to the specimen container of the sperm.' It wasn't a question, but a statement.

'There was a real bust-up between them. Justin said he would give one last try. A final go. Leonora said if that was the case, she'd divorce him. He couldn't afford for her to divorce him. Justin never had any money of his own. It all came from her and he spent it like water.'

'So you produced the sample.' It's not a question. It's a statement.

'I did.' His lips twist. 'And it worked. First time. Like a dream. Faster than anyone expected. Everyone thought the baby came too soon, she was just conceived so fast.'

'But she found out that day. The day I went back for the file. What happened to it? Surely the police must have queried why paperwork was all over the bathroom floor.'

Gordon shrugged. 'I gathered it up, took it with me and burned the whole file.'

My head is spinning and my hip throbs. I'm not sure I can stand much longer, as my legs are buckling from under me, but I can't stem the flow of questions. 'So, you returned while Justin was with his... friend.' I take another drink of tea, desperate to shake this tiredness that is swarming in. 'How did you manage to kill her? How come she didn't put up a fight?'

'I drugged her.' He shrugs. 'By the time the police found her two days later, there would have been no trace left in her system.'

I gasp.

One look at my almost empty cup and I know. It wasn't Siobhan who placed the cup by the kettle with the teabag and sugar already inside. Along with whatever drug he used.

'GHB,' he answers, as though I asked the question out loud. Perhaps I did, although I think I'm incapable of asking anything. My speech slurs and I close my eyes against the black storm clouds forming as my legs give way.

Aware of movement, I'm gently lowered to the floor, the chill of the tiles instantly soaking through my thin nightdress.

My whole body is paralysed, the twitching of my muscles stops and the only sense I have left is my hearing.

Bringing his lips close to my ear, Gordon's gravelly whisper circles through my head, winding terror through me. Terror that I am incapable of defending myself.

'When Siobhan wakes in the morning, she'll find her poor, dear mum dead in a pool of her own blood. She won't want to pursue further DNA tests when she realises you've taken your own life in the same manner her biological mother did. An imitation of that fateful suicide. Pushed too far by Siobhan's selfish pursuit in discovering her ancestry. She won't want to look any further. Even if she insists, the test will only prove that Justin is not her father. Only you and I know the truth and I would never submit my DNA for testing.'

His voice fades and where his hand holds my arm, I feel a sharp jab.

44

PRESENT DAY – FRIDAY, 19 JULY 2024, 3.25 A.M. – SIOBHAN

Sheer terror grabbed her throat as Siobhan perched on the fourth step from the top of the stairs. Her toes, now icy as fear flooded her, curled in on themselves. She'd been perched there for an absolute age while she listened, unsure who it was her mum was speaking to initially.

It could have been one of three men she had met for the first time today.

Perhaps James. Siobhan's surprise grandfather. Although not biologically related.

Justin's voice, the only one she'd really heard earlier, had, she thought, been more cultured than this one.

She'd tossed and turned in bed until she'd heard voices from downstairs. Surprised she'd not heard a sound from Beau, Siobhan kept silent and still so as not to flag up to anyone she was there.

Her heart wept for the pain she'd caused her mum. Regret filled her whole conscience. How had she made such a mess of their lives with one stupid, careless action? Something so thoughtless. Why hadn't she trusted her mum enough to have asked her, instead of acting like some amateur sleuth?

With only herself to blame when her mum took herself off to bed late the previous afternoon just after James had left, Siobhan had been unable to get any further answers. Her mum was too distraught and exhausted, but she'd promised they would speak in the morning. Now it was morning and the quiet murmur of voices had woken her.

The initial surge of guilt faded at eavesdropping, replaced instead with a growing sense of horror. Her phone was on its charging stand in the kitchen, so any thought of calling the police had to be sidelined until she could think of some kind of diversion.

GHB was the last clear word she heard, followed by a shuffle that made her wonder if her mum had sat down. From the direction of voices and movement previously, Siobhan knew her mum was standing near the kettle a moment ago, but as the silence stretched out, she strained to hear.

Siobhan pushed up from the step and crept downstairs, aware of every slight creak and crack of the old staircase. As she reached the bottom and peered around the end of the balustrade, horror snatched at her.

The huge bald guy from the previous afternoon towered over the top of her mum, who lay motionless on the tiled floor.

At first Siobhan's mind would not acknowledge the sight and it briefly occurred to her that her mum had collapsed, and he was attempting to help her.

Until the glimmer of a knife blade flashed into view as the man angled it against the inside of her mum's elbow.

Siobhan's screech rent the air in two.

The man leapt back, taking a few steps away from her mum and crouching into a defensive position, the knife clutched in his hand ready to take on any adversary.

At the sight of Siobhan charging across the kitchen towards

him, he dropped his knife arm to his side and held up the other hand as though that would stop her.

Siobhan snatched the nearest thing to her on the bench, not so much to defend herself as attack the intruder. Surprised at how heavy it was, Siobhan side stepped her mum's inert body, putting herself between the attacker and her mum, and launched the kettle at the man's bald head.

As it struck a glancing blow, the lid flew off and steaming water streamed over him. Droplets splashed back to spatter the exposed flesh of Siobhan's arms and legs, shocking her with the fast burn of it.

His screams, louder than Siobhan's, almost made the house tremble as he collapsed onto the floor, cradling his bright scarlet head in his hands and then tugging at his T-shirt to hold it away from his body.

The back door burst open, and Siobhan leapt at the knife Gordon had dropped, snatching it from the floor to hold in front of her as she took on the next intruder.

'Whoa! Easy. Easy.' James's millpond eyes entreated her as he raised both hands in a calming motion. He appeared to take the scene in with one sweeping glance before he pointed at the kitchen bench. 'Put the knife safely in the drawer, Siobhan, then go and help your mum. The police are on their way.'

'How did you know?' Siobhan slipped the knife into the drawer and then knelt by her mum.

'I didn't. I just had a bad feeling. There's a certain look in a person's eye that I'd recognise anywhere, and I didn't trust this one.' James knelt and ripped the T-shirt from Gordon's body, bringing away with it a layer of skin as he blistered.

Another yowl accompanied him as James bundled up the T-shirt and slipped it under Gordon's head. He was then on his feet, snatching open drawer after drawer until he found tea towels. He held them under the cold water tap until they were soaked, then layered them over Gordon's head and torso. 'Lie still,' he murmured with a decided lack of sympathy as the man writhed on the cold, tiled floor, his screams tapering off into whimpers.

'How's your mum?'

'I heard him mention he'd slipped her GHB.' Siobhan's voice trembled as she ran soft hands over her mum's body, checking for any injuries, any damage oblivious to the sting of her own flesh.

James puffed out his cheeks and reached his phone from his back pocket as he moved over to crouch next to Siobhan and Grace. He faced Gordon but shook his head as he waited for the phone to connect. 'He's not going anywhere. I'm pretty sure he has first-degree scalds. Nasty.'

Siobhan's stomach lurched as her gaze cruised over the scarred face of the man who crouched next to her and closed her mind to what horrors he had been through.

He reached to cradle her mum's cheek in his hand, his tenderness almost breaking her heart.

'What happened to Beau?'

She kept her attention steadfastly on her mum as she replied, 'He drugged him, too.'

As the call connected, James muttered the words, 'Ambulance, please.'

45

PRESENT DAY – FRIDAY, 26 JULY 2024, 4.15 P.M. – GRACE

My hand drops like a leaden weight from where it rested on my stomach to flop onto Beau's hot black fur. I moan as he twitches and for the first time in a week, I realise I have no more pain. Not physically, not mentally, not emotionally.

That may change once I move from this sunbed in the back garden where I am soaking up the late afternoon sun, my faithful dog, fully recovered from his deep sleep, at my side.

For now, however, I am at peace.

James will return tomorrow. He's spent considerable time at the police station answering their questions.

According to James and his testimony, Leonora begged me to take her baby away as she was convinced the child was in danger. When I received news of Leonora's death, I believed what Leonora had said to be true and disappeared with the baby, too fearful of my own life and that of baby Grace to tell anyone, even the police. Especially the police.

Who am I to argue with that scenario? After all, I hate liars.

Our secret has held for more than thirty years.

Sunlight patterns against the inside of my eyelids and I allow a small smile to curve my lips. When the police visited me in hospital, the GHB had conveniently still been in my system, so I was unable to provide a statement immediately. Not until after I'd spoken with James, if you get my meaning.

According to the police, Gordon is still in hospital and will be for some time, suffering from concussion caused by the hefty thwack of the kettle against his temple. The scalding from the boiling water had caused third-degree burns over part of his head and face, and second-degree down his neck, back, shoulders and stomach. If it wasn't for James's quick actions, it could have been far worse than it was. As it is, the police inform me that he will possibly require skin grafts. His protracted stay in a secure hospital may delay his court hearing, but I believe they can go ahead without him should an adjournment be declined.

I hope it does as I don't look forward to the day I have to face him again in court, but I will do my duty to ensure he is imprisoned for the sake of my daughter, as I have always defended my daughter. What he did to me is nothing compared to what he inflicted upon Leonora and what he would have done to baby Grace, because I am convinced more than ever that he would have taken her life too. I close my eyes and I can imagine him laying her small body alongside Leonora's in that deep water. Allowing her to perish.

That would have been the perfect scenario as far as Gordon was concerned. There would have been no further need for explanation with both him and Justin holding tight alibis and the conviction that he'd encouraged, if not instigated, in Justin that Leonora was mad. The nuances had been subtle, but there nonetheless, and even I would have had to admit to the boss's wife showing signs of distress and anxiety.

It would have been the perfect crime.

This way, though, there had always been some doubt in everyone's minds.

I think of James and the agony he'd suffered all for the sake of defending Queen and Country, and my heart can feel no satisfaction that Gordon has brought this upon himself. I would not wish it on anyone. Not even my worst enemy.

Siobhan has taken official DNA swabs, which verify she is Leonora's biological daughter. As if there was any doubt in my mind. The test to see if Justin was her father, however, was negative. Again, no surprise there.

I wonder what time it is as I swat a fly away and squint up at the clear blue sky. For the first time in years, my soul is free, my conscience clear.

The police are currently looking into Justin's involvement too. After all, he is the one who encouraged everyone to believe his wife had committed suicide. He is the one who benefited from her death, in many ways. Somewhere along the line, I have an inkling that he lied about more than just his false alibi.

And I do hate a liar.

He has been asked by the Saville family lawyers to vacate Crest Park and we have been invited to visit.

I don't ever want to return, but if Siobhan wishes to go, I am sure she will be amazed by her ancestry. I wouldn't dream of holding her back. After all, Crest Park will form part of her inheritance once the lawyers sort their way through the trust paperwork.

My daughter could very well end up a rich young woman.

At the cool touch on my arm, I shuffle to sit upright and take a glass of ice-cold water from my daughter's hand. I swallow down a few sips and smile up at Siobhan.

I wonder, if fate had not taken such a massive turn, how I would ever have become this child's mother.

ACKNOWLEDGEMENTS

One of the hardest things to cope with is the death of a loved one. Never more so than when it is fast and unexpected. Such was the case with Beau, my adorable black Labrador who was taken all too young and far too fast. Within three weeks, he was gone.

I took his death very hard as none of my animals have ever died from anything but old age, and for the first time ever my imagination faltered, and I found I was unable to continue with this book which is why the publication was pushed back. For those of you waiting, I apologise.

When you read the story, you will understand the strange connection. I had already written the first part of the book in which not only was Beau featured, but in real life he was diagnosed with the same rare condition as one of the main characters I was writing about. It floored me. The coincidence was unreal.

Speaking to a lady while walking Skye, my Dalmatian, I told her about Beau, and she told me about the recent loss of her husband. I was mortified. How could I feel the loss of my dog as deeply as she felt the death of her husband?

Her words were a comfort, and maybe a turning point.

Grief is a full bucket of water. One more drip, and it overflows. It does not matter what source that drip of water comes from.

I'd like to thank my editor, Caroline Ridding. Filled with compassion, she allowed me an indefinite extension.

As it happened, my imagination kicked back in and once I re-

read everything I had written, I debated for some time whether to continue that storyline and I realised that was the stumbling block. That my head told me not to, but my heart needed to continue.

Fate deals some heavy blows. That lady was right. It doesn't matter where the grief comes from. It is real.

So, I dedicate *My Mother's Lies* to Beau and he got to feature in it a little more than originally planned.

So, now to the people I must acknowledge for their amazing and sometimes in-depth help.

For those who assisted with my DNA questions. I really didn't want to look into my own family DNA, I know there are skeletons in that closet...

Especially Denise Goodhand who went above and beyond to help me in my quest to get the DNA part of this story correct. She allowed me insight into the research of her own family for which I am so grateful and truly amazed. Any mistakes are my own.

In addition, to the following who happily answered my questions and allowed me to get up close and personal:

- Liz Mudd
- Sarah Drew
- Christina Farrlley
- Carla Krae
- Sarah Lannie
- Patricia McBride
- Carol Hellier
- Glenys Wane
- Gillian Connelly
- Maggie Steel
- Karen Brame – who found me through her own DNA research.

Apologies to anyone I missed off as there were so many.

Much as I love to make sure my facts are right, sometimes I feel obliged to tweak things for dramatic effect and most readers would never think twice. Nurses and doctors may find fault, if they look very carefully...

For those who allow me free reign to use their names in whatever way I wish:

- Siobhan Sarah Martin
- Megan Saville
- Pauline McCormick

A special thank you to James (Jim) Mabbott, who wrote from Australia to tell me how much he enjoyed my books and asked if I could name a character after him – even if I made him a murderer! Did I oblige him? My rules are that if you lend me your name, I can do anything with it – and I did. I hope Jim is happy.

Thanks to those who participated in my party game of 'name an item to be included in the manuscript'.

- Tracy Hartridge – record player
- Megan Saville – crochet hook

As always for the wonderful support of Andi Miller and her Facebook group, Books with Friends.

To my new editor, Francesca Best – I think we worked well together. And Gary Jukes, my proofreader, who not only educates me each time but also makes me laugh with some of his comments.

A special mention for Jean Wilson who sadly passed away before she got to read my latest book. Such a lovely lady and a huge supporter of my work. RIP.

Ross Greenwood, for his excellent critiquing and continued support.

Thanks to my family. For always being there for me.

ABOUT THE AUTHOR

Diane Saxon previously wrote romantic fiction for the US market but has now turned to writing psychological crime. *Find Her Alive* was her first novel in this genre and introduced series character DS Jemma Morgan. She is married to a retired policeman and lives in Shropshire.

Sign up to Diane Saxon's mailing list for news, competitions and updates on future books.

Visit Diane's website: www.dianesaxon.com

Follow Diane on social media:

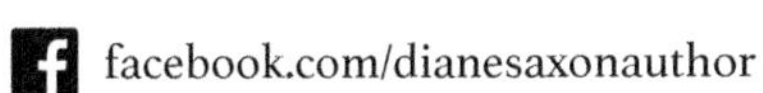
facebook.com/dianesaxonauthor

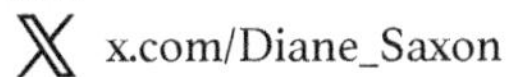
x.com/Diane_Saxon

instagram.com/DianeSaxonAuthor

ALSO BY DIANE SAXON

DS Jenna Morgan Series

Find Her Alive

Someone's There

What She Saw

The Ex

Standalone

My Little Brother

My Sister's Secret

The Stepson

The Good Twin

My Mother's Lies

Printed in Great Britain
by Amazon